INGRID STORHOLMEN is a Norwegian poet and novelist. Her poetry collections have been published to great acclaim since 2001 and she has read at various international literature festivals. Her first novel *Voices from Chernobyl* (2009) won the prestigious Sult Prize and its English translation was nominated for the IMPAC Dublin Literary Award, among others. The novel was also translated into Hindi, French and Estonian, among others, and was dramatized for the theatre in 2015. *The Mother Who Forgot It Was Evening* (2012) was her first book for children. *Here Lay Tirpitz* is her second novel.

MARIETTA TARALRUD MADDRELL was born in England to Scandinavian parents and only began translating from Norwegian and Swedish after chance meetings in India with Hindi poets. Her translations include *Voices from Chernobyl* (2009) by Ingrid Storholmen, *Lynette's Journey* (2014) by Hanne Bramness and *Black Calf @ White Snow* (2022) by Hans Sande.

Praise for *Here Lay Tirpitz*

'Storholmen writes fantastically: taut and plain, but at the same time poetic and extremely gripping. And the characters are believable and complex...she reminds us why literature is important, because it can impart something which cannot be expressed in other ways.'—*Vart Land*

'Ingrid Storholmen has written a great...novel, about the men on board the battleship Tirpitz, and about their lives in war and peace, about their lovers, wives and children. [She] is a thrilling and gifted writer, and shows in *Here Lay Tirpitz* a singular talent and an instinct for converting a large and difficult subject into small and meaningful episodes and glimpses.'— *VG*

'*Here Lay Tirpitz* is a strong, moving and demanding read ... an unusual and powerful book which bears witness to great knowledge, wisdom and a talent for empathy.'—*Dagbladet*

'*Here Lay Tirpitz* is a disturbing and strong anti-war novel. It is seldom that such great sorrow and pain is told so sparingly and inteMnsely. Highly recommended!'—*Adresseavisen*

Here Lay Tirpitz

a novel

Ingrid
Storholmen

Translated from the NORWEGIAN by
Marietta Taralrud Maddrell

Series editor **Teji Grover**

YATRA BOOKS
An imprint of Vani Prakashan Group

WHITE NIGHTS SERIES

First Edition : 2023

vaniprakashan.com

Yatra Books is an imprint of Vani Prakashan Group

Head Office

4695, 21-A, Daryaganj, New Delhi-110 002, India
Phone : +91 11 23273167, 23275710

Registered Bookstores and Offices

Ashok Rajpath, Patna-800 004, Bihar
Coffee House Campus, Mahatma Gandhi Marg, Allahabad-211 001, Uttar Pradesh
Mahatma Gandhi International Hindi University, Wardha-442 001, Maharashtra
36-A, Shakespeare Sarani, Near Rani Birla Girls College, Kolkata-700017, West Bengal

sales@vaniprakashan.in
vaniprakashan@gmail.com

Here Lay Tirpitz

NORLA Norwegian Literature Abroad

This translation has been published with the financial support of NORLA (Norwegian Literature Abroad) foundation.

First published in Norwegian as *Her lå Tirpitz* by Aschehoug

ISBN : 978-93-5518-909-7
Fiction

Printed and bound in India at Thomson Press (India) Ltd.

INGRID | "Look children, Tirpitz lay here during the war," Mother pointed. "Just imagine, a 250-metre long battleship out there in the fjord. Tirpitz was the biggest battleship in Europe, and it was anchored exactly here. Right up against the mountainside, hidden from the English planes by that overhang. Johannes, who is our relative, cycled here and took a photo of it, and was arrested."

Every time we were on our way to Trondheim and came to the narrow valley where the road and railway run side by side, before the landscape opens out and Fættenfjord, Saltøya and the outlying islands come into view, Mother said: "Tirpitz lay here."

Now and then we stopped at the war memorial, situated almost all the way down on the beach, which commemorates the British pilots who never turned towards home, after futile attempts to sink Tirpitz.

Many people I know from this part of Trøndelag have told me that they too heard about Tirpitz as they drove past. If I'm with a visitor from far away, I myself repeat the phrase as we pass the place, and I feel the force in the sentence Mother always spoke. The ship evoked so many powerful memories that it has an effect even now. People remember.

Tirpitz lay here.

The battleship Admiral von Tirpitz, weighing almost 5,300 tonnes, its length of 250 metres and crew of more than 2,500 men, was the pride of Hitler and the German Navy. The ship came to Norway in January 1942. The vessel represented a great threat to Allied convoys with war materials for the Soviet Union, but was hardly ever directly involved in action.

Tirpitz lay for two periods in Fættenfjord, a side branch of Trondheimsfjord, but then it was moved to Bogen in Ofoten, and onwards to Kåfjord in Alta. In the end Tirpitz was moved to Håkøya, where it was bombed by the RAF on 12 November 1944. The ship capsized and more than 970 men died.

Several years ago, I began reading about the Second World War, then more about the war at sea and particularly Tirpitz, and I decided to write a book about those who were on board the ship. Some of them die when Tirpitz is bombed, others survive, all of them are imaginary. I travelled in the wake of the battleship. First I went to Håkøya and the Defence Museum in Tromsø, then to Kåfjord, which has its own Tirpitz museum. Finally I ended up at a veterans' meeting in Heiligenhafen, in Schleswig-Holstein, where I met some of those who survived the bombing and capsizing of the ship in 1944. In autumn this year, 2014, it will be the seventieth anniversary of this event.

"I was a good soldier until the end!" said several of the old men in the Tirpitz Veterans Association. Even if they have long since recognized and accepted who started and lost the war, the soldier's pride is still there. The fish sausage they had in Trondheim must have made an impression, they still remember it. Towards midnight they gather in a circle where the 'Hammock Waltz' is played according to tradition, then the light is dimmed and they hold onto each other and sing 'Lili Marleen' as they did every evening on the ship. Then they are old men no longer, but a bunch of young seamen, they are back on board the Tirpitz.

Winston Churchill:

"The destruction or even the crippling of this ship is the greatest event at sea at the present time. No other target is comparable to it."

I

Germany, autumn 1939

OTTO | I tell Gerhard that he can take over my room and play with my telescope. Then I begin my round of farewells, going first to the churchyard, to Nana's grave, then to Granny and Granpa's. It has always been special to read my name carved on a tombstone, only the birthdate is different. I would have liked to meet the man I am named after, they say I look like him. Granpa died before I was born, Uncle Heinrich's name is on the stone too, he was killed in the last war. In a trench. So it is safer to be on a battleship. We are going far over the sea!

The sparrows are twittering unusually loudly in the bushes in the graveyard. Here most are long dead, only three grave crosses are quite fresh, but no bodies lie under them. They are soldiers who fell in Poland, who sacrificed their lives for their country, my country.

On the way home I hear the cows mooing, it is nearly milking time. I pass by my tree, where I built a hut as a child, behind the cowshed. I have to say goodbye to the aunts and Inge, my favourite cousin, who live in the neighbouring house. I help my father for the last time. Is he thinking like this too? I thought I saw him wiping his eyes this morning when I came down to breakfast, but it might well have been something else.

FRITZ | I take water into my lungs and cough and cough, I am lying in the sea, sailors are floating around me, and when I turn around, I see Tirpitz, capsizing. It is two nights until I have to sign on, I try to sleep again, but it's no use. In the end I go down to the kitchen and drink a little water, but then I remember the sensation of drowning and put the glass down quickly. Then Mother comes in, wearing only her nightdress.

"Don't go!" she says, intensely for her, "I had such a terrible dream about the ship, that it went down."

I stare at Mother, who has now started crying. I have to swallow, as if my mouth is full of water.

"Did I survive, in your dream?"

"I only remember that you called out for me."

CARL | I didn't taste butter until I started in the newly-formed Hitler Youth Group in Munich. Butter! Melting yellow fat on a freshly-baked piece of bread which is still warm from the heat of the oven. What luxury! When my brother and I were growing the fastest, there was always too little food at home. Father kept losing his job. First there was poor food, then there was hardly any food, eventually almost hunger. Now it's "Guns before butter." I agree with that.

OTTO | The warmth in the barn, the sheep lying chewing the cud, it's dark in here, safe and good. Inge and I used to jump into the hay from up there. It was a long way down and not much hay, it took time before we dared. Some of the pigs are stirring, small sleepy grunts, even the old mare is lying down. When I come back, there will be new animals here. We must hope the war is over soon, says Father, but it took four years last time, and the authorities said the same thing then: a lightning strike and then it will all be over. Kitty doesn't leave my trouser leg, she knows something is up. Mother has brought a long sausage up from the cellar, which she wants me to take with me. Nana comes with three pairs of knitted wool socks. I run out to the toilet.

UWE | Admiral of the Fleet Alfred von Tirpitz built up the modern German Navy, and now I am going to be on the ship that bears his name!

HEINRICH | I have eaten in the same restaurant as Hitler in Hamburg, two years after the Führer, to be honest, but I sat at the same table and ordered exactly what Hitler ate. Luckily it was cheap: vegetable soup and water.

OTTO | Our young horse was requisitioned, it belonged to the 'Cavalry Reserve'. Father tried to explain, but I was inconsolable and wept, even though I was big and a member of the Hitler Youth. Out in the countryside my group played sports mostly, not much politics. In other chapters they were given boxing gloves and rubber clubs. Or at least they boasted about it, when we had the big gathering in Nürnberg in 1935.

Father manages to keep me from the medical board for military service for a long time, with the excuse that the farm needs me. They demand that we increase wheat production for the army, which only grows and grows. I dare not tell him that I want to join up and fight for Führer and Fatherland.

The roar of victory, when Germany storms forward, is like the whirlwind in Genesis when it flies across the landscape. That wind will lift our banners when we march.

WERNER | *If you have not sweated at Mix and Genest,*
Slaved at Schwarzkopf, AEG and Borsig,
You still haven't faced the pains of life

somebody had written on the locker room wall. At Siemens, Knorr and Stock you were the lowest of the low, almost a slave for the rich factory owners. At the shipyard it's much better. Not to speak of the wages. It shows that what we are building is important. Tirpitz. Her size is of course top secret.

FREGATTEN-KAPITÄN BIELER | They need me on the new flagship for Battle Group Number 1. They have now finished the fine-tuning at the shipyard in Wilhelmshaven and the crew are being sent to the Baltic for training in firing and manoeuvre practice. At last I get to leave the office. War at sea is 99% sea and 1% war, said the old admirals. They also said that every seventh wave is the biggest. Perhaps it's the same with fighting too, every seventh attack from the Brits will be successful?

HEDWIG | Of course I am proud to have a boyfriend who is going to serve on Tirpitz itself! It's important to join up and fight for Germany, I will try to do my bit.

"Hedwig," Fritz said seriously this afternoon, "meet me at eleven o'clock this evening at the fountain on the west side of Olympia Park." He is so sweet, with the light brown fringe that falls down over his forehead. Must use the lily-of-the-valley soap, put up my hair, he must remember me as elegant, as the most elegant of all. I must hurry, borrow Ruth's new skirt, I'm sure to get it when she hears that it's our last evening together.

Will I be able to wait for him?

KASPAR | I'll be called up to be a soldier soon, I know it. What if I have to kill, what if it's between me and an English soldier? Perhaps he too is a student and has a family, a long life ahead which I will take away from him. I don't know whether I can do it. Mother will find the priest at the door. Everyone is scared of the priest now, where is he going to knock next, with the special expression on his face which gives it all away, long before his mouth opens and says, "Condolences".

If an owl flies over a house, someone will die, I heard once. There is an owl at the edge of the wood here. I have seen it several times recently, it comes out in the evenings. Each time

I am shocked that it has a face, that its two eyes are staring right at me. Now I'll watch where it flies. So long as it doesn't circle over Sigismund's house, or come here.

If it wasn't for the war, I could have got a job in the faculty, my thesis is nearly finished. That's where I belong, not on a battleship.

Now the National Socialist Party has had seven fat years, is there nobody who remembers Pharaoh's dream, afterwards follow seven thin ones, with hunger and hardship? Or perhaps the Führer is stronger than Pharaoh?

I remember something I saw in the paper when such things could still be printed. Someone wrote about King Nebuchadnezzar and his persecution of Jews. It did not go all that well, the king ended up a madman. The writer didn't dare draw the parallel with Hitler, but it was there between the lines. More and more often someone asks: Are you Aryan? It feels like a betrayal to say yes, a betrayal of those who have to say no. In the last war my father fought alongside Jewish boys, no one would have said anything about it then.

OTTO | There is hardly space for the sparkling stone from the garden. Inge, my favourite cousin, gave it to me when we were small, and claimed it brought luck. We are not allowed to take any more personal things than will fit in a little wooden chest as big as Mother's velvet box. I have packed:

- Granny's thin gold cross, which I inherited.
- The press cutting which shows our big prize-winning bull.
- A psalm book.
- Writing paper and two pens.
- The thin felt hat Father always wore when I was a child. I'll put that inside my vest.

“I’m sending my invisible Protector with you,” whispers Inge just before I go. “He has saved me many times,” she says, “I’m sure of it.”

KASPAR | “Do you know what I’ve heard,” shouts Sigismund when I come to show him my call-up letter, “Hitler is a master of black magic! When he was choosing the symbol for the Party, he reversed the swastika, which has always been turned to the right, and that means summoning up suffering and black magic.” “What nonsense,” I reply. “But there’s more,” says Sigismund eagerly, “because Goebbels certainly believes in Nostradamus, oh yes, and both Hitler and Himmler take astrology very seriously, someone told Father. Someone who didn’t want to say his name, but who had been in ‘The German Order’ and ‘Thule’ before Hitler banned them, because he didn’t want anyone who could use powers like that against him. Hitler is called the supreme Wise Man in those circles. The man said to Father that Hitler, both in Vienna and later, was preoccupied with occult theories. One of them was ‘The Theory of the World Ice’, by one Hörbiger. Have you heard of it?” asks Sigismund. “No,” I reply, “remember how people exaggerate.” “In any case it is certain that Hitler swings a pendulum over the sea charts to find out how the Navy ships are doing,” he went on. “The admirals became convinced when Hitler found the ‘Prinz Eugen’, which was on a secret mission, I’ve heard that from a lot of people!”

I go straight home again, wanting to be left in peace. One of Ovid’s lovers once implored the horses of the night to slow down and thus delay the dawn. On this short night, I wish the same. Soon I have to go on board.

FRITZ | I dare not propose. In a bit Hedwig is coming to the fountain, maybe I’ll be allowed to stroke under her blouse, right down to her skirt, it's dark in that part of Olympia Park. Then what do I do, do I take off my trousers, or keep them on? And what shall I do with the skirt and stockings, put them on the ground?

OTTO | When the neighbouring farm was sold at auction I was ten years old and best friends with Manfred, the eldest boy there, who had also thought to be a farmer when he grew up. It was shouted out over the whole yard: "Do I get a hundred? Do I hear a hundred and twenty, excellent quality, handicraft of the best kind." The brass candlesticks which meant so much to Manfred's mother, now strangers stood weighing them in their hands. Soon the animals would go, and Manfred's calf had to be sold too, the one that had a white star on its forehead. Perla. We went behind the outhouse so Manfred could cry in peace, and there he made up his mind that one day he would buy the farm back. That was why he enlisted. To earn money. His mother would get her candlesticks back.

I too think it's great to earn wages. With Father I've never got money for the farm work. In the Navy it's twenty-five reichsmarks every tenth day. I'll save nearly all of it, when I come home, I'll extend the sheep barn.

ROLF | I dream of a house, a little red house in an ordinary oak wood. It's quiet and peaceful there, no people, even though a road goes past it. Then suddenly a lot of soldiers come, they make noise and bluster, against my will I have to go with them when they march onwards. Quickly we come to a battlefield, hundreds of corpses are lying in heaps and I see angels bending over the dead bodies and lifting them up and flying towards the sky and disappearing.

When I wake up, I think about all the holidays when Bernhard and I cycled in the parks, bought ice-cream, took a short trip to check on Lisel when she was going home from the chocolate factory, with the smell of sweetness and darkness hovering around her. All Berlin rejoiced over the Olympic Games later that summer. Cycling slowly over Spree to Alt Köln and looking at the tourists outside the museums, guessing where they came from, laughing at their pronunciation if they asked the way. Cycling on, simply turning wherever we liked. That is the summer I feel nostalgic for, when we could still do exactly as we pleased.

FREGATTEN-KAPITÄN BIELER | Civil war and attempted coup. The Kapp Coup in 1920, it went on for five days, then it was thanks and goodbye to Kapp. Then came the riots in the Ruhr area later that year, my cousin was shot along with many other young people. The Free Corps killed them, but I don't think they faced any consequences. It would become worse, people you knew were arrested, someone at my neighbour's workplace was 'picked up', one of your in-laws' family was taken. You understood that next time it might be your turn, and you ran to the Party office and paid for your membership, aware of the smell of thin, liquid shit running down your filthy soul. From now on you would stink all the time.

KASPAR | Barbusse, Boas, Dos Passos, Einstein, Feuchtwanger, Förster, Freud, Galsworthy, Gide, Glaeser, Gorki, Hegemann, Hemingway, Kästner, Keller, London, Ludwig, Heinrich and Thomas Mann, Marx, Proust, Remarque, Sanger, Schnitzler, Sinclair, Tucholsky, Wells, Wolff, Zola, Zweig. I saw them flare up, saw little flakes of soot with letters on them fluttering in the air and the covers becoming as brown as the shirts of those who were burning them. I was hoping for rain as I stood and stared at the first burning of books, a decent shower so it would be difficult to set fire to the paper. I thought of Heine's words:

"Wherever they begin burning books, they will sooner or later end up burning people." The black soot settled over my life. Like dirty snow, like the brothers Guilt and Shame.

PAUL | We played at piling up heaps of money into tall buildings and walls. Father had bought War Bonds. When he cashed them, he got a disquieting number of notes from the bank.

ROLF | Every Monday and Thursday I brought groceries to the old rabbi who had bad legs. He was the grandfather of Hannah, whom I was in love with. It was as if something inside him shone and filtered out to us around him. I always looked forward to going there, now and then I got a glimpse of Hannah, and it was as if I would get something from him. Something he might say or give me, which I would have a use for when Destiny said: Rolf, your time is now. You have been in a cocoon for so long, now you will be a butterfly, can you feel your wings? That was how the rabbi affected people. Maybe he had said something good about me to Hannah, because quite quickly she became interested. The last time I saw him, he said to me: "You people must change direction, otherwise you risk ending up where you have set our course, and then the world will be in trouble. But perhaps it has to happen, it is said that the darkest hour in the history of humanity will be just before the spiritual awakening of the world begins."

Hannah, what is happening to you, and your grandfather?

FREGATTEN-KAPITÄN BIELER | France occupied the Ruhr in 1923, they claimed we were too poor to pay war reparations. After that the economy became extra tight for most people. I was still going to Officers' College, when Father telegraphed and asked me to come home and lend a hand. Well, what could I do? But when I had finished and got a job in the Navy, it got better, they paid at least.

Stresemann became Foreign Minister, and I thought it would become easier. After a long period of inflation peace was needed. I'll never forget how exhausting it was that a kilo of potatoes cost 50,000 marks one day and 100,000 marks two days later. The feeling when all we had saved was gone, Grandfather's inheritance crumbled away in a matter of days. Shares were more secure than savings for a while, and the most dangerous thing to do was not to use all your money at once. If your month's salary was 65,000, the next week it might only be enough for a packet of cigarettes. If you hadn't bought cheese, meat, root vegetables and tinned food, you were in a bad way. We used to laugh about it, that in those years lunch in a restaurant would become more expensive as we were eating it.

Admiral Raeder, who afterwards became commander of the entire Navy, said to me: "You will have a lightning career, there's no doubt about it." That was a proud moment. When I went home to Irma and told her this, she fetched the fruit liqueur we only drink at Christmas and raised a glass with her officer.

I liked the opportunities that time gave me. I did.

ROLF | "Most people think the Jews have got too much power," said Mother. "They own nearly all the banks and publishers and such. They had luxurious houses right beside Tiergarten, while I and the people I grew up with lived in rented tenements and back garden hovels in Mitte."

Berlin was filled with flags, banners and symbols worn by the Brownshirts. They looked rather splendid. The day that Hitler was elected to form a government and became

Chancellor, they marched through Brandenburg Gate with over 15,000 supporters! Not long after he ordered the linden trees in Unter den Linden to be chopped down.

Everybody bought radios, now that they cost only 78 reichsmarks. We listened to Hitler going on about the magnificent future of the Third Reich. This blended with the sight of benches with signs that said: 'Only for Aryans' and that Father knew that when von Ossietzky got the Peace Prize, he was lying in hospital after all the brutality he was subjected to in prison.

WERNER | It is said that one tonne of a battleship is like a whole year's work for a good worker. I have done one tonne this year, not everyone can show such results. Brigitta is so pleased, we just manage to buy a two-room flat.

Suddenly it is decided that I am to go with them on board to do maintenance and repairs. I am not against it, but Brigitta grumbles, thinks it's safer in the shipyard, besides little Dagmarr is demanding and often ill.

I am looking forward to it. Imagine standing on the deck when Tirpitz steers out!

"Surely you remember the three Prussian virtues?"

**"Yes:
Temperance
Industriousness
Following the Right Line.
What does 'Following the Right line' mean?"**

"If you don't understand it, you are not doing it."

"Oh stop teasing, this is not the time."

"I'm not teasing. It's no laughing matter."

The Baltic Sea, winter 1940

ANDREAS | When you read this, I'll have already gone on board. I couldn't bear to say goodbye. Forgive me, my beloved. This poem is called, 'For Elisabeth'.

The steps outside, is it you
Is it you coming towards me, dear
Can you see who I am
and tell me, afterwards,
as we look into the depths of each other,
When we stand as close as braided branches
and I don't know what I need,
Can you say something to me
about what only disappears
when nobody is looking, as the wind travels over snow,
hides every footprint and never reveals
a single direction?

Your Andreas

ROLF | Ah, baking bread! There's a heavenly scent of freshly baked bread all over Tirpitz, we have our own bakery. Father could never open a bag of fresh bread without saying that in November 1923 a loaf cost 420 billion marks. Then he always added: "Three days before it had cost *only* 120 billion."

Hannah and I laughed at that ritual. Then he looked at us severely and began talking about the robberies of grocery shops and vegetable fields outside the city. "In the end," he thundered, an American dollar cost 4.2 BILLION marks! It must never get that bad again," he used to conclude.

It would get much worse: Jewish businesses were stormed and destroyed. Hannah lost both her evening job and security when the shop was set on fire and the owner was beaten up.

Father often spoke about the Revolution in 1918, how great it felt when the Kaiser abdicated. "But the day they found Rosa Luxemburg murdered, I fell ill," said Father. "I believe the goodness of Germany died then," he went on, "that January day in 1919."

Just after Hitler became Chancellor, I came upon Father in the pigeon house in the back yard. I heard strange sounds from there and went inside. He wept as he fed the birds. "I am grieving for my country," he said quietly. Since then the cooing of pigeons has always made me tense. Here in the Baltic it is only seagulls which make a noise.

FRITZ | How Mother cried when I left! She told me about the time she lost her elder brother Friedrich in 1918. Just days before peace came. If he had been allowed to live a little longer, he could have come home and taken over the farm, and her parents would not have had to sell it. "All the bad things began when my brother died," said Mother. Grandmother never stopped crying, she had a day of mourning every Sunday. She dressed in black and lit a candle in front of Friedrich's picture, baked his favourite cake and cooked only the lunch dishes he liked.

ROBERT | A good classmate from primary school is on board. I have also met someone I used to play football with. Johannes moved from Charlottenburg when I was about ten, but he remembers me too. How about that—meeting two guys I used to know! We have a barber shop and even our own special china with 'Tirpitz' on it.

CARL | My brother was shot by the Brits just before they were evacuated from France. Killing my little brother was one of the last things Lord Gort's men did before they ran away like cowardly chickens. Since then this has become my war. I am ready to do anything at all, if only I get the chance. I hope the invasion of the British Isles comes soon, I'll bloody well be in the vanguard!

GOTTFRIED | Auntie once took me to a Chamber of Wonders. We went from room to room and looked at rarities and treasures kept in glass cases. Beautiful crystals, little Japanese trees, pieces of glass which changed colour in the light of a lamp which revolved slowly round itself. I began collecting all kinds of things that I could have in my own Chamber of Wonders. The other day I found a fine lump of amber on the beach at Rügen when we were on shore leave. The most important thing in my collection is the ancient coin I caught sight of in Oberstdorf during the Christmas holidays two years ago. It was a lucky coin, because the next day I received a letter from Elsa with a lock of her hair. The letter smelled of Elsa. A fragrance like her hair from all the times we danced in Clärchens Ballroom.

When we came out of the cinema with the cabaret music in our ears after seeing Marlene Dietrich as Lola Lola, I dared to try everything. You are lovelier than her, I said and kissed Elsa, and I meant every word. She must have realized that, because she let me kiss her once more. Each time we hear Dietrich sing, my heart winks at hers.

An American missionary, who made a speech at a Salvation Army meeting several years ago, said that in Ethiopia, there is a kind of baboon called "the bleeding heart baboon". On its chest, exactly over the heart, it has fur missing—there is a bare patch, only covered with light skin. When it gets ill or agitated, this patch becomes flaming red and beats wildly. I believe I already know what the baboon feels like. When Elsa came walking towards me the evening I was to leave, I felt my heart shining and so swollen up that she must have seen it through my brand new uniform jacket. "*Nicht zu Müde*". My love, I hope when I get leave…oh, Elsa, what a night we shall have then!

ROLF | In the Nürnberg laws it says that Jews and Aryans are not allowed to sleep together. At first Hannah and I delighted in breaking the law. Later we were simply terrified. Other mixed couples we knew landed up in prison when they were discovered.

Herr and Frau Melchior had their home looted and destroyed. God, how ashamed I am to be German! Father burst out. Mother said nothing. I went around the districts and saw the burnt-out synagogues, and when one of the Brownshirts stood waving a Torah scroll before he trampled on it, I felt scarlet shame beating in my ear canals. Afterwards another one came and set the remains on fire, but the others laughed and said maybe they should have saved the scroll for toilet paper. The shame changed into anger at my cowardice, I didn't dare go over and snatch the Torah out of the hands of the vandals.

Dear Hannah, where are you?

THERES | In the Bund Deutscher Mädel* we have been told to keep an eye on our parents and other grownups, and report if we see suspicious behaviour. I began listening to Mama's and Papa's conversations in the evenings, but it is difficult to know what they are allowed to talk about. And where am I going to live if they go to prison? Now Papa has gone away with Tirpitz, and I don't know when he will come back.

* The League of German Girls

Yesterday my brother said that the children at his school, and certainly at other places as well, have had to learn new prayers: "Führer, my Führer, whom the Lord has given me, guard and protect me as long as I live." And in addition they had to learn them by heart, he said and practised on me: "Dear Führer, we love you as much as Father and Mother. As we belong to them, we belong to you. Accept our love and trust, our Führer!" My teacher has told us that a warm touch of the Führer's hand can cure a cold, yes, and other illnesses as well. Now Hitler rules over a hundred million people.

Out with God and in with Hitler, muttered Mother when she heard the prayers. Should I report her?

CARL | Bloody British pigfuckers! They are more disgusting than blowflies in shit. No, bloody hell, I'm not drunk, don't try to take the bottle away from me! I'm going out to beat an Englishman flat, bash in his mug and kick his fat Jew-arse. Oh, I hate them, they are whores' children, all of them!

\

Dear Otto,

I saw from your letter that you have finished your exercises, and before you really set out for the war, I want to share some thoughts with you, things I never spoke of while I had the chance. It is about gratitude, because that is a powerful force. If one adopts gratitude as a way of life, one gets on much better. When you remember everything good you have around you, it becomes stronger and gives greater pleasure and more security, people become kinder, work lighter, your money grows, and most of all wisdom increases.

Good luck, dear Otto, take care. I sincerely hope that all will go well with you. We are thinking of you, all of us. I would soon have needed you in the timber forest, Gerhard is still too small, and Mother talks of nothing else but that you have to come home safe and sound.

God bless you.

Father

ROLF | At König-Wilhelm Gymnasium in Berlin we often quoted Goethe: "One must either conquer and rule, or serve and lose, suffer or triumph, be the anvil or the hammer." This idea recruited many to the Hitler Youth. Stephan and Gregor joined. Soon they didn't want to talk to "Little Marx", as they called me, any more. They were sure I was a communist because of Father. I and Stephan and Gregor were in the second class in middle school when Father was arrested and ended up in a camp, first in Oranienburg, then in Buchenwald. There he got hepatitis and became completely yellow. Once they thought he was asleep, he heard one of the nurses ask whether he would make it, and the doctor replied that with a protein diet, vitamins, glucose and Metionin he might have had a chance, but here, here he will soon fall into a coma, and then it's only a matter of a day or two. That was when Father entered into a pact with God, he told us. I would become healthy, and so I did. Afterwards everyone called me the Miracle.

Later there was an outbreak of typhus in the camp. It was then Father learned from the doctor that the moment you feel fever coming, you take two spoonfuls of your own urine, that is the only thing that helps. All the same, death was the most usual treatment in there, said Father quietly. He was released early in 1938. Don't know why. Mother said nothing but Father talked about the time in the camps. When we touch on anything difficult or sensitive at the dinner table, she usually disappears out into the kitchen, to fetch the salt. I suspect her of having voted for the National Socialists.

Father has been interned again recently, now in Dachau, I found out in a telegram. He has been too much of a bigmouth. I should have warned him more strongly, you can't say anything about the Party any longer, they have such long ears. Protest is futile, it is you that it harms, foolish Father, and there is nothing I can do.

FREGATTEN-KAPITÄN BIELER | Adolf Hitler inspected Tirpitz in May. It was a great occasion. In the picture sent to us afterwards, he is walking ahead, then come admirals and captains. One of them is looking up, the others, with the Führer at the head, look in front at the endless row of lined-up sailors. Hitler greets them. They are like human pillars, each individual feature wiped out. The uniform buttons are parallel, as if they are all the same height. Their shoes look like white piano keys, in a perfect row. The deck they are standing on is so shiny that the Führer's escort casts a shadow on it.

Everything is still spotless, and they were not thinking about war that day, all the sailors who held their breath when Hitler walked by. This is a game, the cannons, the stocks of ammunition, the drills, they are only exercises we are performing. Clearly mighty Germany ought to have a mighty fleet, of course.

Now it has been war for over two years. I understand that it is full of risks, while many of the young puppies around me still believe they are going to meet all the tin soldiers and wooden ships they played with as children.

ROLF | A priest stands waiting for me when we reach Gotenhafen. Father's heart did not tolerate the stress, he had a major heart infarct and died in the camp.

Father's arm around my shoulder, Father's warm arm has gone.

KASPAR | Even by Prussian standards Father was strict, I wish I had once seen him laugh heartily. The one thing I knew was: I didn't want to become like him.

To become the one I ought to be, I had to stop being what you brought me up to be, Father. If I had played you, it would have been in a minor key. “The mortality of all things moves my mind.” The quote from the Aeneid became my last greeting on your funeral wreath, I couldn’t express myself more personally.

I have not cried yet, several years have gone by now. You won, Father. Your way and nature won. I envy Rolf who is able to grieve.

GOTTFRIED | *Ich tanze mit dir*
in der Himmel hinein.

Elsa used to croon, nearly every night she sang these lines into my ear as we lay close on the same pillow. The night before I was to leave, she sang it several times, and I asked her to think of the words and of me every night, promise me, every single night. In that way you will say goodnight to me. Dear Elsa, let the song bring us together. Don’t forget:

Ich tanze mit dir
in den Himmel hinein.

RICKARD | Orders for mobilization. Now the war is waiting for Tirpitz. It churns in the stomach, the queue in front of the toilets is so long.

Oh, Gudrun, now it’s beginning. I am afraid.

CARL | The exercises are over, they are working triple shifts in the shipyard, the final overhaul of Tirpitz before we set out. Hey, war, now we’re on the way!

We have been drilled and drilled. At last we’re going to join in building the Third Reich. Steal the Englishmen’s empire, shift it to Berlin! Europe is going to be compensated by Germany. The Führer will lead us all the way.

Come on, planes, I will joyfully shoot you down! As soon as the air raid siren is heard, I will be there, ready to squash every single louse in the RAF pilot's hair. Royal Air Force, the puffed-up Brits believe everything becomes so much more distinguished if they put 'royal' in front of it all. Tirpitz has the world's best anti-aircraft guns, I will pepper them, hit the fuel tanks so we'll see free fireworks! Come on, Jew cunts, I'll take you, one by one, as fast as you show yourselves in the sky.

GUSTAV | Lord, let my soul ripen before it is harvested.
Let me receive a whole life's experiences.
Let me receive a lifespan—a human life.

\

"Are you writing a letter to your girlfriend on the first evening? You haven't been together long, I assume."

"Come with us, Helmut is playing the tango on his mouth organ, the dance that yearns for home."

"...and we WILL get home safely," as Valdo says.

"Useless. Frittering away our time, that's how it has been in the Baltic. Nothing but exercises and drills."

"Now we'll get to have a go!"

"Last night there were a lot who pulled their dicks, you who are new just have to get used to the sound of wanking from the hammocks.
And the smell! Athlete's foot mixed with haircream. Dirty feet."

"Are you the ship's poet, you? In the queue for the loo you have time to make poems, or you can do crosswords. Don't be careless shaving, come on, come on!"

"Our ships sunk seven destroyers, we lost three, it said on the radio today."

"I hear the voice of the new guy whispering Our Father, over and over again, are we totally off our rockers here now, or what?"

"Remember, we're going to get home safely."

"The war is sad and heavy
for us sailors on the open sea
For all the time we're sailing
over our drowning destiny."

"Shut up!"

Winston Churchill:

"The whole strategy of the war turns at this period on this ship."

II

Fættenfjord, winter and spring 1942

MARI | A shadow. Is it a ghost, it must be a boat, no, a huge ship, with several turrets! More and more of the ship is gliding forward past the tongue of land that sticks out into the fjord. I can't move, I know I ought to have run to Father and told him what I am seeing, but what if they shoot! So many men on board, as soundless as the ship. They are not allowed to be here, that is why everything is so quiet. I'm not allowed either. Mother's waiting, I should have been home helping her fold linen tablecloths, she needs me to hold the end tightly and go towards her when the cloth is folded. Now the war is coming here.

FREGATTEN-KAPITÄN BIELER | We'll soon be there, Tirpitz is gliding onward easily and happily, borne on the white-crested waves she keeps to 25 knots. What a magnificent machine she is. We are to go north, the admirals decided. Because "the sea off Norway will be the fateful area of the war" according to Hitler.

FRITZ | It's freezing cold standing here in the wind. I've never experienced such tremendous coldness or such a dark January day, but sailing into Trondheimsfjord I want to see for myself, even though I have a free watch. We are steering quietly past a landscape with knolls and islands. Mother's thick jersey warms me under the uniform. It smells of hope here, I feel, survival, home-coming, all the good things I can think of, the smell of the sea spray. We need not fear the Norsemen, only the British submarines and their harrying planes. Fortunately we are safe on Tirpitz, everyone thinks so.

Whatever happens, said Mother before I left, think about us and stay alive, don't sacrifice yourself, it isn't worth it. She looked at me, it was as if she was demanding an assurance with her eyes, I had to promise her to come home, unscathed.

OLAV | The nor'wester bites our cheeks. We are out fishing when we suddenly catch sight of something that comes gliding out of nowhere…an enormous ship! I don't see the name but behind it follows a smaller vessel which says 'Bruno Heinemann' on it. Then come some others which must be destroyers, or perhaps torpedo boats. Instinctively I haul in the net, as if the hooks might snag in something so huge. Must get ourselves ashore. Must report to the right guys.

HEINZ | Before I didn't know the difference between ocean, sea and fjord. Now I have learned that there are fjords in Norway, Alaska, Chile and New Zealand; they are long arms or branches of water going inwards into the landscape.

ROLF | Withered roses stick up through the snow at one of the farms, I see them through the telescope. Minus 17, a lot of turquoise in the colours of the sky. The ground down by the beach is covered in glittering frost. One can see the brightness in the absent light.

\

Source:
THETA
MOST SECRET
"The Admiral von Tirpitz, six destroyers and several U-boats were lying in an arm of the Aasen fjord in Trondheimsfjord on the 29th of January '42. Four of the destroyers have left. There are 100 aeroplanes stationed at Vaernes."

OTTO | We are five cannoneers in my team in D turret and we are four seasons, so to speak. Only discipline keeps us together. I don't fit in here with these city boys who are as nervous as rabbits. The Brits don't know how easy it is to put us out of action, or they would have sent bomber planes here at once. The only consolation is that they are probably in equally bad shape.

I can't stop thinking about the old psychic woman. The one who lived in the brown house at the edge of the forest. We were actually a bit scared of her, but she was often sent for if someone got a septic finger, if goats went missing while grazing, or a thousand other things. One day she came walking straight towards me, waving her arm, hunch-backed and ugly. Witch, I thought, and regretted it at once, she could certainly read minds. I thought, what does she want with me? "Come, come closer, there is something I have to tell you." I stiffened as if the marrow in my backbone had frozen. She took me tightly by the hand and said: "You are going to be on a gigantic ship, and when it is lying off an island far towards the north, in the autumn darkness, you should not stand in the turret." "Eh, what turret?" I said. "Wait, there are several..." she said. "C. Don't stand in C turret," she gazed penetratingly at me and left. Two years later I enlisted on Tirpitz and was to be assigned to one of the cannon turrets. C or D, I heard it murmured when my place was being discussed. "D", I said so loudly and forcefully that they simply looked at me and said: "That's fine. D it is."

OLAV | Early in the spring survey boats came here, and the fjord was charted and reinforced. Then followed smoke-screen practice, laying out of torpedo and submarine nets, and pillboxes for anti-aircraft emplacements on freestanding hillocks. The work was carried out by Norwegian workers for

German and Norwegian contractors. Oh yes, that's the way it was. We had no idea why this work was being done, what all the effort was for. We speculated, but that it was Tirpitz, the largest of all battleships, which was to make its entrance, no, nobody believed that. It was almost an honour, in our little neck of the fjord. "I nearly believed it was the island, Saltøya, that had gone adrift when I saw Tirpitz coming," said an old fellow I talked with.

KASPAR | Just beyond the anchorage lies Steinvikholmen fort. One of the officers said that the place was a centre of power in the sixteenth century, but the last Catholic archbishop who lived there had to flee the country. Yesterday we were allowed to take a small boat and row there on our free watch. We walked around the little island for several hours, even though it was cold. We looked out through the arrow slits, and felt the thick, thick walls. The fort has two towers as well. History breathes out there. I can almost see them in front of me, the men of the Middle Ages, the bonfire with whole roast suckling pig, song and dance, masses with choirboys and incense, kneeling nuns, soldiers and observation posts where a lookout is kept for enemy ships on their way into the fjord. Good to escape from our own time.

ROLF | How they laughed, the two Norsemen, when I pointed in the direction I wanted to go and tried to pronounce the name Vuddudalen. "No, not voodoo, Vuddu!" It's delightful to get out into nature, one is never alone on board. The hammocks are set so close that we jostle each other when it's rough. Now I'm going to go on a long trip, I haven't skied for over two years. I remember the winters when we visited Grandfather and Grandmother and skied all day until we were called in and given steaming mutton soup. My body has not forgotten it. Find a grip on the sticks, rush off, away, below zero temperature and moonlight, can't get any better than that! Must be careful that nobody sees me, we know that the Englishmen have had drops in the area. If I'm unlucky, I'll run straight into a trained parachute soldier, or an over-eager Norseman who wants to fight with a butcher's knife or an old hunting rifle. I can get away from most of them, Englishmen, and in any case, I don't believe there are many skiers on the islands in the Atlantic. Warm under my cap, the snow is creaking exactly as it ought to, and I am free, free, free! I feel my chest expanding and filling with the good winter air instead of the used ship air. Soon I'll set off outwards, down towards the beach and the fjord where Tirpitz towers in the darkness. Good gliding, I'll work up a hell of a speed, but a broken leg wouldn't be the worst now that several of us might be shifted to U-boats. Cramped U-boats, exploding mines. People keep dying that way, lots of them.

Should I throw myself against the spruce tree there, hope for a small break injury? No. Duty. Careful, plough downwards, reach the hammock and simply go to bed and hope for the war to end soon. Above me I see the same stars as at Grandmother and Grandfather's. I ask them to give greetings.

\

Dearest Elisabeth,

Nobody knows the realm of love, the red spots on the map. For what is happening in you, what is directing you to act as you do? No order in the language of love, a language nobody has managed to translate. I know only that love has strengthened me since the day I first saw you, and death has taken my measure since the day I was handed out a uniform in my size.

Love is commitment. Never rest, because even in such a strong love one cannot save the other. A life together, in which we feel more than merely each one of us. Know that you have been the best part of my every day!

Yours
Andreas

HEDWIG | When one becomes pregnant the first time one makes love with someone, it must be a sign that it will be us, that we belong together, Fritz and I. When Mother understood what had resulted from Fritz's last leave, she was not angry. She said it would be all right. It was a relief, because I had been quite beside myself, upside-down and a little crazy. I began tasting the ashes when I lit the oven! At night when I am going to sleep, I imagine that my belly is going to rip, and that I will be broken to bits and die during the birth. Mother calms me down, saying all women at all times have managed this, so you will do it too, Hedwig, even though you are young. I think about Fritz a lot. Haven't heard anything for a long time, but that does not mean the worst, says Mother. It must be fairly safe in Norway. All the same I am anxious that our child might be fatherless before it is born. Because I, who don't even believe I have the strength to be a mother, how could I be both mother and father? I must put my trust in the Führer. Soon we will all be living in the thousand-year empire, where there will be no poverty or insecurity.

I often speak to Fritz's sister. She has not told her parents I am going to have a child, she thinks her father will be angry. Must hope they can help me, a little anyway. The winter is so hard this year. Mother and I have used up nearly all the coal already. I must of course think about a name and the baptism too. I wish Fritz was here, I don't know what to call the child, what name does he like? Perhaps he wants the little one to be named after his grandfather or grandmother, or his uncle, if it doesn't bring bad luck that he fell in the last war. I don't know what he would like. The only thing I know is that if it is a boy, and I get a message that Fritz is dead, the child will be called Fritz. But one mustn't even think like that.

KONRAD | Several days without a proper spread on the bread. Not so much as a little bowl of jam. I dream of boiled ox tongue, a little cheese and egg on Sundays. Salt meat for lunch, bacon and peas, not only fish. Herring and cod. Now I have been thinking about food for a whole day, what is happening to me?

KURT | Look out for periscopes. All the time they are hunting us, the submarines. Seeing a periscope is seeing death. If we discover one, we have to fire rapidly before they have time to shoot torpedoes at us. So often I think I see something.

FRITZ | Nobody I know has come home from the Eastern Front. Nobody! To be able to enlist on Tirpitz is pure luck. Because I want to survive. I want so very much to live, come home and get a job, marry Hedwig, my girl, that is fine to think about. I felt she was the right one, the very first time we met! In her last letter she said that her belly is swelling fast, I can hardly imagine it. Becoming a father. I should have been at home with her, but it's quite impossible to get leave now, just have to wait.

Andreas, on the contrary, sees it differently. Every night he fantasizes about escape, that we must do it now if we are to survive the war. Tirpitz is one of the Brits' main objectives, we know that, they will never give up until they sink us, he whispers. Perhaps the bomb technicians and engineers in England have perfected a new type of bomb right now, light enough that planes can reach us from bases in north Scotland. We are not safe here, we must go away, don't you get it, I don't want to drown in flaming oil. It isn't far to the Swedish border, you know that, you too, don't be so cowardly. Are you going to stay here like another bedbug? In Sweden they take good care of deserters, we can wait until it is all over, then we'll be off home and do ordinary things like walking on a floor which is at rest, instead of the deck which is always rocking. I want to be ordinary again, wear a coat and hat and not a uniform. I want to sleep in a bed, not in a hammock together with over two thousand men who are waiting to be blown to bits. I want to be with Elisabeth again before I die, in two months she'll be twenty-one, I want to be with her then, I love her, and she must get to hear it. I have to run away. Don't you understand, it isn't worth my life and yours, we are meant for something else, something meaningful.

His voice begins to fade, soon he will be quiet, I know him, he has to blow off steam every night, I am his ventilator of course, but if the walls have ears, he'll be severely punished for such talk. Of course I agree, of course I long to be home, and yes, I too believe that new bomber planes will come with death in their cargo holds. I would love to see Hedwig and all the others again. To taste Mummy's Sunday meatballs and stewed apples with real cream for dessert. I too long to do everyday things like taking Hedwig to the cinema and kissing in secret. Or go fishing. Watch Hertha Berlin play home games at the Plumpe stadium.

Perhaps I'll go with Andreas, perhaps the only sensible thing is to flee to Sweden?

OLAV | Quite often English reconnaissance planes pass over Skatval, surely relieved to have survived the anti-aircraft guns on Tirpitz, while we are chopping alder and birch. Other young men are flying over us, they could not have been very different from us. The most dangerous weapon I have seen is Father's elk rifle. A plane flying past, with a mission in the war, and here we stand, in sweaty wool jerseys, looking up, like kids.

I am attracted to the ship, want to be close to it. There are jobs available, such a big ship needs a lot of ants on land, that is what you imagine yourself to be, tiny beside the colossus, like a grain of sugar against a milk pail. Oh yes, the technology fascinates me, and the weaponry, imagine: she has four cannon turrets. I pass on reports of everything I see.

OTTO | I'm hoping for a dry grave. From earth you have come. God, let me have a proper grave with a cross and flowers. To the earth you shall return.

ANDREAS | Must scramble across to Sweden as fast as possible. This night will either be the last in my life, or the first in my new one.

I know where to go. There ahead, beyond the darkness, lies my hope, I have to do it. I go for you, Elisabeth.

FREGATTEN-KAPITÄN BIELER | The atmosphere on board has not been the same since the Bismarck was sunk with two thousand men. The vulnerability at the helm, which was exposed on our sister ship, keeps upsetting our officers. The admirals should have postponed putting the Bismarck into battle until Tirpitz was ready, alone she became too vulnerable. Only nine days out on her first assignment, she sank. Only a hundred survived, it is said.

ROLF | Every free watch I go up on the hill and draw. I have packed pencils and sticks of charcoal in tarpaulin and hidden them all under a stone beside a large sallow tree. I am working on several subjects. The evening light in the sky is delicate here, the spruce trees so dark green that they appear grey, the silhouette of the ship brutally breaks up the ambience of nature, which had been the same for thousands of years, until we came.

So different from evenings in Berlin. We used to sit in the 'Die Neue Welt' beer hall after work, Bernhard and I. Drink ourselves into a stupor, not talk about politics. Let it all disappear. At last we stopped going there, because everyone had to listen to Hitler's radio speeches, some big loudspeakers were rigged up. Hannah didn't risk coming there anymore. Soon there were no places left to hide away. We had to stay at home.

Drills and routines. Cunt and prick talk, detective stories which have been read to pieces, card games, three months in the same underpants. Must draw the other things, the clean ones.

UWE | The alarm. I hear the dogs too, someone must have run away. If they're caught, it's only the bullet in the back of the neck that's left. Deserters are condemned to death. If the right kind of Norseman finds them, they get the same treatment, others will help them in the direction of the Swedish border. It's playing for high stakes with your life, if you ask me.

FRITZ | Felix comes running. Andreas, he shouts, Andreas has run away, it's our Andreas they're searching for, hurry up! Andreas, good lord, how could you be so stupid! They're going to shoot you! I know how angry I'll be, the anger is running down over the cold anxiety and stiffening. I spoke to him earlier today, I didn't notice anything unusual then. Perhaps he was thinking it was the last time he would see me. We who knew each other a little from before and had hammocks close to each other and have been such good friends. Even though I have Hedwig and he is engaged to Elisabeth, we still discuss whether Eva or Rosa was the best of the Broch sisters, or perhaps the lovely Helena whom I suggest in between, and Andreas grins. Now he is running on the mountain here, with the taste of blood in his mouth, surely he hears the dogs, knows they won't lose the trail if they find it. How am I going to be able to tell this to Elisabeth? Deserter. Nobody likes them.

The dogs are quiet now, I don't know whether this is a good or bad sign. Suddenly I think of something, and go to his hammock, and yes, there lies a card to Elisabeth.

\

To Elisabeth, my dearest in the world

You are one of those who calls the sea ocean and gulls swans, and I go around loving you with a heart that grows too big for my body, I am tearing open my ribs to give space to all of you.

When this reaches you, I would've escaped, but don't be afraid, remember that my lucky animal is the hedgehog which protects its soft breast with the sharpest prickles.

Soon I will come home, and then we will love each other to bits.

Yours,
Andreas

BOOTSMANN SPIEDEL | Last week there was a state of emergency, and our boys helped out, walked around on the roads after eight o'clock to see that everyone was obeying the curfew and blackout orders. They often leaned on young people who were only going to visit each other, or people who were running late on their way home from a funeral. We have orders to let such people pass, no grounds for unnecessary provocation.

"Hello, fellows, fresh fish, are you going to buy fresh fish today? Best quality. Halibut and haddock. *Feine fische.*" The smiling Norwegian yodels from his rowing boat, we'll have to send someone down to buy a little, then, to get some peace.

BERIT | Naval Shipyard Drontheim, it's addressed so grandly these days. At Nyhavna, where the gigantic submarine bunkers are being built, there's jobs for cleaning women. So good to get away from home. If it weren't for the war and all the jobs one can get suddenly, I would have had to stay at home at the farm, as a servant for Father and my brothers until Doomsday. All I get there is scolding because the porridge has lumps in it, because the cheese doesn't turn out as good as Mother's, because the bread isn't baked properly. Also, I have to bear my brothers taunting that I'm ugly and will never get married. I ran off when I heard that Anna, cousin of Eline at the neighbouring farm, had got a job at the shipyard in Trondheim.

So handsome he is, the fellow from the big battleship. He was here for some kind of training for a few days, he said, seems a bit shy, clearly interested all the same. He can't know that I have seen him before, that there he stood, the man from my dream.

I recognized him as soon as I saw him, and couldn't help staring. He laughed, came over and said he was called Gottfried.

ANDREAS | In summertime Father and I broke in the foals at Uncle's little stud farm. Got them used to halters and handling. When we came up the hillsides where they were grazing, we could hear the herd coming, hordes of horses galloping across the meadow. A stirring spectacle. A cavalry without riders, immense muscles in play. As if from another era, when the forests were full of wild horses. Father had salt and oats with him, that stopped them. Soon the smallest foals came towards us, as curious as they were afraid.

On the way to Sweden, this is one of the memories I relish. It keeps me going.

FRITZ | After Andreas ran away, frost had settled on the ground and the dogs could not follow his trail. That is why he still hasn't been caught, because suddenly it got cold.

OTTO | We're being watched, obviously we know that. The radio transmitters nearby give the Brits regularly updated weather forecasts, so they may plan when to do their bombing raids. Every single young Norwegian is a possible spy. They are crafty too, I know of a guard who was fooled by a man with a violin case on the back of his cycle. What do you have in it, asked the guard, a radio, answered the Norwegian, the guard laughed and let him pass without checking, but later we got to hear that the Gestapo had caught a man with a radio in a violin case. *Scheisse!*

DIETER | At last an execution on board. Now he'll get it, the cowardly bastard, thought he'll escape from Tirpitz! It's a good thing our border guards got him.

ANDREAS | There's a mattress behind me, and suddenly I

understand why. It isn't to make my fall softer, it'll stop the bullets from ricocheting and hitting the firing squad.

Elisabeth!

FRITZ | Andreas was sunk in the sea yesterday. The body in the water. No ceremony, only silence, hidden grief and shock. We got to see what they are willing to do if we don't obey.

Today it is Palm Sunday with a service at ten o'clock. There will be music and Holy Communion. At home people sit out on benches drinking coffee after Mass at Easter, and it's always sunny in the warmth of spring. My absolute favourite is when the magnolia tree blossoms on bare twigs and we can walk under them feeling happy and light. Instead we are surrounded by snow, there is such a fierce wind that we can't be out on deck, on our holiday.

I try not to weep for Andreas, turn my thoughts towards Mother, she always used to read the story of Jesus' Passion aloud to us when we were small, giving us boiled eggs and Easter lilies. At school we had to compare the Evangelists' versions of the Easter message, see how different they are, all so powerful. I truly try to think through the idea that Jesus took our guilt upon himself and died so that we should experience grace and eternal life. There can never have been more sin to atone for than now. I think about all that is happening, how it must hurt God that our own people shot Andreas, or that the general orders in the Navy are not to pick up British sailors from lifeboats and rafts. We are not even to save those paddling in the water shouting, there might be submarines nearby. They call on the same God as us from the rafts, but he is not to hear their prayers.

Do you want to let Jesus or Barabbas go? How guilty Barabbas must have felt, when he skulked away as Jesus took the cross on his back and started on the way of suffering.

Andreas walked on the mountain here and we are on the Via Dolorosa of the sea, on the way to Golgotha which lies there before us. Perhaps we'll be torpedoed tomorrow, or bombed on Good Friday. No, there isn't much of an Easter atmosphere on Tirpitz.

Wonder what the officers are going to write to Andreas' mother and Elisabeth?

Dear Kaspar,

I have bad news, dearest twin brother, Granny died yesterday. She got pneumonia a week ago and quickly got weaker and weaker. We nursed her at home. It isn't possible to get a place in a hospital any more, they are full of wounded soldiers, but Dr Klein said there was nothing we could do in any case, she was just withering away, as if she didn't want to live any longer. She asked about you the night before she died. Wondered where you are, and if you are all right, if you are in action, in battle. We are all wondering about that. We hope and pray that you are safe. I am glad I am a girl, that I don't have to be in it. I don't think Granny wished to see how the war would end, she said she was afraid it wouldn't go well, and we would all be killed in an inferno, that Hamburg city centre and the districts around us would be bombed and burned.

The priest was here in the afternoon, she took Holy Communion, and we sang psalms together. She died peacefully, took a few very deep breaths, trembled, and then it was over. No struggle in death, fortunately. The funeral will be on Monday. It is a pity you can't be with us and carry the coffin. She loved you so much, Kaspar. Talked about you all the time after you were called up. I know she was afraid for you, she always read the newspaper very carefully to see if it said anything about Tirpitz. It is a long time since it has said anything now.

Are you still lying low? I hope so. Come home healthy, you must promise me that! Kaspar, stay alive, that is the only important thing. I am going to weave a wreath of white lilac and put it on the coffin, Granny was so fond of the scent of white lilac. Then I am going to put a big red rose in the wreath, that will be from you. The ceremony will be splendid, don't worry about it, I know you will be upset when you read this, it is so sad, we all feel it. Helga goes around crying all the time.

Take care, Kaspar, we all love you very much. Greetings from Mother, and Helga sends flying kisses among the tears. May God protect you!

Love
Hildegard

ROLF | You haven't seen spring evenings until you have seen them in Norway. Suddenly spring is here, the days have become so long, the mountains are gilded in the late sun, flocks of geese come in formation, honking right above us.

The weather is clear, good conditions for British attacks, so we don't get much sleep. And listening for planes, who can sleep? There is quite a wind too, which makes the smokescreen less secure. The smoke may easily drift away, and then one of the RAF's hawks will catch sight of us, a huge shining fish, and it has only to take careful aim and consign the cargo to Death.

How many millions of soldiers are lying awake tonight and thinking this might be their final hour? Everyone in the Navy who knows they are sailing over mines, everyone on the Eastern Front who is being driven out, all the civilians who draw the blackout curtains and hope the Blitz-rain will hold off just for tonight, all who are praying and weeping, or staring apathetically out into the night with red sandpaper eyes. There is only one thing that has any meaning, getting through all this alive. Turn homewards, gamble on the world becoming ordinary again, wait for peace, for the white flag. Get a normal life, be able to have a bath whenever you like, read a book, go to a café with Hannah, shovel droppings out of the dovecote, whatever. Anything is better than this, lying every night, waiting. Death breathes on you, an ice-cold breath, is it you it's going to claim tonight? It stands beside your hammock, and you know that now, now it is finished, while the ship takes in water and everything keels over and it is too late to write a greeting home.

In the mornings it is easier, standing looking at the corn sending up shoots, the fields were grey-brown, now they have a green tinge. After another long night of gentle spring rain the land is verdigris green. The early months pass, it will be summer soon, then follows harvest-time, and eventually snow will fall again. What is common to the seasons, what overshadows the small shifts in nature, is the unnatural—war. A world war which is here too. It is difficult not to think of it as one is standing looking at the growing corn. The bird cherry which is coming into bloom.

These are peaceful days. Tirpitz lies at a good anchorage, and we go fishing. It can be nice at times. Hair bleaches in the sun which is up almost round the clock. I have never looked more Aryan. I understand the Norwegians being angry with us and spitting on us when we go ashore for shopping. The men are afraid that we will take their girls, but really we are only longing for our own, back home.

Suddenly there are dark stripes on the fjord, that means rain is coming. How grey it can turn in the bay when the clouds hang so low that they look like fog. I hear the train pass, how lucky are those folks who can simply travel further. The rain will drench our uniforms and make everything unpleasant. Raw and chilly, lying in the hammock half-cold, half-wet, longing for home and warmth and freedom. To get away from this meaningless dance-school discipline. The ship's captain keeps Tirpitz in peak condition, every day we have to polish or oil something which does not need polishing or greasing. They keep us up to the mark, so if we are alert the day the RAF finds us, maybe we'll get to smokescreen the ship before we all become crab food or married to mermaids…

KASPAR | I remember the way the turquoise glass vase scattered the light against the white shelf in Grandmother's rainbow den when it was sunny. Funny, kind Grandmother who was so absorbed in having *von* in her name. It is the rainbow den that I fly to on the nights I toss in the hammock and can't go to sleep. As I am lying down listening for the air raid siren, I try to float home to Grandmother. Carefully I pick up the vase and hold it up to the light, and let the world become light green and a little blue. Grandmother got the vase from her mother, who got it from the Kaiser's sister, and Grandmother didn't dare to even put flowers in it. It was only when she wasn't there that I picked it up, and now she is gone for good.

The thought of throwing the vase out of the window to see it shatter in the street was the most exciting of all. To see a thousand pieces of turquoise glass glittering—that is how I fall asleep at last in the rainbow den and wake up either from fleas or the cold. Grandmother, here I am. Yes, take out the gold-rimmed coffee cups, fetch the fruit cake, and then you can tell the story about when your mother got the vase from the Kaiser's very own sister. Didn't she once come here for coffee and sit in the chair we call the Kaiser's chair, the one we were never allowed to play with?

ELISABETH | Be a Veronica who wipes the forehead of Jesus on the way to Golgotha with the cross on his back! Be a Veronica for every exhausted soldier!

The pockmarks on your cheek, to think that I would find them attractive. It can only mean one thing: I miss and love you, Andreas. Why don't I hear anything from you?

Hope is God's most important gift. I try to remember your whole face, not only the scars, but it becomes more and more fuzzy to me. Might it be because you are dead, that we just haven't been notified yet? Fritz has been home, but didn't come to see me, is that a bad sign? It is so long since you left, and I can't visualize the curve of your jawline, Andreas. I know that your eyes are brown, but don't remember which shade. I think I can say they are a soft brown, like a small animal's eyes, Andreas. You are a head taller than me, but I can't recall how it feels to rest against your chest. Your scent, no. You have disappeared, time has wiped you out. Let me find you again!

KONRAD | Something is moving quickly in the bushes, I stiffen, take hold of the rifle, then I see a boy among the sallow branches, he looks at me, what do you want, I shout to him in a kind of German- Norwegian. "I'm guarding the bird's nest," he says seriously, "I'm afraid someone might harm the eggs."

GOTTFRIED | I have learned "I love you" in Norwegian, now I only have to say it to Berit before we have to go north. Otherwise I must say it to Elsa when I get home, she'll think it's fun. She'll never get to know about Berit. I couldn't resist. Berit was too lovely. It surely isn't so bad either, everyone does the same thing, after all.

FREGATTEN-KAPITÄN BIELER | Berlin has realized it at last. So now we are steering out, on the way to Altafjord, and hunting convoys! That Bismarck went down has become a trauma in the Navy, and the security regulations before we go into battle have become so comprehensive that we have been completely gagged, while the shortage of fuel has added to the risk. We are eager for combat, ready to avenge our sister ship. Impatient, restless muscles longing to be used.

We are approaching cruising speed, passing 25 knots. Delightful to feel how she surges ahead. What engines we have, a gigantic speedboat!

\

"We are here to be of use. Unused torpedoes are a shame."

"But now a convoy is on the way, the ship will be readied, quick, quick, quick!"

"We can go straight at it. Five columns, starboard. Ten degrees. Ready to fire. Charged. Stay on course, Ludwig, the convoy is almost unprotected, I don't think it has destroyers."

"Destroyer, that's an accurate name."

"What the devil, are we turning NOW?"

"I often think about Artemis and the hunter who saw her naked. She turned him into a deer with thoughts and feelings, but not speech. He was killed by his own fellow-hunters, because he could not say who he was."

"Stop chucking your education in my face. We swore the same oath. You're no better than me."

"The finger which crooked itself around the trigger. Tightened. Pressed. Hard inwards. Aimed the finger at the face. The eye."

"Don't remind me of it. He was a deserter, got what he deserved!"

"Where is the bang coming from? The recoil. The sound of the body falling. The gunsmoke which vanishes with the echo."

"Shut up!"

"Didn't even get to lean over the rail, it ran down my uniform, grey vomit, the stink persisted, I had to get a new uniform."

Bogen, summer 1942

FREGATTEN-KAPITÄN BIELER | On the way south from Alta after the brief attack which was broken off far too early in my opinion, we run into bad weather. I am reminded of the story of Rainer who was swept overboard by a wave and lifted back on board again by the next one. He became religious afterwards, talked about having felt the hand of God, not so strange, that.

This must be the Deluge, how it rains! Can we use Tirpitz as an ark? I joke with the others on the bridge. Should we collect two of everything and begin again?

It wasn't so bad that time, the weather forecast was exaggerated. For a bit of a change, on the free evenings I go to the officers' mess to listen to the radio, always such good music, melodies like the sad '*Ein Soldat am Wolgastrand*'. Best of all is Zarah Leander with '*Kann denn Liebe Sünde sein*'.

On 8 July we arrive in Ofoten after the tour into the Arctic Ocean, a bit shaken up after the unfortunate attack from what was probably a Russian submarine. The most humiliating thing is that the Luftwaffe could claim the entire victory after the Brits, in a panic, must have spread the convoy out. Here in Bogen it is midsummer and peace.

OTTO | The cries of the seagulls pierce through everything. They shriek so often and so much that the sound continues ringing in my ears at night. When at last I have dozed off, I get woken up by other birds which already begin the day at about two o'clock because it is so light. It gets on my nerves, but who is one to complain to? Ship's captain, sir, I'm going crazy from the seagulls, would you kindly remove them?

KASPAR | I remember the woman who unexpectedly said to me several years ago: You're going to be surrounded by greenery. She was known to be a healer, when she thought about people they became well, but she always had to lie down afterwards, because the pain went through her. Now I have the greenery around me. I have never seen anything greener than the forests in this part of Norway.

I walk around like Rousseau wandering in the forest of St Germain. It emits a smell, no, fragrance. The air is full of it, replete and heavy. Suddenly it is as if I can see myself from outside. It is only my body which has put on the uniform, not me.

Later I see the mackerel clouds through the porthole, they are tinged pink and coral-red by the midnight sun, the clouds calm me down, and slowly I get to sleep again, even though it is difficult when there is so much light, I might as well have sat on the deck reading a book, now in the middle of the night! This must be what Gogol means when he writes about "white nights", or is it Dostoevsky, I can no longer remember what Granny read to me, I am so tired.

The summer here is abnormally intense, the birdsong is experienced almost as noise in the nights, up on the hill sits a persistent woodpecker, every single day it pecks and pecks, I don't understand how it doesn't get a headache.

FRITZ | *Die Wasche liegt im Spinde*
geordret, blank und fein,
wie mich's gelehrt zu Hause
mein liebes Mutterlein

If I read the verse from the linen cupboard at home enough times, I usually calm down. Clear weather is bombing weather, and I can't sleep at night either. The sun stands high in the sky at two o'clock in the night—it's abnormal. Switch it off, dear God, switch off the light! Only this verse can take away the restlessness. It lets me smell the scent of sundried cloth. There are only a few days until my leave. Soon Hedwig is going to give birth.

BOOTSMANN SPIEDEL | It is a distant thought that I was in the group of artists *Der Blaue Reiter* in Munich, we were well known at that time, long ago, at any rate Vasiliy Kandinsky and Franz Marc were. I was more on the fringe, only seventeen or eighteen years old. It was a hard time when Franz invited the *Die Brücke* group up from Berlin. The evening the joint exhibition opened, we nearly came to blows. How important all that was! All the same it didn't take long for me to forget all of it. The last war put an end to the whole of *Der Blaue Reiter* in no time, and Kandinsky had to go back to Russia. I myself was called up, there was total mobilization, and after some months in the Navy I had forgotten all I knew, and my hands had become calloused and stiff. The fingers which had been used on the trigger felt wrong to paint with. Besides, the subjects I saw from the cruiser I was serving on were gone the moment that we went past. After a while my sense of colour disappeared too, then I simply wanted to put my service weapon to my temple. The war needed me, I heard, and I just had to learn to accept that my time as a painter was gone. Home again I didn't make contact with Franz, instead I sold my artist's materials for a bargain price to a young boy devoid of talent. The Navy swallowed me up, suddenly I had become a junior officer, and then it was war again, and I ended up here on Tirpitz, where nothing happens.

But today I had a magnificent experience. For the first time I experienced what Kandinsky always talked about, that music has colours! Synaesthesia, his and Schönberg's great idea, which I understood nothing about at that time. I and some other officers were asked in by Öberfahnrich Röll, he was playing a gramophone record when I came in. The piece was unknown to me, but there and then I saw that the cello parts were cognac-brown, and the violas deep burgundy. The oboe almost milk-white! When the French horn came in suddenly, it became dark green around me. I rubbed my eyes and wondered whether the others were in the same state, but nothing suggested it, they just sat with their cigars and small talk. The feeling was so violent that I blamed a headache, which was as good as true, because my head was expanding itself.

In my cabin I feel the joy coming, I have the ability as well! Afterwards, whiplashes of sorrow that the wars have taken the art from me, that I find myself on a battleship and not bent over a large canvas while I listen to music and paint the colours in the movement I hear. I see a picture right in front of me: I want to paint Castor and Pollux as young men on horseback, when they come to talk to Simonides, and thus save his life while the house topples behind him. The riders will be blue, blue and in B minor.

OTTO | The cornfields stand so beautifully on the plains beyond the fjord here, no sign of weeds. Food sways in the wind, a reliable dance with strong ears, heavy and yellow, which in time will be bread, will be porridge, will be life sustaining God's loan, as Granny calls it. It will be a good yield here, although we are so far north.

From the deck I can see corn-crows gathering in the twilight, some of the farmers have been threshing today, sun-yellow field-gold cut and bound up and set on poles, quite different from what I am used to back home, but the corn-crows are the same. There must be hundreds of them, the trees are black with birds. Granny used to say they hold parliaments, that they have a queen crow who makes decisions. Strange to stand here thinking about her, while the scent of ripe corn comes in small puffs of air, right out here to the ship. I should have been at home helping out now. Gathering straw into heaps and setting fire to it, like when Gerhard and I were small and always played Indians, while the orange and remarkably close August moon sailed slowly up across the sky and one could see the first weak star lighting up.

CARL | "You have a heart of iron and lead in your blood. You monster!" he said. I lashed out. After the fight I got respect, not friendship. Now they would risk their lives if they said anything sarcastic to me or anything nasty about me. I want their fear, creeping, grovelling, one look from me and they would piss themselves. Yes, that's what I wanted. A bit too much. Too quick to use my fists. Degraded like the Hitler Youth leader in South Munich. Devil in the cunt! Far from women and parties and cars, yes, everything you can only dream of without power, because I'm not that pretty, or that clever, smart, important or rich. Only power differentiates Kaiser from common man, countess from fishwife.

KASPAR | The danger is that you begin to identify yourself with the enemy, that's what they want us to unlearn. When you see them, you realize the similarities they share with you and then think about them soon dying, and that it is you who have them in your sights, ready to fire. It's the Brits today, us tomorrow, don't forget that.

During shore leave I meet grey Russians mumbling prayers, they drag themselves past me on the road, but one of them raises his head, defiantly. I think of Goya's picture 'The Executions 3 May 1808'. It is said that the painting saved Goya himself from the death sentence. He shifted over to Napoleon's side, and when the Spanish king returned, his life hung on by a slender thread, right up until King Ferdinand saw the picture and let Goya continue as court painter. The force in the picture I can remember clearly, the man in the white shirt with his arms outstretched as if to be bound on a cross, but also the struggle, strength and bewilderment mixed together. The picture smells of terror, now I am able to sense that smell in reality. These Russian prisoners must have escaped from the road-building, they know they are going to die, that only the executioner is waiting, 3 September 1942 it should say on this picture, more terrible than anything Goya could have painted. I meet the gaze of the prisoner with raised head, and greet him, hoping the guards do not see it.

ROLF | Udo in the hammock next to me is a typical "March-Violet", as we used to call it, the sort of person who joined the Party because he profited by it. Not on political grounds, he says, oh no, but think of everything one got hold of!

It is true, precious stones have never been cheaper, Mother bought some too, without asking questions, many people wanted to sell, all who were leaving the country. Collections and collections of jewellery. Brilliant. Pink pearls. A set with sapphires, with the genuine blue colour, said Mother, not the cheapest dark ones, no, lovely, pure blue. I took my savings and bought a piece of jewellery for Hannah, she just looked bitterly at me, turned and went away. I wanted to shout that I hadn't bought it from a Jew, but what did I know about the fellow who sold it to me, perhaps he was a middleman who wanted to earn money from those who had to go.

I am trying to think of all the walks I went on with Father. He knew the names of the birds we saw, I only remember a couple of them. Am I going to forget him in the same way? All

I can now remember as "Father", his handshake, hair colour, voice, is it going to disappear like the names of the bird species that have slipped my mind? Is something mine only when I remember it? Father, the landscape I am standing in, looking at. The peace I have lost.

\

"What are you going to do during your leave?"

"Try to get spliced with Otto's cousin, Inge she's called."

"Really'.

"Remember the bet, a piece of cake for the one who gets married first!"

"Not everyone has your way with women."

"Here are only ugly men, without money."

"You gamble yours away!"

"None of your business, right?"

"Nasty cough you have there, had it a long time?"

"It's no problem. What are you smoking, by the way? Felt slippers?"

"Cold feet?"

"Best girl in Berlin, my Diana, but marriage, no it sounds a bit too much to me. Think of having to come home sober every evening."

"Can't we swap leaves, then, since you don't need yours?"

"Bribe me with a box of cigars, then we'll see."

"Watch your balls, you bloodsucker."

"Maybe her cunt will be occupied when you get home, so say the rumours."

"Only talk of women with you. To come into the base. To Wilhelmshaven. That's my great dream. Then all the pipes will play. Rejoicing from land. Hats thrown in the air, and women waving white handkerchiefs. An admiral standing to receive us. Flags and banners."

"My son will get the battleship I have begun carving out of wood. And my daughter will smile and cry when I come home, so I won't have to."

"Where are the caramels, get out the sweets, it's going to be a long watch."

"Do you remember when we crept up along the coast, the Kiel canal, Elbe, the Baltic Sea, it seems so long ago. In war one year is like ten, one day like a month and an hour like a day, at least."

Fættenfjord, autumn 1942

FREGATTEN-KAPITÄN BIELER | Since we came back it has been peaceful. There will be a major overhaul of the anti-aircraft guns soon, everything has to be perfect, because we have to reckon with an air attack. The ship's captain is sure of it.

OLAV | "Migratory birds" they were called, the German spies who travelled around mapping the area in the years before the war. They were so interested, and very friendly of course. We were easily fooled that time.

I hadn't learned anything that could help me, knew nothing about smuggling information, encoding, the security of secret meeting-places, killing techniques or cover stories. Completely blank about everything which might be useful in the Resistance Movement, as were the others too, so we simply had to begin somewhere. Teach ourselves to deceive. Oh, yes.

We had developed a signalling system for raids: if the people at Dale have put two milk pails out on the step, it is a full alarm, if Jarle has set up corn poles in a triangle, or Solveig's cow stands tethered on the west side of the farm, then we must hope the travellers to England are well hidden in the goat barn. Oh, oh! If the barn door is standing wide open, then you should not come in here. If the boat is lying upside-down, you should turn round and go away slowly, never, never run.

CARL | Half speed. Keep on course. Starboard 063.

Torpedo 1 and 2 ready for firing.

FIRE! FIRE! Wait, hold your breath. Three out of four hit. Now it's breaking loose! New destroyer on port side. Half speed astern. Put the engines in slow speed.

Quiet. Don't blink, don't breathe, fire!

Starboard 30.

Then the practice is over, we only have to go on waiting.

Tirpitz, the predator of the ocean, is resting.

"It isn't possible to sink Tirpitz. Damage yes, but never sink. An unsinkable colossus at sea." They often proclaimed these slogans. It's a good lifejacket. The ship can't sink. But there's far too much time for thinking while we wait.

KASPAR | *Ich weiss nicht, was soll es bedeuten,*
Dass ich so traurig bin;
Ein Märchen aus uralten Zeiten,
Das kommt mir nicht aus dem Sinn.

The others have found out that I know a lot of poems by heart, in the evenings they gather round me and listen while I declaim 'Die Lorelei'. Afterwards Helmut may hum Liszt's 'Hungarian Dances' or something from Chopin's 'Fantasie-impromptu'. If he is in the right mood, the boys can also get him to whistle stuff they like, 'Blumenlied' or old soldiers' marches.

GOTTFRIED | It will be hard to keep myself away from Berit, but I have promised myself to think only of Elsa now, the letter from her changed everything. I am going to be a father. Responsibility. Honesty. Elsa deserves it. She is so pretty. I remember the first time I saw her, I could count her pubic hairs through her tight-fitting skirt, and that was surely intentional. And her gold lamè dress last Christmas. Elsa had packed herself like a shiny gift. The only thing I wanted was to lie with her. I could not wait, should not wait, because she said no with her mouth and yes with the biggest lips. Now, now I take you! Bites and kisses and caresses and…

Let me play with you, you lark from Litchenstern! Let me lift you up and run with you, straight home to bed! Soon I will hammer my pile-driver into you, you can rely on that, my lovely Elsa!

UWE | The smarting, almost burning pain, on the verge of convulsion. My blue, full balls long only to empty themselves. Ease the pressure. A long squirt.

I can't die without having made love with a girl. I think about it several times in an hour. But where will I find her? I don't want to go to a brothel!

JOHANNES | Now I haven't heard from Sonja for three months. She can't have found a new one, no, I don't believe that. The other alternative is just as bad, that she is dead, but then the chaplain would have come and told me. Perhaps it is only that the post to the Front takes priority over ours? She promised to write once a week, every Friday evening. Tell me whatever you like, so long as you write, was one of the last things I said to her, on the platform. It was like in a film, fog and darkness and drizzle, the trains hooting and lit up, there we stood like so many young couples, I'm going to war for you. I twisted her hair around my finger, I believe it hurt, but she let me do it, we kissed, a little carefully, there were so many people there, but I said I loved her, and she should wait and write. Could she have betrayed me? Dear Sonja, just a greeting is enough.

FRITZ | The child is sleeping. Completely at peace, I stand here for a while peeping attentively down into the cradle, seeing the little cheeks moving, as if he is thinking of food, milk and mother's breast. Now and then a frown passes over the tiny face, is he dreaming? What could the dreams of such a small child be like, when it has no language and the world is no larger than a breast, a change and sleep, sleep. Perhaps he remembers the birth itself, that it was painful to push his way out, it was painful for Hedwig anyway, from what I understood from her and the midwife. The boy has soot-black hair, and our friends tease Hedwig that a gypsy must have come by nine months ago. I just laugh, recognizing so much of my family in the sweet face, the shape of the ears is exactly like mine, only so incredibly smaller, and above the eyes the boy has a feature from Mother.

Now he's stirring, just a bit, and I hear something which is neither a call nor a cry, but a sound, still so far from a word. Oh, I am going to miss you, as I have already become so fond of you. I'm leaving tomorrow, dreading going to Norway again, odd that it is so exhausting to lie about idle and inactive. Very sorry I couldn't be at your christening, little heart, and can't go on holding you in my arms when you are crying and Hedwig is completely tired out. I love walking around in the corridor outside the bedroom, carrying you, back and forth, and looking out of the window and seeing the neighbour's old ginger tomcat on the way home from a raid at about five o'clock. Pressing your screaming body protectively against mine, feeling how it struggles to get out enough air to roar, howl, kick agitatedly with your thin legs. You must have a pain in your tummy, your whole body is tense. I am not upset by your crying, knowing it will pass, soon you will calm down again, and I can give you to your mother. The legs move, I hope you'll be a footballer, a big striker for Hertha Berlin! Now you are going to get milk and sleep again, but I won't get to sleep. Because I'll be lying listening to your breathing in the dark, and trying not to think about the war you are born into; there are so many, who were once as small as you, being killed and maimed.

Dear God, protect the little one from the horrors of the world, his father has to go on board out there.

INGE | Mother was so exhausted that she couldn't even manage a smile in the picture in which she is presented with the 'mother medal'. For "having given ten children to the Führer," as they said.

Dearest Gottfried,

You proud Tirpitz on the waves of the sea
May good fortune and happiness follow in your future

I miss you and thank you for your warmth, you showed me a confidence I had never felt before. You are my man, maybe it sounds strange, but that's what you are. You opened me up, saw who I was, and I was able to experience love.

You say that Tirpitz has returned, may I see you soon?

Yours
Berit

OTTO | The air raid siren is wailing. Oh hell! The smoke is seeping out, planes are on the way, new bombing attacks. The Brits want to get us, but soon we'll be hidden in artificial fog, we just have to wait. I am glad I am on deck and have a chance of swimming to land if we are hit. Under the decks it can be a pure death chamber, the boy in the engine room is doomed to die if the bombs hit, although I know how strong steel is, I've seen it in the smithy back home. Our armour-plating is twelve centimetres thick, it can stand a lot, I shouldn't forget it. I wonder what they are thinking, the Englishmen, sitting there in planes packed full of bombs, are they thinking the ship is full of nineteen-year-olds who have as little wish to die as they have? Are they afraid of our weapons, that we might get them, that the Luftwaffe will come and help us? I'll stand here and write a letter home while the bombs are falling, the last thing I will do is to write to Father. I have enough time, haven't heard the planes coming in over the fjord yet.

They will soon be here, people are shouting. The moon is up, so the Brits can see us easily if the smoke thins out. If it blows away, they'll get to hit us, sink us, and I'll write the last letter, they'll find it on me, before we are buried in our uniforms.

ERICH | Hit! Direct hit! I hear how the lad pounds on the anti-aircraft cannon, slapping and clapping it and shouting: "You got it, you devils! Up with the German Navy and its weapons!" The order is heard once more: "Fire!" It resounds in our ears, everyone cheers when our shooters get new hits against the planes which are coming in formation.

CARL | The planes are doing a bunk! Bloody bomber swine. We got them properly. The sound of our anti-aircraft gun makes me proud. That was real war! For five minutes.

GUSTAV | After the attack there's a dull mood, nobody is able to smile. We have had a demonstration of how vulnerable we are. I am sitting with Martin, Kaspar, Otto and a few others in the mess, we're drinking beer, but conversation stumbles, silences. Suddenly I am reminded of one of the Christ legends Grandfather comforted me with when I was a little boy and afraid of something or the other. Now I tell it to the others:

A boy was out playing, he was too small to be a shepherd, but he walked by himself and dreamed of having his own flock of sheep when he grew up. Suddenly he could not recognize where he was. He must have gone quite far, because he had counted his sheep again and again in his mind and found out whether they should be fairly brown or completely brown, or hardly brown at all. He thought about the names they would have, and imagined the stream he would have to find for them, and all the trees he would bend so they could graze on the leaves. Mother would be pleased with the good cheese their milk would yield, and the wool she could make clothes with. All this he had dreamed about as he walked, and now it was becoming dark around him. But he was not frightened. Far ahead he could see a little hill in the dusk, and he decided to go towards it, because then I will get a good view and survey, he thought, and can make up my mind whether I want to turn and try to find my way home or if I want to go even further out into the wide world. He came up from the back, a fairly gentle slope upwards and not difficult to walk even though it was getting increasingly dark. But the boy was not afraid of wild animals, or Roman soldiers or evil spirits, no, he felt light and happy. Then suddenly he saw three crosses ahead, and understood that he had come to Golgotha, because that was where they used to crucify people. Perhaps somebody is hanging there now as well, somebody who is actually dying at this hour, what if I get to see it, won't my friends be amazed! It really looked as if somebody was hanging on all three of the crosses. He had nearly arrived now, and even though it was almost completely dark, he could see the bodies which were nailed firmly to the crosses. They must be terrible criminals, thought the boy, and it must be very painful to hang like that. Perhaps they are murderers and thieves, he shuddered as he got closer. He could see a clear glow around the cross which stood in the middle. As if it shone out of the woodwork, or was it the body which was sort of shining from inside? He sneaked forward in the dry waste ground of the hilltop, so that he could look at the faces of the men who hung there. It was strange, the radiance around the cross in the middle only became brighter. The soldiers, who were supposed to guard the prisoners, were all lying asleep, and the boy crept even closer. The one that the light came from spoke to the boy, clearly marked by suffering he looked straight at him and said: The Lord is my shepherd, but you shall watch over the Lamb of God who takes away the sins of the world. I am still far too small to take care of the flock of sheep, said the boy, but just then he felt a wind blow through him, lifting him from the ground, and at once he became much bigger and stronger and full of power. The Lord has enlightened you, said the prisoner with the burning eyes, from now on you shall guard the flock. God's sheep are many, and several will go astray, therefore you need to keep watch. The boy felt himself braver than ever and stared hard at the prisoner, and said: I will guard all God's sheep for all time. Then a light appeared around the boy, the same light that shone around the prisoner, and there the boy looked straight into heaven, where God the Father of All sat upon his white shining throne and held out a golden shepherd's crook to him. From that day to this, that shepherd is watching over us, you do not see him, but he is walking beside you in the darkness and shining with his staff, so that God's little sheep will not be lost.

Nobody gets up to fetch more beer.

FRITZ | Only for a few days was I able to see him. Wrinkled and smooth at the same time, and infinitely soft. Small as small can be. His smell, I saw how Hedwig sniffed it in. How calm she became in her face when she breastfed. She said that she believed we humans are right-handed so that we can hold infants on the left side, where they can lie and calm themselves to the sound of heartbeats. It is said that a newborn can hold itself up by the hands, I believe it. The big joints, worthy of a football player, and the mouth mumbling for food, sucking. Hedwig's transparent face. Pregnancy gave her curls, the heavy brown hair with red glints in the right light, suddenly curled itself around the temples, so pretty. Noble. Now she had been put to use by life, I believe she felt like that. I looked into the little one's eyes the few times he opened them. Had he been here before, his gaze seemed so old? When I was leaving, I tried to pour all the love I felt for him into one container, where he can get care and tenderness when he needs it. I put my hand on his head and felt a note come, a harmony with the child which seemed unbreakable. A pact. I watch over you. Watch over me.

Dear Father,

Now it is soon my birthday. I want a cat. Or skates. Great-grandmother and Grandfather are coming, and little Wilhelm has become big Wilhelm, he says so himself. God takes care of us. Both big and small. You too.

With love,

Theres

ROLF | Mother hasn't sent a single letter since I joined up. Nearly all the others get greetings from home. The postman shouts out the number and surname, many people stand waiting. I see how Heine beside me begins to cry soundlessly as he reads. The tears make small streams in his face. My crying is on the inside of my face, I can feel it dripping behind my eyes. Every time I have cried everything stops and starts with the questions: Why don't you like me, Mother, what have I done wrong? Don't you love me? Didn't you want to have me?

Caresses remained stuck in her fingers, the flowers I picked for her did not yield smiles and thanks in return. On my first day at school, when the other children came together with proud mothers who had combed their hair with water, and led them to the big stone building, which had such high doorways that a little child felt it was being devoured, Mother didn't come with me. Not a single question about how it had been, when I came home. There was no sign of life from Hannah in the post today either, but I have stopped expecting it.

HEDWIG | Have you had a letter? Wait, then I'll put the coffee on, and we'll read it slowly as we drink a cup.

OTTO | Felix, Ludwig and Rudolf are dealing in the black market, everyone knows it, spirits and tobacco at outrageous prices, but it is too tough to report them. After all we need what they have now and then. The Norwegians are the most eager customers, every Thursday those three go ashore to deal with the Norwegian fellows.

We often sit playing poker for money in the evenings. It is forbidden, of course, but the officers don't care to enforce such things when we are lying quietly waiting for weeks on end. One evening we had a visit from a theatre. We organize evenings of songs and cabaret ourselves, and now and then I am the master of ceremonies. Amazing how much fun we have. How good we are at letting things be ordinary and normal. Even having to sleep in a hammock for a couple of years.

KASPAR | The mountains around are creeping into the clouds which look like puffs of wool, perhaps they are warming themselves? The light is overwintering somewhere else. Give me something snug, something with water, childhood and fur.

I left my heart behind at home when I came. So it wouldn't be forced to kill, said Gustav. When I come back, I'll put that pure heart back in its place. I wrapped some cloth around it, so it would keep clean.

GOTTFRIED | I always carry the note with me, only once a month I read it. Not to wear the paper to bits and keep the power in the words. 10 October 1938 we got engaged, and every month on the tenth I unfold the note: "Gottfried, my true love, I love you more than anything on earth" in Elsa's childish, round handwriting.

In the evenings Zarah Leander sings *Eine Frau wird erst schön durch die Liebe* and *Nur nicht aus Liebe weinen* until we are crying. If I simply think of Elsa, a warm thin pulse of blood moves out into my cock, in milliseconds it lifts itself as much as it can in the tight uniform trousers.

CARL | Max has been on leave and brings a bottle of Weinbrand-Verschnitt out from his kitbag. Now it'll be summer again!

ROLF | When we lay in Fættenfjord the first time, I always ran off into the woods when I had leave, in early spring, carpets of white flowers with green leaves covered the ground in the narrow valley. I went inwards and upwards, snow was still there on the north-facing slopes, but it knew it had lost. Damp crept into the shoes, like a tree taking up water with its roots. Birdsong intense, a wall of sound, as alive as alive can be. The spring was violently in place here, wild life force, I have never seen anything like it back home.

Yesterday when I went on a long ski trip, I heard twigs crackle suddenly. My first thought was that my rifle was still lying on board, while the danger was here in the woods. The animal came closer, breath stopped as if it was also scared. I thought now I'm dying of fright. Then I saw something big and grey, was it the Devil himself? High above me, from a head with antlers sticking out, an eye looked at me. What was this? I tried to swing round with skis on my feet, and fell at the same time as the animal turned. I set off down the hill, towards the fjord and the ship, and the animal ran into the forest. I was completely white when I came back, said my friends, who thought what I had seen was probably an elk. Norsemen call it the King of the Forest. All day the fear has been sitting tight in me, like clothing I am unable to take off.

FREGATTEN-KAPITÄN BIELER | Butter biscuits dipped in tea with an equal amount of milk and three teaspoons of honey, feeling the biscuits melting on the tongue, there is still pleasure in life, even on the night watch. In a few hours it will be harder to keep oneself alert. For something to do I transcribe the weather forecast which they are sending by Morse code from land.

Go on, or we'll go under, is what we are trained to do. The German Navy should always show initiative, but we are only waiting. Rotting. I notice it in the sailors.

"Spoiled provisions for the ship's food, that's great!" "Sit down and shut up!" yells Stabsoberbootsmann Schulenberg.

"It'll be night watch for you." I don't understand how he lets himself be provoked, I let the incident pass. Suddenly I begin to think about something Hermann, the neighbour's six-year-old, said last time I was home:

"It's a pity about the German eagle. It's far too big for my birdcage."

KONRAD | I don't get full, try to stop thinking about food, but it doesn't help, little meatballs pop up in my head, thyme-roasted potatoes with bacon-wrapped chicken fillets, éclairs with vanilla cream, or a crunchy green winter apple! We eat in groups on board, and I nearly always end up last, and have to wait while the others sit in the mess. Often there is little left. At home I could eat five meals a day, here there are three. Never possible to wangle anything to take with oneself up into the hammock at night either. I have managed to buy a little from the Norsemen on land, dried meat or carrots, but it doesn't help. Hunger comes and overpowers me. Might I have worms in my guts? I could ask at the sickbay, perhaps I might get an extra ration? Soon it's Christmas, hope we get something better then, at any rate. I look forward to nighttime, I often dream about food and may wake up almost full, after eight pieces of bread with cheese and saveloy with salad and tomatoes!

OLAV | Inside Fættenfjord lies a large German armada, oh, yes. Imagine being able to use a word like armada, a word taken right out of the history books.

Shall we row over there and find out if we may come on board? It is Saturday evening, perhaps both cigarettes and drams are handed out? Birger looks at me with a wondering glint in his eyes, oh yes, the longing to do something exciting shines out of him. Imagine if we had been born in Germany, then we could have been in the Navy now. Norway simply capitulated.

BERIT | That dark look of yours before you looked down at the ground, you couldn't bear to look at me. You must understand that I love you, Gottfried, but do you know how painful it is when everyone scorns me? And soon you are leaving, all of you, and we can't be together any longer. You don't know that I have seen the picture you have hidden in your wallet. Elsa, it says on the back of the picture. Did you believe that I didn't sense something?

I saw your tears, you love me, I know that you know you will miss me, you saw that I mean what I say. You cry easily, don't like to miss anything, but we have the world against us, and I have to be realistic and move to a place where nobody knows me before it shows.

UWE | Walter always has something to show off when we are sitting drinking. Amulets for health and good luck in war, little battle-Madonnas which he got from the Catholic priest before he left. Stones with great powers. Magic charm incantations. Before he lived as a farmer in Mesopotamia, he tells us, he lived in the land between the rivers that we learned about at school. In Africa too, there he was a woman, a depressing and tormented life, to be sure. After that he was in Hungary, he carries on, living as a castle musician and intellectual with old books around him, he can remember his own death, how he just fell forwards, his head landed on the book he was reading. Which book, I ask. Dante, he replies. *The Divine Comedy.* It was a worthy end, I say, laughing. Later he lived in Mexico, as a newly-wed stableboy.

It seems as if he could have gone on for a long time, I have never heard anyone talk like that before. Previous lives? There is something fine about it, that the soul lives on in new worlds. That death is not the end, or that one doesn't stay in heaven forever. Now when there are so many dying, many hundred thousand Germans, it is said, and many more Russians, of course, there must be a lot of souls looking for new lives to insert themselves into. Maybe I am only here for the time being as me. Uwe, from Moabit, 72 kilos, Navy seaman on Tirpitz. Maybe I am only on the way, in an interval, maybe all my dreams come from previously lived lives? The remains of something. The idea is great. I don't want to be lost in the churchyard earth or on the bottom of the sea if we are torpedoed. I want to be thrown out into orbit, like a drop of water on the way to the source.

OTTO | I often think about the walks with Grandad in the forest on the day before Christmas Eve, we closed the marten traps. Animals have peace at Christmas, but not us, even at weekends I am listening for bomber planes. How I long for home!

\

Dear Brigitta

Today it is Christmas Eve, and I imagine you and Dagmarr on your way to Christmas Mass. You are in the brown fur, she is in a sailor dress, while the church clock is already chiming, and snow covers the whole town, a cold wind comes in from the sea. At home it is warm, and the Christmas dinner is ready in the oven. I wish I could have gone there with you!

Warm Christmas greetings,
Werner

KASPAR | I am a person under the uniform, but totally without legal capacity. Even bedtimes, trips to the toilet and smoke-breaks are decided by others. My shitting is dictated.

I don't want to be here, I want to celebrate the holiday with my mother and sisters, I haven't chosen to be on a battleship. May the war end during the next year!

GOTTFRIED | At home we would usually have gone from joint to joint on a New Year's Eve like this, had a beer and maybe a shot at each place. Laughed and danced in the elegant rooms, the dance hall in Mitte with silver-coloured walls and mirrors on the upper floor, mirrors where one can see the shadows of ghosts. Once I lured Elsa up to smooch. Before it was Silke I used to take there with me. A large gypsy orchestra played wild gasping Balkan music, in which the instruments shouted at one another and asked where are you, trumpet, here I am, clarinet.

That's how New Year celebrations used to be. On Tirpitz, holidays and ordinary days are the same. Here we lie hiding ourselves while joy is visiting other places. I want to have a little fun before I die, says Felix. Come on, boys, let's sneak ashore in the dinghy and find some girls. "I have to try screwing before I die", whispers Uwe, but I'll stay behind. Elsa, my Elsa. Silke. And Berit!

Hey wait, I'm coming after all.

KURT | Not to overlook a single periscope, a plane as small as a bird, or a surface ship on the horizon, is my duty. They call me hawk-eye Kurt! But now the eye is tired, the third hour on watch is the worst, it becomes hard to believe what one is seeing. I am my eye, what the eye sees, is me. The card I drew the evening before I left was the hanged man. I managed to forget it, now I see it again, there's a man hanging from the mast there. Stop being silly! Think about something from home instead! I miss the scent of the linden tree blossoms, the light over the Landwehr canal on summer evenings. The heavy willow trees which bend towards the water. The church bells, Grandfather's sundial. The L-shaped apartment, and Adelheid on the Ferris Wheel.

OTTO | Nothing is sadder than a burial at sea. Valdo simply became ill, now he lies sewn into his hammock with lead weights so as not to float up, we are standing lined up at the rails while the dead seaman is lowered overboard. The rites of burial at sea are brief, the priest reads from the Bible, the ship's captain says a few words. We sing a psalm. Then it is done. Just like at Christmas it feels too little. There is no Christmas spirit even though we get extra drams after the Christmas service. It isn't a funeral without the family present, it should be earth that is thrown on the coffin, not water.

There's a stink below deck, perhaps a rotting rat.

ROLF | You have not seen all shades of grey until you have seen a fjord, some days one sees the whole spectrum of blue. The best thing on board is to be ordered to fish. Fishing with a rod from the main deck, cod and pollock mostly, occasionally we get other fish I don't know the names of. Following the line down, seeing the bait disappear into the blue-greyness, knowing that there is life down there. Smooth silver-coloured fish swimming towards each other, veering aside with a little flick of the tailfin, noticing the bait, snatching it. The cod is cowardly, it gives up as soon as it feels it has been caught. All wriggling decreases quickly, it simply hangs there and knows it has lost, soon it will be boiled in salt water and served with potatoes, margarine and, at best, chives. The pollock fights!

Strange that it is like that, but we find the same thing among people. Some hold their hands up or wave something white, others run away, refuse to engage with the situation, still others want to change their own fate, it is they who attack first, who don't hesitate when they aim at your head. Which category do I belong to? I would rather avoid getting into a situation where this is revealed, it is dangerous to be brave, deadly dangerous. Sticking the knife into the fish's head, twisting until it becomes still, the blood the same colour as mine. Cutting off the head and slashing open the belly. Pulling out what has functioned as a perfect machine, the arteries which have fed the heart with oxygen, food on its way through the digestive canals, gills which floated so lightly in the water, the bladder's functions abruptly broken off. The gulls get their share, I sling the bait out again.

The veins on my hands have become so clear, I do not recognize them, they are old hands, someone else's hands.

Hannah.

The big bomb birds with burning eggs in their bellies, they are coming soon.

PETER | Since I was promoted to postal censor, I know quite a lot about the ship's secrets and have to be extremely careful about what I write in letters home. I try to confine myself to descriptions of nature, the weather and life on board. What we are busy with, sports activities, singing evenings, religious services. Actually I only want to write about how scared I am, my desk is right above the ammunition store. It will be a quick death, at any rate. Hardly any human remains to collect.

One does not see one's own eye. One does not know one's own death. That's how it is.

GUSTAV | I thought a lot about what it is to die, noted in my book. Probably I wasn't well, I see when I read it now, but death becomes so real after an air raid. I want to prepare myself, not just meet it with surprise.

Can one pull the man out from the grave and allow him to complete his lifespan?

No! Because "death is the last enemy"!

No! Because "death is devoured, victory is won."

God counts us one by one. One person. Never the mass.

Now I am trying to think with more reconciliation about death. Yesterday I wrote a sort of poem:

After death I wish to be laid
In the palm of the Lord's hand
and calmly feel grace breathing
forth new breath.

LOTHAR | I've fetched beer for Peter and myself, now I'm going to tell him about Thomas, I want one of those around me to know. Peter is often in the ship's library which I was given responsibility for, when I was relocated to "lighter duties", as it is called, after I came back from France. I like Peter, he reminds me a bit of Thomas. We fought side by side, Thomas and I, I begin, and feel my voice faltering. Taking a big gulp of beer, I carry on: We had done so since our village was ordered out, the order had respected it, wherever we were moved around. Had I been an officer, I would always have put relatives and friends to fight together, it would have been much more effective, because then they would protect each other and be willing to die for the other one, and not least take revenge for the one who fell, to the last drop of blood. Then it would have been *our* war, not the war of someone in an office in Berlin.

Thomas was strong and fearless. Those are good qualities for a soldier, but it is not these qualities that get you home safely, it is the best who die, and the most cowardly who save their lives.

We had advanced quite far, because each day we were certainly getting closer and closer to Paris, but all we saw was land and a long river. It was hot, nearly midsummer, we went towards a stream, Thomas and I, there were no encounters that day, the Frenchmen were lying around licking their wounds, we believed. Thomas held the canteen down in the water, calling: Father, shall we bathe afterwards? It was as if he was eight years old again and wanted me to come with him to the beach because it was such a great bathing summer this year, as he said. I passed him my canteen, asking him to fill that one as well, so I need not bend down, my back had been grumbling recently, mile after mile with heavy kit, I was one of the oldest.

I felt the wind from the bullet which flew past without a sound, or perhaps my ears didn't want to hear the bullet that killed my son. Soon the stream was red, the blood was quickly washed away, but all the time more and more blood came. Now it was a whole stream of blood, and when Thomas fell in, straight down into the water, only then did I react. Slowly I lifted him up, held him in my arms as if he was an overgrown child. Someone shouted to me, but I could not hear, the stream ran inside my ears, and I stumbled onto the bank there, with my feet in the water, and my upper body wet with hot blood.

Thomas' eyes opened, rolled around, tried to focus, the wide sky over the plains in France would be the last thing he saw. His gaze couldn't reach down to mine before it faded, something disappeared, I saw life leave him. Thomas was dead. I felt his body become twice as heavy, I collapsed under that weight. I rolled down into the stream with that dead son of mine on top of me. Later they told me that saved my life when the French advanced immediately afterwards. I lay there feeling the water running past, without resistance, it wasn't cold, it wasn't clear, it was nothing, it was only a motion, a streaming, and a heavy black body. I didn't think so far, I was thinking nothing, not about how I would tell Ute about this, or how I could manage to get out of the stream, how I would have the strength to push Thomas aside. I did not hear the battle, heard only the trickling, as if I'd become a water creature.

I was woken up by the cold, something heavy was resting on me. Thomas. Some time went by before my thoughts could take it in, but it was Thomas. He saved my life that day. When at last I got up in the twilight and hoisted Thomas onto my back, I knew that no French bullets could wound me. I saw a grove, some trees at any rate, went in that direction, wanting to find a place to lay Thomas down, a little clearing, preferably with soft grass, where I could spread my jacket over him. The last part I carried him in my arms, a bundle with long legs. I will never forget how heavy my feet were, as I staggered forwards, I didn't think of the enemy. As soon as I came into the grove, someone came running towards me, good God, Lothar, are you alive, I heard someone say. No, I replied.

INGE | The woman laid two fingers on the dead child's head, swore an oath.

Did she want to see the child again? Hold it, feel how cold it was? She could not give birth to a fatherless child, was that why it went wrong? Did she become so frightened that the child died? I will hide my tears while she is drinking a herbal decoction to make the milk stop flowing.

In the block on the other side lies one called Elsa, seven months' pregnant, who has found out that there is no foetal heartbeat any more. She knows she has to give birth to a dead baby. I know it too, because it was I who was at her house today, saw her belly, but not a glimpse of the face under the thin sheet she was trying to hide behind. Gottfried, she sobbed, he must come. There is a hard stone inside her. Hard and silent, that is how silent silence is: when there is no longer a foetal heartbeat, when there is no longer any movement, when there is a stone inside the belly. And that you have to give birth to. We may not meet again, Elsa and I, but I won't forget her. She must think about the stone at night, feeling that it has fallen further down in her belly. That her body is a coffin. Tirpitz sinking in amniotic fluid.

\

My dear Bernhard

You promised to come home soon, but leaves are cancelled, you write, why so? Now waiting is becoming a struggle. I am getting more and more fed up with Mother-in-law, she treats me as if I was an employee, and orders me to do one thing after another. I have enough to do with the little one, I can barely stand up to answer her. Come as quickly as you can. It's a quiet war here at home too, but our boy is so well-behaved, so good, you should see him now!

I will pray for you

Yours

Lisel

UWE | We always drink "submarines" when we are on land, a glass of spirits sunk down in a large glass of beer. You can't manage all that many submarines before you go down, to tell the truth. Then we hope for free time and good weather afterwards, so we can lay on the rear deck in the sun and recover.

RUDOLF | That lass there is broad enough in the hips to give birth to my kids, don't you think? What do you reckon, shall I make her an offer?

GOTTFRIED | Frida, Lotte, Anja, plus those I have really loved: Elsa, Berit and Silke. And Herta, the one night I got a chance! The boys like me to speak about women…I exaggerate a bit then.

BERIT | I had such expectations for us. I thought you would stop me and say that we must not give up. I remember when you said: "Dearest Berit, when I think of you, the wine in my glass begins to boil!"

Here is your ring, Gottfried, it wasn't gold after all, do you think I didn't notice? It's kicking in my belly. The foetus is shrugging, I close myself around it, feel the warmth of an imagined child's hand in mine.

OTTO | Since the air raid us fellows in D turret have become friends. It's like farm work, we have to do it together. Comradeship helps us to hang in there. To make an extra effort for your friend, let him get through a task a little more easily. If we do it for small things, I am sure that we'll do it when it really gets serious too. It's comradeship that makes us hang in there. Not fooling about or splitting hairs with the others, I learned that in the harvest.

KURT | Look, look, a heron in the snowy darkness!

PETER | This is violet, not lavender, or a lilac scent. They like perfuming letters, women. Now and then it smells of cooking fumes, home, daily life. Some use coloured writing paper too. Pink with rose scent. Too much, if you ask me, but the boys are pleased. Some of them come nearly every day asking for letters, and I have to answer no, not today either, but maybe tomorrow. "*Für Mutti!*" they call me and my shelf. I wait almost as eagerly as them. Gradually they become more and more subdued, and at last they give up. Some letters are heavy, often from mothers who have put in a few biscuits or some coins, as if the sailors were still kids, and not at war. Tragic news comes too, then the priest has to take over. No, lavender and violet are the easiest.

GOTTFRIED | What do I remember about Berit? That she has a mouth that turns to chocolate when I kiss her, I feel like replying to Uwe. Maybe I'll contact her again. If I feel up to it, it might be a lot of fuss, but the chocolate would be good.

OTTO | I long so much for the peace inside the cowshed, the calm around large animals, the cows lying in the stalls, the prize bull rattling his chain a little. The empty gaze of the sheep as their jaws move, the mixed smells of hay and muck, the restless trampling of a heifer which is about to calve. The darkness and animal warmth. I want to go home, dear God, let me go back to the farm. To my cat and the brook with the good water, to all the strips of field I know the names of. Let me come HOME! I must have said it aloud, because Bruno hushes me from the next hammock, he too knows the animal warmth, and the joy of harvesting the earth before the rain comes. The thick yellow layer on the milk, going out to pick up the potatoes we need for lunch, funny old Gerti who is allowed to go and help with whatever he can manage and understand. That I would miss him too!

KASPAR | "Abraham's willingness to sacrifice Isaac indicates God's willingness to sacrifice his son, isn't that so?" Gustav only wants to discuss theology all day, merely needs an ear, not an answer. Both we Lutherans and the Jews have the same forefather in Abraham, he goes on to say, and I glance around to see whether anyone is listening to what he is saying. It isn't popular to point out such things, and well he knows it, surely he only wants to provoke me, I don't reply. We must have forgotten that now, he says, much too loudly, yes, the Muslims too count Abraham, or Ibrahim as they call him, as their patriarch, through the bondwoman Hagar's son Ishmael, yes, you surely haven't forgotten that it was he who was Abraham's firstborn, he says loudly. Does he really have to shout like that, of course everyone knows the ship is listening, that someone always hears and reports it. The forty years in the wilderness were a small test for the Jews in comparison with the one that awaits them now, he says, have you heard about the ghetto in Warsaw? The camps that are filled with Jews, some say they are being killed with gas and burnt. Stop it, I say firmly. I have relatives in Poland, he goes on, they have told my sister about what is really going on, but that nobody says anything, that people just move into the empty flats where the Jews lived, without asking about them. Now at least he has lowered his voice. Don't say another word, I beg him in a low tone. In the beginning was the Word, he says defiantly, carved into tablets of stone! Let's talk about something else, I try mildly, but he almost roars back: Religions inherit from each other, the scapegoat becomes Christ, the lamb that takes upon itself our sins. The prophet Jonah who sees the evil in us. … I don't know why I haven't got up and left, perhaps I am afraid he is going to jump overboard or something. Three days and three nights in the belly of the whale, exactly as long as Jesus was in the kingdom of the dead. We are in the belly of the whale too, I try to say, attempting a joke, here on Tirpitz, but he doesn't want to hear such things. Everyone is to go into the new Ark, he says and looks at me, everyone is to go, Jews as well. They are still waiting for the Messiah, he continues, quite inconsequentially. Perhaps it is time for him to come now and help them? Hush, I say, shut up. Jesus is a symbol of God's grace. Jesus never broke with Judaism, he goes on, so why should we do so? Blessed are the pure of heart, for they shall see God, he says quietly, and my conscience pricks me, because probably he is one of them, the pure of heart. Blessed are they who are persecuted for righteousness' sake, he whispers, for theirs is the kingdom of God. Then he bangs on again: When the Romans drove the Jews out of Jerusalem, he begins loudly, but I hear this is dangerous, so I interrupt him. Can't you talk about something else, please, and suddenly he starts quoting from the Koran. There it is written that if you save one person, it will seem as if you are saving all of humanity. If you kill one person, it is as if you are killing all of humanity. Think of that, he shouts at me.

FRIEDRICH | We laughed and cheered when we found out that Intelligence had picked up that Churchill called Tirpitz "the Beast"! Now we'll come and get "Tommy"!

OLAV | Two officers are lodging with Jensine and Knut, one evening I popped in, one of them said: Hitler is our God. We die so willingly for him. Hitler has such concern for all of us. His heart bleeds for every single soldier who falls. I feel shivers down my spine when I think of it. The officers are nice enough in everyday life, and Knut has said that they are the best protection that one could imagine. The Germans will take care of our farm, he said, now that they are living here, all the bomber planes will be shot down long before they come near us.

I'll never forget the expression he had on his face, the one who is called Innerhofer, when he said that about Hitler as God.

A grown man who believed that Hitler bothered himself about him, as if Hitler was father and the officer his child. It was so terrifying that I made an excuse to go and see to a cow with milk fever. I did not calm down until I came into the warmth of the cowshed and the cat came and rubbed itself against me. I remembered some words from Ibsen's *Brand* as I sat there on the milking stool: "Your God is an extravagant god. He craves many souls." So does Hitler, indeed he does, it is souls he has taken, I was thinking as I poured out milk for the cat and shovelled muck down into the gutter. It's the souls of the German people he has stolen, that is why they come here, that is why they want to take the whole world. They will never give up, not before Hitler is dead, I am sure of that. One of the maintenance men, Werner, he is different, I could almost have become friends with him.

FREGATTEN-KAPITÄN BIELER | The alarm is sounding! Unidentified planes, so much for the free watch. One must rely on luck, I hear the sailors saying constantly, it isn't true, it all depends on an absolutely military attitude. Is it this attitude they lack, those who have been fighting so long over Stalingrad?

Here Tirpitz has contributed simply by our mere existence. The Brits are so afraid of us that they have stopped the convoys, our boys must be pleased that the Russians aren't getting regular supplies of tanks, machine guns and other materials. They ought to thank us, thank Tirpitz!

MAX | Cheers for the German advance! For the Third Reich. For Führer and Fatherland. The party will last as long as we have something to drink toasts with.

\

Dear Fritz

My beloved, through the distance itself we touch one another. I find you nearest to my heart.

Do you remember Tanja, the neighbour girl, now she is dead, she and her parents, a bomb fell right on their house. They sat eating and hadn't run for cover when the air raid siren went off for the third time that afternoon, now they are blown to bits, all three. To bits! It was our doctor who said it like that, shaking his head, there is nothing left to bury.

We are all safe in the bomb shelter, but they keep coming closer now. I hope you are all safe on board! I will write a longer Christmas letter to you tomorrow. How quickly this year has gone by. Alfred has become so big.

Yours forever
Hedwig

UWE | Love is a solitary thing. All my youth I loved Klara. Only Klara, but she never saw me, she didn't even once look my way.

Love is a thing no one else knows about. Whitish, almost invisible.

Red sun in the wine we drank in the summer of '39. The sound of bullets to come. I didn't dare speak to her, Klara.

GRETHA | Wilhelm got this maths problem in school yesterday: "To build a mental hospital costs six million reichsmarks. How many detached family houses at 15,000 reichsmarks could be built instead?" It's unbelievable, and now they are coming to measure Grandfather's forehead height and nose, he understands nothing about the cold instruments they lay against his face. In the end they find out that he is Aryan after all, but somewhat senile, it's tragicomical.

JOSEF | Tuberculosis, and Spanish Flu before that as well. Coughing. Blood on handkerchiefs which are hidden. Mother, weeping, burns the christening robe. Father's look when he has to take Great-grandfather's colonel's uniform and give it to the flames. We know what he died of anyway, consumption asks neither about rank nor achievements, says the neighbour woman when she sees Father going to the bonfire with the uniform. He has stretched out his arms to be furthest away from the contagion, but it is too late, we are all coughing.

I survived, certainly only because I'm going to die in the war, it happens like that in my thoughts, nightmares still wake me up, Mother floating around in her white nightdress, beside herself she shouts again and again: She is dead! She is dead! She is dead! I understand that my little sister has become an angel, as the neighbour woman had mumbled might happen.

I know too that Mother will never have another good day, whatever I do.

GOTTFRIED | I see her before me: hectic, hair like a wild bird's nest, the hand holding the pen sweating as she concludes her letter to me with: Kindly do not correct this letter with red pen, my German is bad. Oh, my beloved Laila, nobody makes sweeter mistakes than you. A life with Laila would be an eternal party. Don't forget Elsa, then, shout the boys, and the one in Trondheim, Berit. There's a stab in my chest for a moment. Elsa hasn't had such an easy time since she lost the baby, but what can I do from here? What a bunch of monks you are, I shout, laughing. Now you'll see that I'm back in the saddle! Glory, what would one do in wartime if there were no women to conquer?

FREGATTEN-KAPITÄN BIELER | Admiral of the Fleet Raeder sent Christmas greetings. The young officers were proud that the highest man in the Navy had remembered us as we lay here in Fættenfjord. By the end of January the Navy already had a new chief, Karl Dönitz. He wrote in his first directive that our life belongs to the State, that our honour lies in fulfilling our duty, that we have no right to a private life, but must show an unquenchable spirit of sacrifice to win the war. I felt dull when I read it, but this is what we have to live with.

KURT | On her birthday, 12 June, we went to the funfair and rode on the Ferris Wheel, it was so high and went so slowly that one could make a child there, it was said. I proposed to Adelheid when we were at the top. She raised her painted eyebrows and looked more surprised than happy, before she pressed the joy button inside her and shouted Yes! so loudly that people in the other carriages heard it. We laughed and kissed and cried and laughed again, and I will never forget the dull evening light and the lamps being lit. Afterwards we bought candy floss and soft drinks, and Adelheid began to hiccup, and we laughed all evening. We didn't get serious again until we were on our way to her parents to tell them. Suddenly I became nervous, but when I saw the smiles between her mother and father, it all evaporated, and we ran off to my parents at once, and there it was bubbly and everything. They rejoiced in our joy, and I know that I will never be happier again than I was that afternoon and evening. Because we didn't have time to get married before Poland was invaded and I had to go. Christmas leave was cancelled, and then Adelheid died, in one of those big air raids on Berlin's suburbs.

\

"Look, Johannes is sitting in there by the wall, is he crying?"

"Shall we go over there?"

"No, leave him in peace, he must have had news of a death, or maybe Sonja has broken up again, I saw a letter came for him today."

"News on the radio just now, civilians killed in Hamburg, isn't your family from Hamburg? Don't you have relatives there?"

"Use paraffin on the crablice! Pull down your pants now, it's the only thing that helps. That's how it goes after shore leave."

"Ow!"

"No new orders, we just lie here using up fuel. And waiting for air raids."

"On the last night, home on leave...it was like eating perfume..."

"Her cunt beat like a heart all night."

"Hey, can't you try to let go of Mummy's apron strings?"

"Shut up!"

"The tide is turning, does it mean the fortunes of war have changed?"

"Idiot."

"Oh, endless flag-hoisting ceremonies."

"Come again, quickly, quickly, quickly!"

"Remember, no yuk-yuk with Norwegian girls, you're going to be a father!"

"Did you hear what Martin said in the game of 'What shall I do when I get home again'? 'I am specially looking forward to seeing my wife's burning bush, I hear it speaking to me all the way here!'"

"Why is there nobody who wants to speak of the dead?"

Kåfjord, winter and spring 1943

FREGATTEN-KAPITÄN BIELER | A cup of hot cocoa on the bridge. We are on our way to a new anchorage. Knowing both those who are on watch and those who are sleeping is my responsibility. Several mothers have written to me and asked me to bring their sons safely home. At the same time, one has to show initiative, a commando group in the wartime Navy should attack, not only wait.

My belt has become too slack, I must ask for new holes to be made. My stomach burns, I can't tolerate coffee any more, it must be an ulcer, but I can't abandon Tirpitz now, there's a new order coming soon, we have been notified. Everything is uncertain.

KÅRE | Tirpitz came in March, just before I was to be confirmed. Soon Scharnhorst and other smaller ships followed. Consequently my area housed one of the largest gatherings of ships in the war, who would have believed anything like this? At Strømsnes! What are the odds on that?

We know there will be bombing. Obviously the Brits will make the attempt from bases at Murmansk, there will be explosions between the mountain and the fjord, if their aim is even slightly off then, it'll be us they'll hit. We are frightened all the time. Mother's relatives from Kjøllefjord refused to come to my confirmation, Uncle Oddvar is involved in something secret, I heard through the bedroom door once when Mother pulled Father in there after she got a letter from home. I was angry with the Germans who ruined my big day. They are Christians too, with Luther and all, said Mother, how can they behave like this? I'm not allowed to go dancing either, because these days there are mainly German soldiers at the parties. You shall and must stay at home, says Father. No question of anything else. They are terrified that I might get to know any Germans. Better dead, says Father. I know he means it.

Tord from the neighbouring village who is two classes below me, comes running into the yard to warn us, he says they have seen Germans setting out, they might come here. You had better take cover, now it's serious. Perhaps they have found out that we are hiding Uncle Oddvar here.

Tord is almost crying, begging us to hurry. Father and Uncle Oddvar run straight into the forest, each taking his pitchfork with him. We children stop dead, frozen stuck to the ground, lime under our wooden shoes. Mother shakes us, looks into our eyes, begs me, the eldest, to take the others with me across the river, don't go over the suspension bridge, says Mother, you are too visible there, cross further up, get yourselves to Anne and Peder and hide yourselves in the barn there. I wake up suddenly and ask what she is going to do, what about Karen?

My little sister, Karen Eline, was born with her head wobbling from side to side, always drooling. The weird, hoarse, fairly strong sound she makes, which may mean anything at all, only Mother understands whether it is 'yes' or 'no' or 'it hurts'. She must hurt a lot. Father has made a sort of rolling bed with four little wheels from a pram for her, so she can lie with her head propped up and come out with us into the garden. Straps across her thighs and chest so she won't fall out. Mother hardly goes away from her, only for a short while, then Father or one of us others sits with her.

I'll stay, says Mother. We'll stay here, Karen and me. They can hardly shoot a cripple. Mother is trembling so much that she has to hide her hands in her apron. Off you go now, all of you, but be quiet, don't talk to each other before you are on the other side. Get going, children, go now, run! Pray when you have time. Pray for Karen.

Lars climbs up the knotty sallow tree which is so unusual and old that we call it "the sallowfellow". From there one can look down onto the farm, he is almost dumb when he jumps down, then he clears his throat and says that he saw several motorbikes with sidecars driving onto the farm, there must certainly be twenty Germans, he believes. We cover our ears so we won't hear the shots we are waiting for.

KASPAR | In a letter to Hildegard I give Tirpitz the title "The Lonely Queen", because there is something majestic about her as she lies, huge, stately. And completely useless. It isn't ships like this that a modern navy needs, but submarines, that is why we keep lying idle. While our brothers bleed, we're playing football in the evenings or sitting in the ship's library and trying to make time pass. We are almost 12,000 German men in the Alta area now, I have met Viktor again, who is Papa's lawyer's son, and Magnus, whom I played with every summer holiday in Bremen. Could have been fun if it hadn't been a war, the news we get is not cheerful. We shouldn't complain that too little is happening. Because where a lot happens, the soldiers don't survive.

FREGATTEN-KAPITÄN BIELER | Submarines can attack in a herd, like a school of fish. Out with the divers, the submarine net should be as tight as a herring net. Huge silver-grey fish we're going to catch. Don't let there be any holes or cracks. The net should spread right down to the bottom. I know our sailors complain that the discipline on Tirpitz is tougher than on Lützow or Scharnhorst, but after all we are the flagship, and a little rivalry between ships is good. There is little else to think about here, many sad faces to see, the sailors become slack, last time we were out on exercises, they became as seasick as landlubbers, in waves only as high as two to three metres. We ought to go out and test our muscles properly soon, but shortage of fuel is always the answer if we try to talk to the admiral. He just sits in that mahogany-panelled cabin of his, smoking cigars. Pity the Brits are holding back the convoys, we could have done with a triumph now. Those splendid Arado planes of ours stand rusting, like this whole iron box, which the sailors call Tirpitz, is doing. The only hunting we are doing is of rats, one gets five marks for handing in a dead rat. Pathetic! I think of ship's captain Topp's New Year speech: "Tirpitz is still the strongest and sharpest sword in Germany's arsenal." It is no longer true. And now Rommel has had to give up North Africa.

HEDWIG | Death comes in the morning. With the light the planes and poverty become visible. A bag of potatoes placed on the stairs in the morning, a little extra meat on the ration card. Coal from Fritz's parents. That saves us.

Grandmother's weaving, she threw in red and pink threads and wove a tablecloth which I was to have in my home. I am grown up now, and a mother. I want to create a home which Fritz can come back to, and Alfred can grow up in. Since Grandmother died, I have put away the tablecloth, must save it and all the love which can be found between warp and weft, in the colours and the pattern.

I hope Fritz understands that I can't use the prettiest thing. There are Easter lilies on Grandmother's grave, a little snow has fallen on them, they look so offended.

INGE | First a miscarriage caused by the shock from a volley of shells, then a new birth. Luckily an easy delivery, the baby is full-term, and it's alive! There lies the brownish afterbirth. I ponder words I feel are great. Afterbirth, placenta, "mother's mouth". The white fat around the child. Blood from the vagina. Scissors in sterile water. Cotton wool to dry the mother with. I go on the morning rounds at the clinic before the night duty is over. The child lies dressed beside the mother, its little head is still elongated after the journey through the birth canal. The face is the last to be born, they say. She is pleased that I have come, I may hold the baby, it whimpers, a low moan. A newborn's voice practising speech.

A birth and a miscarriage. Life and death, and life that opens itself again. I go home, the turkeys in the backyard here are too heavy to fly, their clueless eyes look at me. To prophesy a bloody rag. Their heads wave at half-mast on bodies which need time before they can accept a new hope, little cocoons which are bursting.

JOSEF | Such a fine boy, Wilhelm, missing the children gives me pain. Is Gretha able to help them enough with their homework? Wonder how tall Theres is now? What does she think about the war? That she should grow up in a war, we didn't know that when we took her home with us from the clinic, wrapped in the white woollen blanket.

ANSELM | On the outskirts of Alta we meet the Lapps and buy reindeer cheese from them, they have a little camp there. How strong the cheese tastes, but one gets used to it. I am one of the few who has contact with the Lapps, it is funny to see them coming driving with the reindeer. One of the women dares to smile at me. Her brown eyes have a lighter, amber-coloured ring around the pupils. I have never seen that in anyone else. She is refined in her heart. If only everything had been different, I would have proposed to her, something inside me says that I could have lived together with her, lived well with her. In the evenings we can hear their songs, from the Lapps' tents, the sound of open country and winter-spring. She teaches me a special song, a *joik*, says it is mine and will follow me. I try to remember it. Some of the others are afraid of the Lapps, say they can cast curses on us, bad luck and death, yes even make the ship sink. For me the curse is falling in love, whether it is cast on me or not.

HELMUT | *Hörst du mein heimliches Rufen*
kennst du meinen heimlichen Schmerz

I walk slowly past the barracks in Alta and listen to the soldiers singing. Then there are spontaneous war cries: We'll fight to the last grenade! Long live the Führer! Long live Germany!

ROLF | When I get home, I'll bring lemonade, cakes and a book to Tiergarten and sit there reading all day. That's what I dream of! When I get home, I'll go to the Philharmonic and listen to my favourite cello concerto because then it feels as if they are playing on strings fastened directly onto my spine. When I get home, I'll have a milk coffee at the restaurant outside Hotel Adlon, look at all those promenading along Unter den Linden, sit commenting on their clothes, the gestures of the customers, smiling and watching. When I get home, I'll invite Hannah to a picnic by the canal one sunny day and watch the swans and boats and eat cherries and see who can skip stones furthest out in the water.

GUSTAV | Sun in my eyes, the warmth finds its way in under the uniform. What we could not believe in when the days lay in darkness, now it, the sun, is shining strongly, almost faithfully, and I feel happiness sniffing at me again.

PETER | I look back regretfully at the hard physical labour on the railway, instead of sitting on a chair all day. It was meaningful, what we were doing, Hitler gave us a job and something to eat. My brother took over the farm and became obsessed with farmers belonging to the most genuine race in the whole nation since they tilled the holy German soil. When I came home for Christmas, he had painted the *Blut und Boden* emblem, with axe and sword, in red over the whole wall of the barn, the one that could be seen from the road. He spoke only about the Harvest Thanksgiving the Party had put on. And our old priest came in uniform and said that Hitler was sent by God to save Germany. Everyone looked as if they agreed. But now I think the earlier landmarks, the ones I could rely on, have begun shifting themselves. It must be the waiting that does it, I didn't think this way when I worked on the railway and dropped exhausted into bed and fell asleep before I reached the mattress.

KASPAR | The Jataka Tales of the Buddha's previous lives which our governess used to read to me and Hildegard, I remember them so well. Today I wrote one of them in my notebook:

> *Buddha was born again as a dog, and together with other stray dogs he was accused of having eaten the leather on the king's beautiful harness, even though it was really the purebred palace dogs who had done it. The king decreed that all ownerless dogs should be killed. But the leader of the dogs, who was the Buddha, said: Are you not using the four evil methods, bias, ill-will, ignorance and fear now when you are judging? Such methods are wrong and are not fitting for a king, because a king should be unprejudiced and impartial. Then the Buddha made the palace dogs drink*

buttermilk and eat a special grass so that they threw up and then it was found it was they who had eaten the leather. The king was both surprised and grateful and said: I will never forget this, and from now on all ownerless dogs will stand under my protection.

The governess was always respectful when she read about the Buddha. While some of us were drinking beer last night, I repeated several of the tales. Gustav and I, at least, were ashamed of ourselves.

ROLF | Perhaps it is the appendix? We are standing helplessly in the field hospital with the boiled water they asked for, and looking in at the doorway while the surgeon operates. It's going well, this time. Last week they had to amputate an arm. The stink of rotten human flesh is the worst thing I have ever smelled. It must be offered to Neptune, they said, and asked us to throw the arm overboard.

I suddenly remember the smell at Gregor's house, it didn't smell bad, but it was different from our house, and I could never get used to it. Once I was to sleep over there, but changed my mind, and his father had to walk with me through the dark roads and all the way home, where Mother, ashamed and angry, took me in, I was too old for such behaviour. I always wondered whether there was something wrong at their house, something they didn't talk about, something sad, I noticed it particularly clearly in Gregor's room, because there were two beds there, I never dared ask about who had slept in the other one. Several years later I came to hear that Gregor had been a twin, and that twin boy had died when he was five.

KASPAR | When Helmut discovered the piano in the hall, he sat himself down at it, and before we could say anything, we were listening to Schubert's piano trio in B sharp. The Scherzo from Opus 99 with the rondo in the last movement as the great climax, I don't know how many recognized the music, but several of us were completely knocked out afterwards, that anything so beautiful could be found in a world that was going under.

My dearest Papa

I miss you a lot and wait every evening for you to come home. Mummy too. And Great-grandmother and Grandfather. We have got a dog! A yellow bitch puppy. Do you get good food? Jesus will take care of you. You are the nicest Papa in the world. It is a pity you have to be away. I hope the war is soon over. Come home to us! I am drawing the puppy so you can see it.

Yours
Wilhelm

UWE | 21 years old. Today, and the third birthday I'm celebrating on board Tirpitz. I don't exactly know what is happening, perhaps my friends have prepared something to surprise me. Perhaps one of the officers will say a few words. I hope so. Back home in Moabit the cherry trees and almond trees generally bloom in rivalry on my day, and Mother gathers and uses the flowers as confetti which she throws over me while the others sing and the candles on the cake are lit. That's how it has been since I was a little boy, and then I would have to search all over the house for my present. One year it was hidden in the chimney, another under the potatoes in the cellar. Once I found a present in Father's wardrobe too.

I long so much to see them. Good, good Mother, how afraid she must be for her boy. They must be thinking about me, sending good wishes, and would so much have wanted to throw flower confetti over me today. Here, in Norway, it is still more winter than spring, it snowed earlier today—imagine, it's snowing on my birthday! It must be a bad omen, at home they may be wearing shorts and summer dresses now, here we still have to have several layers of wool if going on the deck for a long time. It's a dog's life! But still a life. Thank God that I can experience this day, and then I pray that I may survive the war, and that my twenty-second birthday will be celebrated at home. Amen.

Well, just look, here come the boys, they're singing and looking sneaky, Sebastian is holding up a bottle of brandy, perhaps it will be a good celebration anyway? Cheers!

CARL | And I have two Norwegian girls at the same time, says Gottfried. Maybe three. Ha, do you have them together in the bed as well, then, sniggers Albert. No, they don't know about each other, you pig. Look at Uwe there, he is totally shocked. Come on, tell us, says Albert, which one is best and why, all the details, please, that's what we need! Well, one has big round breasts and the other small and pointed ones, Gottfried begins. Laila has a mass of red hair on her pussy and Berit has hardly any hair at all. Where is the hair? asks Uwe. Glory, I bluster, you know that, surely. No, says Uwe mildly. Don't say you went to war a virgin, roars Albert so loudly that several more come over to us, this is entertainment. In Alta there is a floating brothel on a converted passenger ship, there you can learn one thing and another about how the world goes round. A really good brothel, no Jewish girls there, but willing Norwegian women who know how to value men in uniform.

MARTIN | My hero is Leonhard Euler, the blind eighteenth-century mathematician. I was so impressed he was able to demonstrate that 'the bridges in the Königsberg' problem could not be solved. That with the seven bridges in the town, whether it was possible to cross all of them only once. I will remember Euler's figures all my life, because it is approximately like 2,7182818284590452353602875! On Tirpitz there isn't much time for mathematics, but I make some problems for a couple of the others now and then. Brain exercise, you may call it, but I feel that I am weakening myself, that all the physical work takes away ambitious thoughts, all desire for speculation. The worst is that the deep concentration one needs to get in and be able to look clearly, squarely at a mathematical problem is lost in the noise and interruptions. How I long for concentration like that again.

KURT | Floating horn mines, the greatest of all dangers at night, the word 'mine' is so innocent, sounds almost soft. Our Father, keep your hand over us. Keep watch together with me, help me to see the mines before they run us down! Mustn't panic, think about ordinary things. Polish my weapon. Watch. Rest. Polish my weapon. Watch. Rest. Polish my weapon. Watch. Rest. Polish my weapon. Watch. Rest. Swab the deck. Wash the galley. Brush my uniform. Watch. Rest.

OTTO | A crowd of pale scarecrows walk towards me when I am on land. Russian prisoners. The grey mass goes on towards the construction work. Quite different from the Cossacks I imagined when I read about them as a boy. Dobra, dobra, or something like that, they mumbled when I threw them the half-packet of cigarettes I had in my pocket.

The same evening I saw one of the officers raping a girl behind the cinema. The next day I acted as if nothing had happened. She couldn't have been more than fifteen or sixteen years old, we are not to do such things, but I dare not report him.

UWE | I had thought the first time would be beautiful and gentle. With Klara. Careful, a little solemn. But here there were many standing in a queue, and it was only to get one's pants down quickly. There was a heavy smell in the room, of something familiar, almost nauseating. I didn't know what I should say to the girl lying on the bed, luckily she was young, some are as old as your mother, Albert had warned me. She raised her arm and reached for me. Obviously we didn't have to talk. Close your eyes.

Klara.

\

"Alarm! All men forward on deck. Close the hatches!"

"It was only a drill. Yet another practice.
The ship's captain is timing us."

"The wake will disappear while you're watching it."

"What the hell does that mean? Navy clairvoyance?"

"So damp that mould grows, could have grown mushrooms down here, think of that, you chef!"

"Dream of fresh bakery and cocoa with cognac."

"Shut up, baby's bum!"

"What are we on course towards, the enemy?"

"No, towards three weeks of gales."

"Wet sea."

"What?"

"I love this ship! The sound of machines."

"The ship is alive!"

"Smell the aroma from the
officers' mess! Something
quite different from the food
in our mess. It's the cook's
assistants who feed us, to tell
the truth."

Svalbard and Kåfjord, autumn 1943

FREGATTEN-KAPITÄN BIELER | Special assignment. We're going to the Barents Sea, prepared the ship for ice, full dress, hot drinks every three hours. Operation Sizilien is the name of the attack on Barentsburg. 8 September we'll get to see Spitzbergen, according to the plan.

ROLF | You haven't felt cold until you feel the frostbite from snow which hasn't even appeared yet. In the Admiralty in Berlin it is certainly nice and warm. They can order in mulled wine if they like. It is said that one can smell ice. Now I know it is true. Fimbul, the eternal winter.

When we woke up this morning, frost lay like a bridal veil over the ship, all around us, it is like looking straight at a watercolour which is painted with a lot of water on the brush.

The light on Svalbard, the sun over Spitzbergen! Here lie the polar bears on their beds of snow. The noise from the glacier which is calving, ice floes float like cork. The mountains of birds, that such a thing should exist. Colonies of puffins. I could never describe it to anyone, perhaps paint it, give a picture to Mother.

A hill of walruses. Their noise. A blast, strong and supple, like themselves. The whales' sea. What an experience! And I who had hardly left Berlin.

On the way here we saw a big herd of orcas, they are too far north, more than normal. We are too far north as well. The hunt for the convoys is our whale hunt.

The inland ice is in motion, the glacier shifts, I can almost see it moving. It crackles, breaks, hollow ice castles. I feel like the great explorers. The life of fur-trappers. The whaling stations we sail past are abandoned now.

The ancient history the glaciers could tell, plants which have frozen in, stones which may originate from when the stars were young. Permafrost. A word I remember from school, now I recognize it. There can't be war about the ice, there is peace in the ice, millions of years of peace. The wild patience that turns resin into amber.

KASPAR | Suddenly I saw something white in the water, a whale, a white whale! Moby Dick at Svalbard! Captain Ahab's albino whale? No, more of them came, now I saw that the white whales were only about five metres long, and it was a big herd of them. Oh, that one second when I believed I saw Moby Dick.

FREGATTEN-KAPITÄN BIELER | Popping up like this at Spitzbergen should be as surprising as the kettledrum beats in Haydn's symphony, the ones that wake up the concert-goers. That was the plan, according to the admiral.

Actually we didn't achieve all that much, but good grief, how it was used in propaganda. None of us recognized ourselves, but when we came back to Kåfjord there were several iron crosses for Battle Group 1. We on Tirpitz got more than four hundred. Scharnhorst got only 150, so now there will be envy.

OTTO | "Tirpitz triumphs in the attack on Spitzbergen," it says in the newspapers at home, writes Mother. Well, we know we only fired cannons at empty houses, closed-down worksheds, slag heaps and shit. We want to go home and fight, save our own, take care of our family farms and country, not win ignominious victories. Just the same there was a real party when we took war booty from Svalbard for ourselves, there was butter, chocolate, spirits and cigarettes.

The fog makes our clothes damp on deck, it is clammy, raw and hangoverish. Shit! Nobody can thrive in wet clothes. Rumour has it that there's TB on board, is that what's going to do me in?

UWE | Safely back inside the torpedo net, and in front of us lie Nymph and Thetis on the lookout. Two old Norwegian ships, which we have taken over and rechristened. No British planes reach here till Kåfjord, either from bases in Scotland or the new ones we hear they have set up in Archangel. We shall survive the war, and sail home to Wilhelmshaven in great triumph! Then it will be our turn to get flowers from the girls.

FRITZ | I couldn't sleep last night either, I looked at the clock, first when it was nearly two, then at ten to four, afterwards I must have slept a little, before the wake-up signal, which every soldier is always woken up by, however tired one is. I am cold and feel terrible, it will be better when I get moving, but out on watch when nothing is happening, I get tired, try to think about football, about which place Hertha Berlin will get in the series this year, but it doesn't help. Painful to fight the sleep in oneself, when everything is screaming for rest, when the brain beats faster than the heart. The punishment for sleeping on watch is too harsh for me even to think of, and I pinch my cheek to keep myself awake, shake my head and snuffle like a horse. Yawning on the sly because of the officers who come walking by. Don't shame your uniform!

Are little Alfred and Hedwig asleep?

KASPAR | Then "Holy Mary, pray for us" is heard, the Catholics on board drag it out too long, this isn't a monastery. God does not exist on Tirpitz, this is the ship that repudiates God, here no prayers are required. You don't win a war with prayers.

\

Dear Mother

We have autumn colours on the trees already, it is really lovely here, Mother! Yesterday I saw two reindeers crossing the road right in front of me, they were more afraid than I was, so don't worry. I have many good friends, one has just come on board, I know him from school. I hope all is well with you.

Love
Rolf

FREGATTEN-KAPITÄN BIELER | 22 September. In the morning there was a totally astonishing attack by British mini-submarines. They were not many metres long, but they caused an enormous explosion! Tirpitz was humiliated and lifted into the air like a dinghy. We lost one man and the ship's captain Meyer has been sent to the field hospital after a nasty fall. Complete chaos on deck, gradually an alert officer got the distribution of guns and hand-grenades organized, but it didn't help. How did the Brits manage it? We're going to be out of play for several months! Sea expertise, that's the truth.

REINHARD | I saw something steel-coloured. In shape like a small submarine, then it was gone. But inside the net. They said I must not imagine things, but I shouted that if I am going to die, I want to at least to know how. Maybe the ship was in danger! I saw it first, will I get a medal?

OTTO | Fritz died. We saw his coffin lowered slowly overboard because it was hard to transport it to the church. We usually try to forget death, but now it knocked on our door and showed itself.

HEDWIG | The scream is stuck, grief is a note my voice does not have the power to reach. Moving house does not help, every place lies at the same distance from death. To the war churchyard where Fritz lies buried, it is as far as the moon! In dream I carry you out. Blood drips from your eyes. You see no longer, you are on the way to another place. Only Fritz died in the submarine attack. Out of over 2,000 men on board, why did *you* have to die?

FREGATTEN-KAPITÄN BIELER | "Today we shall grieve, tomorrow a new day begins, then we shall go on. That is how you honour a fallen comrade best. He received death, all of you got life, therefore be worthy of that gift and use it as well as possible, for yourselves, for others and for the land of your birth. See for the eyes which were closed forever, speak for the mouth that forever has stilled, live for the courageous heart which sacrificed all."

He came on board hardly eighteen years old and quite fresh, and unusually enough asked to speak to me, and unusually enough I went along with it. Fritz he was called. He had with him a letter from his mother, Frau Neurath, to the one who was responsible for him, a letter in which she asked me to take extra good care of her son. The boy could not swim, and was frail. She ended by praying to God to preserve the ship, me and her son.

He was the only one who was killed by the explosion from the mini-submarine attack. Now I have to write a letter to his mother. The admiral became quite grey-haired after the attack. I noticed it during the flag ceremony. He has become silvered by grief, I thought, solemn and oppressed as we were in the days that followed. Tirpitz has become a cripple.

KONRAD | The oil we leaked is still floating on the sea here. I dare not have a smoke.

\

Dear Elsa

I will always be yours, Elsa, only yours, until death separates us, and if the war goes on like now, I am afraid it might happen quite soon. Some days ago we were attacked by mini-submarines from England. It was by a hair's breadth that time. Obviously I am not allowed to write this, and if anyone reads it I will get disciplinary action, but I want you to know, beloved Elsa, how bad it is, how near-death it is. I admit I am scared, don't want to die apart from you, my plum, my heart. Hoping intensely for Christmas leave. There is talk about us being divided up into groups of 600 men, perhaps I will be among the first who are allowed to go. Then I'm coming straight to you!

Kiss,

Gottfried

SONJA | On my way out of the hairdresser's, and there is nobody to look nice for, all the men are gone. Setting it is useless. Such bad luck to be young at a time of war, when there is nobody to dance with or wave at. What is going to become of me, an old maid like Aunt Gisela? Who scarcely gets a visit at Christmas?

CARL | A man has to hang in and share the fate of his country even when it is difficult. As long as Germany is at war, so, bloody hell, I am too. I can't think of anything worse than losing the hatred.

WERNER | I grew up on the bank of the Danube before I moved to Wilhelmshaven. I dreamed all my childhood about following the current of the river. From the Black Forest to the Black Sea, to the huge delta between Ukraine and Romania. All the way through Germany, Austria, Czechoslovakia and Bulgaria, 3,000 kilometres, 2,888 to be precise, my dream was that long. Instead I am stuck sitting on a target of a battleship which is lying at anchor most of the time.

"Monte Rosa", the workshop ship, is coming with a crane and equipment and several hundred new mechanics; we few who work on maintenance can't repair this damage by ourselves. The sailors look at us, want us to get the ship in order again, it was grievously weakened after the mini-submarine attack, I could have wept when I saw the result.

UWE | My sister, Katharina, was brain-damaged and was killed in a gas chamber before the war broke out. Mother and Father were given merely the urn and a bill. We were their angels of death, Lotta told me, we led the children into the gas chambers, it is important to keep the people pure and strong.

She came to the field hospital in Alta, as a nurse. I had broken an ankle and an arm, wounded during the attack by the mini-submarines and stayed in bed quite long. She was the kindest out of all the nurses, I was half in love with her.

Gradually I understood that Lotta might have participated in the killing of my sister.

OTTO | The most dangerous place to stay on a ship is in the turret, directly above the ammunition store. If the powder catches fire, then it's thanks and goodbye, but we have to stay at our post, whatever happens. That's the procedure, and we are drilled to keep to it until the final end. Tip for a useful Christmas present, I heard Carl say today: Give a coffin! I always carry Father's soft felt hat with me, inside my uniform jacket over my heart, I have got it into my head that if I lose it, Father or I will die.

ELSA | I can't be bothered to wash my hair and make myself up in the mornings any longer, why should I, there's no Gottfried coming to see me anyway. There was a self-torturing pleasure in feeling that I smelled, that I looked ten years older in the old golf jacket when the stomach no longer stuck out. The meals I cooked just became simpler and more disgusting, soon I hadn't the energy for anything but sandwiches, hot food was too much trouble, and the cups remained sitting in the basin. Perhaps the exhaustion was caused by the foetus dying, I didn't remember anything anymore. Lethargy.

Then Mother stood at the door, uninvited, and looked at me and the mess in the flat. She began to scold and cry at the same time, turned and ran away, an hour later she was back with green soap and fresh chicken meat, figs in a little box, six eggs, leeks and tomatoes. Real coffee as well and a piece of the cherry cake I've always liked. God knows what she must have sold to get hold of all this. She heated water for bathing and washing, I sat apathetically in a chair without opening my mouth. What's the point, I wanted to say. Mama, don't even try, nothing means anything now, but I hadn't the energy to protest. Soon Gottfried will get leave, said Mother, you must build yourself up until then.

I slept for nearly half a year. Gottfried never got leave. Then came a letter from the government, I was requested to apply for a job in a weapons factory. Now us women were to be "man's working and fighting comrades"! The fog vanished, it was the best thing that could have happened to me, I got more and more responsibility, soon I was in charge of my department.

Just before Christmas I came to work and saw that the factory had been pulverized by a bomb. There was not so much as a chair left, not a work overall from the wardrobe, not a bolt, not a screw, not a spot of oil. I cried hysterically, knowing that everything was over for me too.

\

Dear Uncle Oddvar,

How are things in Kjøllefjord? Has Grandfather's pneumonia got better? Do you go fishing these days? Here all is well, Karen has been a bit sick, but it usually passes. Mother asks me to greet you all so warmly! Otherwise there's a lot of activity at Strømsnes. Monte Rosa has come with more than 888 repairmen for Tirpitz after the destruction the brave dwarf-submarines did. The Germans are working round the clock, it is obvious they haven't given her up. We can only look on, says Father, and know that as long as she is afloat, new attacks will come. Ugh, it is horrible to think of. We are coming to visit on Boxing Day, you must tell Grandmother.

Live well and be careful (you know what I mean)

A very happy Christmas

Love

Kåre

MARTIN | Sabina has hung red Christmas baubles on fishing lines from the ceiling, it looks as if they are floating. Defying gravity. She is trying to tell me something. I have been home on leave for several days, but she talks only about mundane things. Says we must go out and buy gifts. She acts as if it is possible to buy anything now, as if the shops are full, as if there isn't a major war going on. We must buy sherry, she says. It isn't allowed to be so distant from real life! Does she believe we can get hold of imported fortified wine nowadays? Ships are used to transport war materials, not sherry or Madeira. I want to shout that at her, but think twice about it, think it's best to let her live in the bubble, inside the red Christmas bauble. I put on my scarf, let's go out and see if we find anything then.

OTTO | How far have they got in the Christmas preparations at home? Is the pig slaughtered? Are there any pigs to slaughter? Candles to dip, gifts to make? I wonder whether Gerhard is good at helping out, and Father, he is good at carving meat, cooking steak and chops. How our Christmas will turn out to be, I don't even want to think about it.

A telegram from home can't be more than thirty words, only about personal family matters. I read again what came today:

> *Dear Otto, all well home, we expect to hear from you soon. Can you send a few words? Merry Christmas! Hearty greetings from Father, Mother and Gerhard 20 December 1943.*

ROLF | We are responsible for decorating for Christmas and I have appointed myself in charge. That is how I can go ashore and fetch moss and twigs. I get to feel snow underfoot and think about the Christmases at Grandmother and Grandfather's when I was a child. Besides, I escape the cleaning. We shall have red garlands of crepe paper and plaited baskets and a large Star of Bethlehem made out of yellow paper, which is to hang beside Hitler's portrait in the mess, where it is written: "Our leader's struggle is our struggle. Our leader's faith is our faith." The celebration will be a success. The orchestra began practising Christmas carols long ago, that is important, the songs will bring us home, and then the priest will speak. Afterwards we must have something entertaining, so that we don't keep sitting there snivelling. I have asked an officer to come as Santa Claus and give out extra rations of goodies to all the sailors. Then there will be jubilation, and then it is time for the telegrams at the end. Will we get one from Hitler himself this year? In any case from the Admiralty, I am sure of that. I wonder whether I'll get a greeting from Maria from Potsdam, whom I have just become penpals with, she writes so well and sincerely. I long for her letters, does this mean I no longer believe that Hannah is alive?

FREGATTEN-KAPITÄN BIELER | I have got hold of a foxfur jacket, I will send it by field-post parcel home to Irmchen. She wishes for one, and fur clothes are easy to get hold of here and really quite cheap, I don't think the Norsemen know how expensive such things are in Germany, but they are quite dumb too. They need us to control them, if there is to be growth and progress and development, that is certain in any case! I don't know how many airports we have built out in this country, and harbour constructions and railways, they have a little to learn.

KASPAR | The Christmas carol 'Old ballad of Mary', the folk tune from Thüringen I know well, that gets the feeling going, it is like pressing a button, and tears are there and have to be swallowed, hidden. Obviously it becomes even harder when we hear 'Silent Night', because then it is Christmas, as it has been ever since Gruber set the melody to it in 1818, when the organ had been eaten by mice and the congregation needed a new song, that is how I remember the governess told it. Surely it wasn't only I who let the tears run discreetly when the priest led the Christmas devotions with music before the meal. About the shepherds on the ground and their faith and courage to follow the star into Bethlehem, and the three wise men who also followed the same star. If we simply follow our star, it will go well, concluded the priest, we who have Jesus need never be afraid of anything.

Later it becomes jollier, after a few drinks. We start up, all the men's voices blending in the chorus:

O Tannenbaum, O Tannenbaum
wie treu sind deine Blätter!
Du grünst nicht nur zur Sommerzeit
nein, auch im Winter wenn es schneit
O Tannenbaum, O Tannenbaum
wie treu sind deine Blätter.

Late at night, only the spirits are left, when both the mixing water and common sense are used up, then the word 'mutiny' comes on the table. Though high on spirits, the word is only murmured, before voices are raised, it is Walter and Jochen who talk the most, who are deepest in overconfidence. Obviously Hitler has become mad, they say, everyone knows that, Germany is in great danger, a mutiny on Tirpitz itself will start a people's revolution against him and the Party. Against the whole war which has run wild and will kill all of us and destroy Germany. By taking over the ship, we can get people to listen to us, we can hold meetings and talks. When we have broken away from the fleet, more will come and follow us, be sure of it. People will come to know about it, and support us, nobody can conceal that Tirpitz has broken free!

The mood has changed, everyone is suddenly clear-headed, they stare at Jochen as if he was standing with a gun pointed at them. It is completely silent until Johannes goes up to Jochen and says: You are alive only because none of us has denounced you yet, remember that next time you feel the need to talk like that. It is time to finish, men, tomorrow nobody will remember this, agreed? We nod and break up, only Jochen and Walter are left sitting there. When I turn around, I see that Jochen is crying, Walter is patting him on the shoulder and looking around, he looks at me and makes a silent prayer with his eyes.

UWE | To wake up and know you said something stupid yesterday, that you took the floor, spoke uninterruptedly, that you mocked Bernhard. That you tried to kiss Emmeline. Klara comes up in my mind, as she always does when I feel ashamed. I come up with more and more tortures. Dammit, that I should have drunk so much yesterday. Klara. Why do I have to ruin everything? Klara. Will Emmeline be bothered to speak to me anymore, at any rate I won't get the job with Bernhard's father which we have talked about. So long as they don't say anything to Felix, he'd be so jealous. Klara.

Bruno doesn't speak to me when I come downstairs, was I so bad yesterday? I ask. Worse, he says, aren't you ashamed of yourself? But I am, I say flatly, I really am. "Fairweather Nazi," you called Bernhard, do you think he'll accept that, should he accept it? No, no, I say. Do you have any headache pills, I ask, but Bruno just looks at me, says I deserve the pain. I shuffle away, free watch luckily, lie down carefully in the hammock. Klara, Klara, it is completely wet. Oh, no, I must have pissed myself.

HERBERT | Have you ever fucked a Jew? asked Hans, teasing maliciously. No, I said. I didn't dare to add it wasn't the race laws that were the hindrance, but that Esther was never interested in me.

PHILIPP | Scharnhorst went down on Boxing Day, outside North Cape. Many who were originally on Tirpitz went down with it. Only 36 out of the crew of about 1,800 men were saved. There must have been living and dead men bobbing like corks in the water.

At the evening meal, there are four biscuits and a little chocolate on our plates. A pail of pea soup pops up. They are trying to restore our spirits.

FREGATTEN-KAPITÄN BIELER | When we heard the announcement about Scharnhorst's defeat, the fact that none of the ship's 80 officers survived made a strong impression on me. Many must have committed suicide. One shot himself in front of the picture of his family in his cabin, related a sailor who was saved.

Since we ourselves have had our wings clipped, Scharnhorst has sunk and reports of the bombings at home increase, the mood on board becomes more depressing all the time. In addition the dark season wears us down. It is long between smiles.

I have started walking around with my identification sign around my neck again.

ROLF | New Year's Eve on board: sausages and rum, mouth organs and festoons. Loud wishes for a speedy victory. This is perhaps your last year, if the war does not end. Can't live like this, this isn't living. Drowsiness like being drunk, a white dough of exhaustion, a sticky mass one hasn't the energy to bake, you sit there stuck, forgetting everything else. The easy things. The foot which lifts itself up with pleasure from the floor because it wants to be in the air, in a dance. Music which never ends. Thoughts that think by themselves, because you can't let them go. The tight pain in the head, lack of sleep. Scharnhorst which is not mentioned.

GUSTAV | The kind old priest at home said to me before I left: I have been in a war myself. I know how easy it is to begin to doubt when one sees all that suffering. What saved me when doubt came was that I continued living like a believer. It is wise to keep on saying your prayers. The Holy Spirit will protect us in the faith when we ourselves are not able to do so. I remember he said that in a mild tone. Then he cleared his throat a little and continued with greater force: Keep your hopes up high, young friend. While we are living on earth, we can count on God fighting against evil. That gives hope to humanity, remember that when you need to. Hope is a help in the struggle. You will come back, don't be afraid. Don't be afraid, let it be a sentence which rings in your ears when it gets tough. Because God has lit a fire which is shining ahead, that is where you are going, remember that.

UWE | I don't want any more, dear God, take me away, don't let the others see me like this. Take me away from this ship!

My best beloved on earth!

You don't answer my letters, Sonja, not even the Christmas letter. Answer, but don't say you have found someone else. I can't come home and find you with another man. Then everything would be in vain, Sonja, it is you I want to come home to. You are the only one worth fighting for.

Johannes

FREGATTEN-KAPITÄN BIELER | I myself take his watch and wedding ring, his wife will get them. I read 'Our Father', it never does any harm, even if grace is denied him. I suspect suicide, but haven't said so to anyone. There are many ways to lose a soldier. The coffin is lowered carefully. The ship is silent and heavy.

Fugit irreparabile tempus—time flies beyond recall, even on board Tirpitz, although we have been lying here in Kåfjord all winter, waiting. The captain is anxious about discipline weakening since we are never tested in battle. The men are drilled as often as possible, but we must go out soon, staying still is demoralizing for the seamen. Dissatisfaction increases, yesterday Oberfähnrich Röll yelled out that they must direct their complaints to Rhadamanthys! If I remember correctly, he is the court of appeal in the Underworld. That does not bode well. When I came in to Röll afterwards, he sat listening to Mahler's *Das Lied von der Erde.* We did not say anything, but it was there between us, all the beauty the war is destroying. He related that there is a quotation from 'Lamentations' scratched on the wall in the field hospital: "Is it nothing to you, all ye that pass by? Behold, and see if there be any sorrow like unto my sorrow."

OTTO | The only thing he said, the one who apparently committed suicide, was that he was an East Friesian from Emden. I am sorry I did not ask him more. It is hard to remember someone you have not known, but I feel it isn't right for him to be forgotten at once. If I die, I hope they will have a ceremony. One minute's silence at least, the whole ship with caps in hand.

When the war is really over, we'll go out and have a beer, says Ulrich encouragingly, the first round is on me!

FRAU NEURATH | Fritz stands all alone in the photograph, in white shorts, striped cotton shirt and a rather too grownup expression for someone so small, he is only six or seven years old. Now he is buried in Norway. The road goes through memory. I remember you, that is how you are still alive. Soon I will come to you.

ROLF | Long nights, little light. Boredom is called Patience. The Bismarck Parade. The king and the jack. The days are dealt out, that's how one survives. Watch, free watch, night, food, watch, free watch, night, food, watch. Another year has gone by since I was home. Another year has been stolen from me. From 21 to 22. That should have been my time. Free, free to think and to love, consider and experience. I see no end to the war. The only thing I know is that the hours are vanishing, eating up the days. Patience. King, jack, diamonds and clubs.

HARRY | The waiting subtracts from the war, remember that, said the Oberbootsmann, he is the ship's philosopher and is probably right, but wrong at the same time, because the days are also subtracted from life. Dying of waiting. O let me shovel coal instead!

SONJA | Hearing your voice against my ear, it is asking what I want you to do. Stroke downwards, slowly, slowly, when you get near the warmth, my dampness, separate me with your finger, look at me, bend down between my legs, your tongue is as careful as the finger was, I pant. Bite. You are hard, hard against me, you lift me up and show yourself, the gleaming limb. I'll soon get to taste, take it into my mouth, wash it with my tongue, the tongue goes all over, and you take pleasure in it, stroke a rough finger against my bottom, look at me. You pull yourself out of my mouth, then you are inside me, and it is the only thing I want, stay there. Move there, thrust, thrust, thrust. I wait for what is coming. You hold back when I want to speed up, slow beats, you explode and I overflow.

Faithlessness which just then was necessary. You can't deny me that, Johannes. I must. I had to.

KONRAD | In the asparagus season, that's when I'll go home! Do I like the white or the green best, that is a question I can lie thinking about for a long time. I end up with the white, with gammon and hollandaise. Always beer. I order the barman to bring two bottles of Berliner Kindl at the time, they are so small, after all. With the green asparagus I want scallops. The Reisling should be exactly eight degrees. When I am really hungry, I fantasize about schnitzel, with lashings of pepper sauce and thick chips. Two more beers. For dessert we'll have apple strudel with both ice-cream and custard. It is a good thing I tell Günther about it, he gazes thankfully at me, with half-closed eyes, so good, he murmurs, raising himself up in his hammock and saying solemnly: When we go home, I will invite you to a restaurant, and then you will get apple strudel with both ice-cream and custard.

OTTO | Matthias is enthusiastic now, he is showing me the fine chess set he has made. Each piece more elegantly carved than the last. He has painted tar on half of it, and now, free after many long evenings' work, he wants to play with me. Do you know, he says that the total number of possible chess games should be higher than the quantity of rice grains in the world? I'm not very good, the best I can hope for is a stalemate, and that, according to Matthias, is only for sissies. But tonight he shall have a game. To have time for such things in a war is almost absurd. I will cheerfully lose at chess, Matthias, I am sure. Take the white pieces and begin.

UWE | Well, I've become a sort of kid brother in the group, I don't exactly know why. The others are always asking me how I feel, if I am happy or scared. One may mix happy and scared, I was thinking as the organist played Bach chorales during the service in Alta church yesterday, so loudly that it deafened the air raid siren.

BOOTSMANN SPIEDEL | The young Norseman shouted after me: I am the steel, you are the sledge hammer which beats me. You are not destroying me, you are hardening me! I ought to have arrested him, of course, but something about his eloquence spoke to me. I let him go, but tried not to think any more about what he had said, certain thoughts one can't permit oneself. David and Goliath. I don't want to go there.

WOLFGANG | I am lying in my hammock, it's impossible to fall asleep, the night doesn't work any longer. I doze, suddenly I see the hillside up to our house in front of me, I stop at the place where the horse always insists on a rest. Further up I can see the warm light from the kitchen windows.

KASPAR | Life on board Tirpitz is like a bookcase. The notebooks at the bottom don't talk to the dictionaries on the first shelf, the dictionaries don't exchange anything other than essentials with the novels on the second shelf either. The poetry on the third shelf has not greeted the Bible or the Psalm books on the top shelf for a long time, and the bust of Goethe on top no doubt speaks only with the Nine Muses.

ROLF | It is a long time since you stopped noticing the smell of your own underpants. You no longer remember what it felt like to put on clean clothes every day. It is so easy to slide into indifference. Run when the others run. Stop when you are ordered to. Where did I let myself go, will I ever get it back?

I write about this to Maria, from her reply I see that she understands what I mean. Imagine falling in love with someone you have never met.

HEINRICH | Sharpen your bayonet, soldier. Polish your gun. Soon you might meet the worst death—your death.

\

"Post is the only thing I want, letters from home, from my girl."

"Well, we all do."

"No, only you, you cunt-otter!"

"Do you know what I heard, a new boy in C turret is totally gambling-mad and wants to bet on everything under the sun. Yesterday, when he had no money left, he ended up with Russian roulette, but fainted when he heard the first click. This is absolutely true."

"Remember what Socrates said about death:
If it is like an eternal undisturbed sleep, it
is nothing to be afraid of. But the whole ship
suffers from a sickly fear of death."

"Thanatophobia."

"Hey, what are you guys talking about?"

"Have you heard that Johannes and Sonja are engaged again, yes, she was sorry, you see!"

"Did that idiot take her back?"

"I know the kind. She won't be faithful
for long, I'm sure of it."

"I understand him, it's better to have somebody than nobody."

"Hey, drink this, liquid courage."

"I always keep this note in my pocket: 'To my dearest. Now we are under attack. Know that I am thinking of you.'"

"Who said that?"

"The fellow with the Vandyke beard,
he who brings bad luck."

"It's sure to go well this time too."

"As the French say, it's only the
first bottle that's expensive, cheers,
cheers!"

"Cheers!"

"What are the most beautiful words in the German
language?"

"Right, they are 'take off your clothes.'"

"I never get used to the mountains here, before
I came to Norway, I had hardly seen a hilltop."

"Agreed! The mountains ought to have
been moved away, they don't need to
be here every day, anyway."

"But they give good protection against attack."

"Yes, well that's what we're waiting for.
The Devil's empty nothingness raid!"

Kåfjord, winter and spring 1944

FREGATTEN-KAPITÄN BIELER | Yesterday we raised anchor for a test run, we went out after almost half a year of repairs. The crews on the other ships saluted us. The Titan has stood up again.

JOSEF | My shoulders ache, one never sleeps well in a hammock. No support. In my dream there was a child who called Papa, Papa, all through the night. I don't know whether it was Theres or Wilhelm, or someone else's child, perhaps it was myself, I remember only the shout which came at irregular intervals, far in the distance, it was as if the child was out in the street or on the stairs. I need time to shake the night off me. The best thing is work, and today we are cleaning. Hoping for a day without an air raid siren.

OTTO | I am so utterly fed up of being lied to. If you ask a Norwegian the way, always go in the opposite direction from what he says, he is always trying to trick you. But last week, when I went to buy eggs and came to a farmer's family who were sitting round a table, I became quite dizzy. How I missed Mother and Father! I believe they understood that. In any case they let me buy some. That evening we made eggnog, then it turned into a party. I also traded some excellent fishskin shoes for half a litre of spirits and fifty grams of tobacco. They were so elegant. Right up until they got wet in the slushy snow. *Scheisse!*

CARL | In the class photo we stood side by side, Sven and I, and now he too has ended up in the Alta district, it's bloody unbelievable! I have heard he lost his brother in the Ukraine. Does he remember I teased him? No, dammit, that was over ten years ago. In the class photo you can see the scar he got from my ski stick, I haven't dared to look properly whether it's still visible. In the café I notice he keeps peering at me, but so far he hasn't said a word, not even greeted me, perhaps he wants to act as if he doesn't recognize me, if that's what he wants, that's fine with me. Or has the hare become a hunter?

BOOTSMANN SPIEDEL | Just recently several little boats have come out to Tirpitz with shouts for "Doctor, doctor", and each time he has gone off. Delivered breech births, diagnosed appendicitis, splinted legs and treated burns with salve and clean bandages from our store. I know it, because I have often gone in the boat as a guard. He is a good man, our new doctor.

KASPAR | First boat to Narvik, leave at last, a bus, then a train to Oslo. Norwegian prisoners are sitting in the other carriages, being sent to the camps. The train remains standing for a long time at a station. I peep out, and see a crowd of women and children standing on the platform saying goodbye to husbands and fathers. The red light stays on, and some of the soldiers shout out to the station staff, who change it to green, while people run beside the train and hold their loved ones by the hand as long as they can. The crying ascends from quiet to loud sobbing as we pull out of the station.

HEINRICH | Pity I didn't get a long enough leave to go home to Germany like some of the other lucky pigs. Oslo is boring. Everywhere there are women standing queuing up for food, they don't even look at us. Hans, who likes buxom women, gets fewer and fewer to choose from.

KURT | So tired that I haven't the energy to hold my head up. Everything becomes grey and foggy. I ought to ask for a replacement although there isn't much left of my watch. Lookouts on Tirpitz have to be sharp, the safety of everybody, including those on the bridge, depends on me.

SIEGFRIED | Idiot, don't sleep on watch! Remember they can send you to Russia, or in any case a month in jail, look alert, I can't always be coming to wake you.

BOOTSMANN SPIEDEL | Dozens of auxiliary troops in the air force fell in the last attack on Cologne, among them my younger brother Oskar. I read the telegram again and again. Oskar is dead.

A letter came from him many days later, it must have been delayed in the post, it was as if I received a letter from someone on the other side, but the contents were very ordinary, typical Oskar:

> *At 22.45 came the first alarm, then we went to bed again, and at 2.10 we had to get up again, 3.30 came yet another alarm, and at 5 o'clock I was woken up too, then I didn't have the energy even to try to sleep, whatever happens we have to be ready for breakfast at 7 o'clock.*

KONRAD | The stink of unwashed uniform. Sweaty bum-crack. Foot fungus and nail fungus next to each other. Warts. Forget it, we have to endure all.

GOTTFRIED | How can I know that Elsa is waiting for me, that she isn't betraying me now this very minute, this second? It gets suffocating in here, I run out on deck and stare into the soft blue night, the ship is completely silent, is it only me who is awake, only myself who is awake in the whole world, and perhaps Elsa in Berlin, in the arms of another?

UWE | Today Father is fifty. I've sent a telegram, but I would have liked so much to actually be there, seeing the gifts and Father's happiness! I know they are thinking about me, they are sure to drink to my health, but what use is that, I want to be with them. "Bloody war," as Carl always says, bloody hellish fucked-up SHIT war!

FREGATTEN-KAPITÄN BIELER | He has completely flipped, that is obvious, how he is going to gain control of his nerves again is outside my grasp. Talking to him seems like a farce, he struggles and lashes out about himself, what shall we do now? Should we chuck him overboard, like a rabid dog? He stands by himself in a corner, shouting "Stop! Stop! Don't touch me!" waving his arms about. Now it is no longer the Brits who are his enemy, but his own demons. Wild eyes. Only a needle can calm him down. There are so many ways to lose soldiers, it never ceases to amaze me. What are we to write to his parents?

KASPAR | We are sitting talking instead of resting. Jochen says he has lost faith in the Third Reich. Shut up, I shout, that is mutinous thinking, you can be punished for talking like that, and you know it. He looks at me with a tired gaze, don't say you have never thought of it, he says a little lower, now that we are not going to win this war. Submarines and planes disappear, the same happens to cruisers and destroyers, after Scharnhorst there's only us left, almost. It can never work, just admit it, the leadership at home makes one mistake after another. It's going to hell, and what are we going to do then, afterwards, if we don't get blown to bits by British bombers?

What do we have to come home to, tell me that, you who were just now on leave. To believe you can come back, and everything will be as before, is so laughably naïve that it's not like you, says Jochen. It is time to wake up, it becomes bloody well more and more unbearable to me to be on board and never achieve anything but swabbing the damned deck. It will be over soon, before winter comes, the war may end.

CARL | Remember, then, there were 700,000 fewer unemployed people in one year, something we could thank the Führer alone for, I hear Jürg speaking at length about it. He started in the Hitler Youth in Munich at the same time as me, and now he has been promoted to officer, while I am still a seaman. The devil take Mother and her bragging, she is sure to have convinced the women in the block of flats that I have become a *Leutnant zur See* at least. I can't be bothered to exert myself like Jürg, and in any case not suck up to people, he's an arse-licker, he is. I'll bloody well say that to him afterwards, so he won't start imagining things, I knew him long before he became an officer and I know he's not such a great guy!

I've had enough of this war! Do you hear, you people in Berlin, I am so damned fed up, don't have the energy any more to stay here looking out for periscopes or listening for planes. Now it's bloody well enough—we have kept on for nearly five years. Put an end to it!

HEDWIG | Mother-in-law died last night. Sleep turned quietly into death, grief over Fritz conquered her life force. We could share that grief, it brought us together. Morning is for the living, there is a radio programme on, activity in the bathroom, clothes pulled onto a warm, moveable body. And onto a cold, stiff body, for the last time. A blouse. A flower in her hand. A candle. No more, now there is no more.

I go out onto the veranda and look down at the crater from the last bomb. Before, the men in the street always used to gather in the square, playing chess on boards which were carved into the tables under the big willow. Talking about politics, but more often about the weather, about each other, sitting quietly, telling a story about a woman in the neighbourhood who has had eighteen children, or about a poor man who personally went to the Kaiser and complained of his distress. Then they would laugh a bit together, before they got up one by one to go home and eat lunch. Now the square has been bombed so completely that one can't imagine there was a gathering place here. There are hardly any men left either.

FREGATTEN-KAPITÄN BIELER | Hardly anyone gets the Knight's Cross any more, at any rate not in the Navy, what have we to show off, damaged and gagged as we are? In Berlin they must get the Great Cross simply by looking out of the door. But what are they thinking of doing down there, now that we are surrounded and isolated on the Eastern Front? In the Mediterranean the Americans seem to be winning island after island.

Someone has smuggled an enemy propaganda pamphlet on board. A kind of home-made newspaper, in German even. It tells how we treat Jews and other prisoners, of our losses and the advances of the Brits and Americans. I feel I can almost tell from the faces of the seamen which ones have read it. The newspaper must have been on board for a few days before it came onto my desk. How am I going to rebuild morale among these men who have never been able to test themselves, who simply walk about here on the most expensive vessel in the world, and wait?

I must put this over the loudpeaker:

Heilige Glut!
Rufe die Jugend zusammen
dass bei den lodernden Flammen
wachse der Mut!

UWE | I get a day off the day Father is buried in Berlin, only two weeks after his fiftieth birthday. The whole morning I sit in my hammock gazing at a picture of him. Until Otto comes and drags me with him to a quiet corner of the mess. Here is coffee, he says, and then you can tell me about your father. Start with the first thing you remember about him, how old were you then? In that way I got to empty myself, it does good to talk, much better than crying. The image of Father comes so close, in the brown trousers he always wore at home, all the times I sat in his lap and he stroked the line on my forehead where my hair began, again and again. Or when he and I sneaked down into the cellar and tasted the Christmas baking Mother had hidden, I must have been four, it's my first memory of having done something wrong. Father in his study, don't disturb said his back, but then he always came out and played ball with me just the same, or called me in and gave me a sheet of paper and a pencil, and then I got to play architect or bank clerk or someone working in an office. Office manager, said Father, that is good. It's necessary. Then we laugh, Otto and I, then I cry a little, and then Otto says amen and then the funeral is over.

\

Dear Elsa

Hang in there. Soon I will be with you again, I think I will get leave next month, if nothing special comes up. Be there, with bottom bare!

Towards you, towards you, towards you, whisper the train rails. Towards you, my love, I'm coming!

I have sent my shadow ahead, soon he will be knocking on the door and stroking down your back.

Love

Gottfried your boy

UWE | I don't want to   I don't want to die
I don't want to   die   Help me

Are you there   Lord!

BOOTSMANN SPIEDEL | 3 April '44. Massive attack, 100 planes, 15 direct hits, I have been informed. At 9 o'clock we sent over the communication: "All doctors and surgeons to Tirpitz." They will have a terrible job, it's a bloodbath here on the deck, the sailors were shot down by machine guns, then exploding bombs. Those that didn't hit made a geyser that spouted water many metres into the air. I haven't seen anything worse.

OTTO | The worst was seeing 122 empty hammocks where friends lay yesterday. I want to go home!

In addition there were 316 wounded when they had counted large and small injuries. When I hear the figure, I think about St John 3.16. Is this to be a mockery, God, of how much you loved the world, sort of?

And Uwe, who had become our kid brother! Blood and splinters of bone everywhere. Even the grand piano in the officers' mess is blasted into kindling wood. And Siegfried from Thüringen, with body parts torn from each other. He had a premonition, I remember it now. One night when he was going to bed, he said he sleeps in a deathbed. As if he was already lying in a morgue.

I want to go home!

ROLF | Tear the eyes out of my reflection in the mirror. The eyes have seen too much! Give me new ones. Those I have, I will send by post to Maria, my beloved pen pal, I am sure she will put them in water, so that they will have something to cry with.

KASPAR | According to orthodox belief it takes forty days after death for the soul to get where it ought to. A soul halfway to its destination, what is it thinking then? Is it afraid? Perhaps death is as it says in the Bible, that the walls fall down and the prison opens itself? Is it like that for Uwe? In any case he does not have to wait any longer.

BOOTSMANN SPIEDEL | I remember when I told the sailors Aesop's fable about the boy who often cried "Wolf, wolf", and that day the wolf came nobody believed him. We must always be on guard against bombs and mines, every air raid warning must be fully respected. They must run in the pattern we have imprinted in them, otherwise there will be chaos.

It is your life that you lay on the poker table, every time. Now everyone has seen that the wolf really can come in the shape of a submarine. At night I dream that I have puppies in my belly, I can feel them squirming.

MARTIN | "When you stand there gaping like that in the nor'wester, your cock gets so cold, you are so hollow inside—everything goes through you and out of the little pip you have between your legs!" Carl laughs loudly at his own joke, I have stopped caring long ago, because an idiot like him can't shut up for a second. I look forward to not having that fool around me all the time.

BRUNO | We usually go to the loo together, Mathias and I, he is full of stories. We always sit until someone comes and shouts, it is so peaceful on the john. A bit draughty in winter, but just the same a peaceful pocket on the ship. Mathias talks, and I laugh.

RICKARD | God, let me have something other than herring for lunch!

ROLF | Rain is falling towards a lantern, every single drop is gilded. Won't die now, the cloud cover is protecting the ship. Tonight no bomber planes will come. I am alive like the clouds.

One two three four five six seeeeeven, say the goldfinch, the next day there is sun again. I peek into the bushes, or into the tree trunks, that is where one sees them, the small birds. I am free, on land. If only I could draw the birdsong.

OTTO | Today a hundred men were allowed to go ashore. Two hours' leave in nature. White clover, it smells like the winter hay at home. Shall I take the time to look for a four-leafed clover, or shall I walk so far that I can't see the ship anymore? Feel like an ordinary man, on a visit in early summer, the air is so pregnant, full of scent, of sound, of dandelion fluff. Flowers and birdsong invoke God today, so that I will remember how good life is. So small and precious.

Flies buzzing, midges. The face puckered by bites. Whining, then silent, and then you know it is sitting and sucking your blood. Daylight all night. The light opens itself up, you can swallow it. It seeps into your veins, fills you.

Dear Heinz

Dear "Bootsmann Spiedel", as you so pathetically want to be called at home too. If you die in the war, then I won't have to:

- *Listen to your complaints that my cooking is too bad.*
- *Spend every single holiday with your mother in the country, where NOTHING AT ALL happens.*
- *Always smooth things over when you push people away from you with your brusque behaviour, which only comes from insecurity, an insecurity that weeps on my shoulder nearly every time we come home from a social gathering, and have offended somebody again.*
- *To therefore have to dread every single party and dinner invitation, or other social gathering, which I otherwise enjoy so much and miss.*
- *Spend my time ironing shirts, something I hate.*
- *Be afraid of getting pregnant, and therefore have two children to take care of, one small and one big.*
- *Be interrupted when I am trying to tell our friends something, to be corrected, and then you take over and finish the story and lap up the laughter.*
- *Pretend I like it when we lie together.*
- *Get yelled at because you ALWAYS know better than me.*
- *Have my toes trodden on when we are out dancing, but smile and pretend you are good at it.*
- *Listen to you getting sentimental, all the tears, shit and quarrelling which come every time you dip into the dram, several times a week.*
- *Buy bottle after bottle of expensive and heavy cognac and haul them up all the stairs because you have claustrophobia and have to live on the top floor with a view, something that makes our rent so expensive that I have to give tuitions, but your talent would be disturbed by teaching lessons.*

– *Become bitter, drawn and ugly before my time.*

I would have liked to live my life as I wish. But I would always have missed you and loved you and certainly have been torn asunder by splinters of regret. Because it is you who are my heart, I don't understand why, but it is so, and I hope so intensely that you will survive and be safe on board Tirpitz, and that the war will soon be over, and we can be together again!

May God who gave me you, save you for me.

Your Regina,
who will never send this letter

OTTO | Hansi was sitting in prison when the Navy needed him, so he and many others were set free. If it had been for theft or something, it would have been fine, but Hansi was sentenced for raping women. He likes to boast about it, and none of us dare tell him to shut up. Not with those muscles, not with that sadistic smile, always with a dangling cigarette butt, ready to mark with a burn all who show off. How he hassled Fritz while he was alive! Now it's Bruno who is suffering. You saw it in Hansi when he came on board, that he wasn't an ordinary thief, something in his face gave him away. What a society we are going to have when the war is over and all the soldiers go back to ordinary life. Will it be like taking off a spiritual uniform, or will the violence have stuck, as it has done with Hansi?

When I was about ten, I remember there was great excitement in the village when a little boy was suddenly sitting playing with a human bone, a thighbone I think it was. It turned out that a French war grave lay there, people had completely forgotten it. But the earth did not want to forget, and raised the bone up into the light of day.

MARTIN | We know what they are up to, obviously the ship is big, but it's too small for secrets. They fuck each other in the arse. Everyone says so, I wonder if it can be true. Look out so they don't take you in the toilet, laugh the others. I always look out for them.

BRUNO | My eyes flicker, a reflex from when we could have been eaten if we hadn't found a way to escape. There are no such possibilities here, I am standing in a corner, and Hansi and three fellow conspirators stand round me. I know what to expect, so I bend my head a little backwards to protect myself from the hands that are on their way to my throat, the blow does not strike as hard as it was intended. I must grab the chance, take the initiative, hit back before the adversary regains his balance. Hit now!

I hesitate, too scared, there are three of them, it is only to wait for the next fist or shout, hope there's an officer nearby, someone from the watch crew, but they have chosen the place of attack with care; on a ship where one is as good as never alone, they have found a forgotten corner near the stores. I'll be lucky if anyone comes here. There's a buzz round my ears, and when the blow meets my mouth, I feel something knock loose, a tooth.They broke my front tooth. Blow upon blow follows, kicks, I fall on my knees, try to protect my head with my hands, I feel something wet, spit for sure, then I don't remember anymore.

"Hey, there, don't be sad, put on music over the loudspeakers,
let's hear '*Deutschland, Deutschland über alles*!' And then a little dance music afterwards, then morale rises several notches.
Remember, we ARE going home!"

"Couldn't we simply have proper sea warfare again! Not just going downhill, trotting along easily, grey sea."

"The sea is the real enemy, all seafolk know that."

"Trust your luck."

"We are travelling from Hades, from Hades, hey, hey!"

"From Hades, from Hades, hey, hey!"

"It's letter distribution now!"

"Come on."

Kåfjord, summer 1944

OTTO | The farmers are cutting the grass all around the fjord, the nice smell of dry flowery hay reaches right up till here, small puffs of summer and normality. I would have given anything to be with them. At home this is done much earlier if it is an ordinary year. Mother always comes out with lemonade in a little milk pail, and then the only thing to do is flop down on the hay stack, roll onto one's back and rest in the midst of timothy grass and sunshine.

CARL | We are always hungry, the whole bloody time, if this had been a job we'd have gone on strike. What is this to offer young strong men? A little thin soup, without meat! We know the supply ship has engine trouble, but it should be damn well possible to send a new one. Milk gruel will probably be next. Listen, officer! Angry and hungry soldiers are dynamite, you must know that?

How long do we have to stay here in the north, when we are needed in the Atlantic? The hour of destiny is upon the Third Reich, and we who are on board the largest battleship are not to be part of it, that is bitter. What did you do in the war, Father, a future son will ask. Well, I swabbed decks. Women's work dressed up as discipline. There you have my contribution. Someone who is so keen on coming to blows. Fighting. Perhaps I should be pleased to be able to wash and not be killed. Or am I becoming completely soft from soapy water?

KLAUS | It must be one of our own, because suddenly I see the plane making a swastika in the sky. A sign, we are going to win, of course we will.

GOTTFRIED | Anne Marie is teaching me the names of the flowers in Norwegian, saying "reinrose", "lapprose", "multeblomst", "rødsildre". The names scramble into each other, become sounds. I gaze at her little three-sided mouth, "blåklokke", it says, "prestekrage". That's the one which people with lovers don't love, she says, smiling. Do it, then, I say, strip the petals one by one and see. I daren't, she says, what if it will be "love"?

MARTIN | How many potatoes must I have peeled since I came on board? Hundreds of thousands? I'll do a multiplication and work it out. Now we are cooking meatballs, they'll be jubilant, one and all. They are sizzling in several large pans, the red mince quickly goes grey, afterwards brown. At last, good. One gets bored of potato peeling, it is almost like a punishment, although the Führer says that every link is equally important. The cooks are clever at making the food last, and just when the boys are about to get bored, they throw in great quantities of mince and yell "meatball time!"

ROLF | Rain for a week now, at last the scenery suits the way I feel, dark and wet. I have to go out, my shoulders are screaming, discomfort in the legs, now I can't sit here any longer. I must have air. Variety, something to stretch my eyes towards. The birds have stopped singing. Soon it will begin to smell of rot, rust in the mouth.

In the latest number of "Der Schweinwerfer" you may read: an exclusive interview with the ship's captain, an article about reindeer from a Lapp camp, with pictures! The results of the shooting match between Tirpitz and the gang from the cruiser, did we get revenge for the embarrassing loss in the football cup? Follow it, follow it! We also have stories and poems by our own poets, the popular column Five on Deck, a crossword and seven questions, the winner will get a cigar. Best of all, naturally, is that we have the addresses of several young girls who want to become pen pals with someone on board our proud battleship. Here 'first come, first served' applies, so hurry up. For those with the writing itch, we request as before that you may begin sending material in already for the next issue of the ship's newspaper. We particularly call on people with drawing skills, we would like to feature a drawing of Tirpitz here among the mountains.

\

JOSEF | What shall I buy as a birthday present for Gretha? A new radio would have been excellent. On Saturday evenings we could whirl round to the Strauss waltzes they usually play at nine pm, we wouldn't even have to go to the dance hall. Only ourselves, the children in bed. Then the red eye will shine and the song will be belted out, my love.

MICHAEL | Before it was victory after victory and constantly extra news bulletins. Now it is suspiciously quiet. When even Goebbels can't manage to come up with good news, it surely doesn't look so good.

ROLF | The seaweed smells, a summer withdraws, leaving behind oppressive air, brown algae, I feel restless in this in-between weather. It is as though there is a hurry for something, but I don't know what.

Cloudberries they call them, some yellow, cloud-shaped berries which all Norsemen are obsessed with, unbelievable how good they taste, like floating sunshine and mountain summer. Lots of berries available here, the cook has sent out twenty men to pick them. Yet another summer without leave, luckily I was allowed to get off the ship and walk here for a few hours, but when one leaves the deadening routine of the ship, one begins longing. Maria. She pops up first. Such a guilty conscience. Perhaps it was friendship I felt most for Hannah?

Once when Grandfather was a sailor somewhere in South America, he had an offer to buy freedom by paying for a bird to be released from a cage. If only I could have bought my own freedom! Instead I have to go back on board. On deck it is as quiet as if the rest of the world did not exist. Perhaps it has gone, without us noticing it. The sound of nothingness. It is ringing in my ears.

When I am back the signal for a radio announcement from the Wehrmacht breaks in, and now the ears are quite open: "Enemy planes have violated airspace and bombed central Berlin, civilians killed and wounded." Anyone I know or am related to? Mother?

OTTO | What is war, well, it's avoiding getting pneumonia. Avoiding getting shot, and if the ship is torpedoed, jumping over the rail at the right moment. War on Tirpitz is to endure the waiting. You can bear it more easily if you have someone to talk to. Sunday evenings with a free watch and maybe a cup of coffee on deck if the officers are in a good mood, inspires us to more confidential conversations than we otherwise have. Friedrich tells me about his brother, who is a tail-gunner in the Luftwaffe. A tail-gunner on a bomber is one of the most dangerous things you can be in war, everyone knows that, Friedrich as well. I have heard that the Air Force itself reckons a tail-gunner survives four attacks, then the statistic says it's over, they get shot, and the tail-plane falls off, but the pilots manage to eject themselves out in parachutes.

Friedrich talks for a long time about his elder brother, as if he wants to keep him firmly in mind, he does not know whether he is still alive. He says that his brother always had a little suitcase with a change of clothes and a hundred marks lying ready in case he had to travel to Dresden, where Friedrich went to Engineering College, at short notice. I am not strong, says Friedrich, all the others in the family suppose I get on fine, but my brother knows me and knows it doesn't take much before the world becomes too big for me. Before everything goes black. When he notices that I have fallen down into a hole, he takes the ready-packed suitcase and gets onto the first train. Can you imagine how much that means? Knowing that he always has the suitcase ready? Friedrich gets up. Something is dragging him down, I notice it and make up my mind to take care of him now when his big brother can no longer get the suitcase and come, but is perhaps on the way to be shot down over England.

KASPAR | When at last I got shore leave and came down the gangway, I did something which surprised me completely. I knelt and bowed my head and kissed the ground as if I were the Pope. So unspeakably glad to be on solid ground.

ROLF | One has to raise one's line of sight to follow the first red and yellow tones up over the slopes, fever eating up the mountainsides. So beautiful that it shouts inside one, it is as if the colours have chosen to exist through me. I must show Norway to Maria some time.

\

Dear Hildegard,

I must write to you, because last night I dreamed that the ship capsized and men lay in the water screaming and swimming in oil. I woke up, sweating and cold at the same time. I felt the claw of death against my throat. It will not go well. Hildegard, I feel like Cassandra, you remember the Trojan princess, the one who is psychic and sees that the huge wooden horse is dangerous, but whom nobody believes when she shouts it out. It is like that for me too, I can't tell my dream to anyone. Then I might be arrested for agitation, the whole ship is nervous these days, there have already been nearly twenty attempts to take Tirpitz out since I came on board. The latest, which has weakened us terribly, was now in September. I wrote to you that I dreamed about an attack from tiny little submarines, but when it actually happened, I could not go into details, we are not allowed to mention such things in letters. Now it won't last any longer, I know it, the ship is so damaged that the Brits can easily take us. Hildegard, most beloved twin sister, you are the witness to my prophecy. Cassandra was also a twin, I recall now, strange how much I remember from our governess' mythology lessons, it's as if my brain has become clearer lately. Helenus he was called, the twin brother. Both became psychic as children when Apollo's holy serpent licked their ears as they lay sleeping, do you remember that? Cassandra experienced it as a curse, that I well understand.

Hildegard, take care of Mother, I know you are strong, much stronger than me, I'm going to pieces as I sit here writing, my anxiety is so overwhelming it obstructs my breathing, when I know what is coming. I will end now, dear one. In a few weeks you will know for certain. Tirpitz will go down before Christmas.

Greetings to Mother and Helga and say that I love them infinitely, and you.

Kaspar

KURT | Man overboard, man overboard! Good God, he can't swim! Bloody hell, people, jump in after him, save him!

FREGATTEN-KAPITÄN BIELER | We won't find him. Once he was as small as the children on land who are playing football. Completely unorganized they run after the ball in a swarm, like insects. They are five, six, no more, and suddenly one of them is crying, not knowing why, but immediately afterwards they are all laughing at one who fell down in a funny way. They have forgotten the ball, the goals as well, winning has no meaning, they are together, playing, letting themselves run from one to another, without thinking, simply floating around in a jumble. I see the same children become men, become soldiers, they are still running around, don't know what their aims are, who they are fighting against, what the enemy looks like, and what they are supposed to do to them. We won't find him.

OTTO | *Scheisse*! Tonight too it will be bombing weather. I have a cigarette on deck, trembling. Breathing space, a moment of peace, even though people are walking past me. I draw it slowly in, blow even slower out. If only I could blow out enough smoke to make a cloud around us, the evening sky has cracked open, remains of the sunset in red and a little pink, five or six pale stars. The British pilots will find their objective easily tonight. Perhaps the planes are on their way in over the coast at this moment?

Not to know when you are going to die is God's grace to humanity, remember that, Grandmother used to say. Remember to live while you are alive, was Grandfather's response. Now at last I understand what they meant.

WERNER | The rumours come from those who were wounded after the Murmansk Front, they say that nobody who is badly wounded will get to return to Germany. The seriously wounded never come home, far out in the sea they get an injection and are shoved overboard and disappear into the sea. Cripples must not shame Hitler's ideal kingdom.

EUGEN | "When Germania arises", proclaims Heinrich. Do you believe that, you swine? Listen to yourself, Germania, whatever that is, you tell me, idiot, I say. Hitler and Speer can no longer build their utopian city. Besides the swampy land under Berlin will never stand the strain of the triumphal arch and the other enormous buildings which are planned. They will sink, like a ship, only more slowly.

GUSTAV | I have a sore inside each palm, a kind of eczema or rash, red and malignant. Then they burst and I bleed, not that it actually hurts so much, but it is noticeable, as if I had two stigmata. Marks of Christ's nails in my hands. I dare not go to the ship's doctor, this is both too small and too big. I am afraid I am about to go mad. I daren't look at my feet to see if I have marks there too.

We are souls who are having a human experience, not humans who are having a soul experience, the priest said yesterday during the Mass. When I ended up beside him in the beer hall later in the evening, he said that the four qualities which a mature heart contains are compassion, inner harmony, steady nerves and infinite love. If you can manage to keep these pure in a war, you are a saint, but certainly a poor soldier.

CARL | Germany's biggest cannon is called Great Gustav. We usually tease Gustav, how's it going in Great Gustav's trousers, is the cannon loaded? Have you anyone in sight? He goes red, but that wimp has to stand a little teasing, dammit.

FREGATTEN-KAPITÄN BIELER | I see it in the crew. They are losing respect for me and the other officers. Thinking we are not aggressive enough, I know it, but it is their safety we are thinking of. We want to avoid more standard letters to mothers and wives. If I express it like that they will understand. Every night I hear the accusations of the dead sailors: You had my life in your hands, and you threw it away.

Now the hunter itself is being hunted. Can we protect Tirpitz much longer? I doubt the promised support of the Luftwaffe, they don't have enough planes in the area.

JOSEF | You must be worthy of your children's tears. If I die, I hope Theres and Wilhelm don't remember the slaps, or that I locked them in the potato cellar.

HEDWIG | During one of the many bombings in our district, I saw a mother being hit by a shard of grenade which cut off her head while she was breast-feeding, the baby was still drinking milk from the dead mother. I can't forget that sight. Suckling a dead mother. Pastor Ruhland spoke of something equally grotesque: 'One day a woman came dragging a dead man to the church office and demanded that I should marry them. She was definitely shell-shocked, to comfort her I did it. I married her to a corpse."

GERHARD | We sing battle songs nearly all evening. There hasn't been much singing since we lost Paris.

KURT | Sleep presses the backs of my eyes and wants to get out, simply close the body and consciousness down and let me rest. I don't know how long I have been on watch, but it is more than the four hours I ought to have. I can't guess why I am not being relieved, I am so tired I haven't the energy to care. It is dangerous to be as indifferent as I am now, it is not certain I am alert enough to see the first signs of a submarine attack. A periscope which is up and breathing, an overgrown snorkel spying. The thought of the Englishmen hardly scares me at all, I am too exhausted.

FREGATTEN-KAPITÄN BIELER | A young sailor stopped eating, he couldn't manage to get the food down. When he was forced to do so and threw up, he had to eat his own vomit. I did not agree with that order. In this case it is not a matter of lack of discipline. Soon he looked like a grey ghost, with two huge dark eyes. He withered in front of us. In the end he died, he weighed 44 kilos then.

KASPAR | When I hung over the gunwale and peered down into the black sea, I suddenly recalled the quotation from Nietzsche which I used to think was so magnificent: "When you look down into the abyss, the abyss is also looking into you." Fear grabbed me by the neck, it is here you will disappear. The abyss. Total destruction.

HERMANN | The smell from the ventilation vents. The stink of humanity, wet clothes and dirty sailors. On land the trees have lost their hair, become bald old men.

OSWALD | New equipment is coming soon. I am among those who are going to go to Germany for training and surely have a chance of greeting those at home. After the watches we lucky soldiers, who live in barracks on land, can spend the evenings in the café in Alta with girls you can treat to coffee-substitute and cakes. The competition is strong, certainly 22 soldiers per girl, and I am not all that pretty. Often I am left sitting with one of the older soldiers who talks incessantly about it being his second war. We on board Tirpitz are nervous wrecks the whole bunch of us, I hear another one say. The Brits are coming up with new weapons all the time, dwarf submarines and constantly more types of bombers. And it's us who are their trophy.

By the end of the evening only Åsta is left. Toothless Åsta. She does not look at me, knows that I am sitting and considering whether she is worth it. Do you think I would be bothered to look at your sheep's dugs and fleshy belly and feel your dry cunt, eh? I heard one of the others say to her. Perhaps she is diseased too, no, it can wait. There are surely plenty who will have me when I get home. Not much competition there when so many men are dying, there it is I who will get to choose. Good night, Åsta, I say, go home now. When she gets up, I see she must be over forty, she will not have an easy time ahead, that is for sure.

OTTO | We are sitting smoking and playing the "What am I going to do when I get home again" game. It is important to have Dieter with us, he has the best imagination, come on, we say, what's the first thing you're going to do then, Dieter? I will, he pauses, considers, smiles broadly and says: Oh yes, then I will eat my dinner in the wife's lap! Will you have her cunt as a table? shouts Max. Is it clean enough there then, wonders Wolfgang.

GOTTFRIED | I didn't get to say goodbye to Anne Marie. When I got back to the ship, it was all decided, we are to go south. Perhaps I can write, I say to myself as I get ready for the night shift. I camouflage my tears as a cold.

\

"The Führer's gaze looks at us. Tirpitz is more important than our lives."

"I can't handle all the news nonsense from Berlin, we don't need to know any more than what's around us, I have always said."

"Twelve torpedoes are lying as clearly as shining babies, we are proud fathers."

"Co-ordinator, the admirals have divided up the sea into quadrats, in hunting territory."

"Have you written your will?"

"What the hell kind of question is that, keep away from me, you bring bad luck. Scram, scram, I said!"

"Oh, the smell of our smoke at top speed, after so long. Now we have to be towed, it's humiliating."

"Don't think about it. Sleep while you can, as much as you can, so your nerves will hold when it is necessary."

"Oberfähnrich Schoenbach slides through the ship like oil. Look out, straighten your back!"

Håkøya, autumn 1944

FREGATTEN-KAPITÄN BIELER | After the 15 September attack, when a direct hit by a bomb destroyed the bow, Tirpitz is reduced to a floating battery. We are being towed to Håkøya near Tromsø, where it is so shallow that she can't sink. It has to be admitted, in reality we are no longer seaworthy and probably won't ever be again. We are to lay here until someone else comes and bombs us. A gigantic coffin, that's what she is. The others in the officer corps don't realize how badly off we are.

PETER | I have been promoted to orderly, running with messages between the big boys, and get to know more than I would like. The end is coming close now.

KASPAR | We have started calling life on board "On a mission to heaven". After reaching Håkøya, more people than I understand that it is only a matter of time.

I can only be killed once, in one place, and so I might as well die on Tirpitz as in my cellar bedsit near the university which is sure to be smashed by bombs as well.

JAMES | I am soon boarding my plane to lead an operation I know is risky, I have been asked to write a will. I have spoken with a priest, phoned Mother and asked her to give my love to Mary. I am calm, but excited, almost light.

Tirpitz is the goal. We all know how important it is. I light a smoke, look at the sky and notice how wide and open it is, wonder whether it is because I may die soon that I experience it like this.

In front of me I see an ancient washerwoman, she has a stick, is obviously suffering and walking slowly on the way out of the base. Quickly I am up beside the woman, stop her, take her wrinkled hands in mine and say: I am giving you my youth.

ULRICH | Alarm, the blue and yellow air raid flag is hoisted, I hear them beginning to secure the watertight bulkheads.

JAMES | Should I hesitate now, when it is really important or simply empty all the misery and death I have over the German devils down there? Tirpitz is so big, there is only space for half the ship in the telescope!

I hear the bomb hatches opening.

WERNER | Now the flares are here, they are dropping a lot of large, shining bombs at the engine room. Silence, just before the bang.

PETER | I remember so well when it occurred to me that I might die. Frightened, I ran down to Mother and Father. They looked at each other, comforted me, carried me upstairs, laid me down and said you don't need to think about that. It repeated itself every night. In the end they became cross, thought it was just something I was saying to stay up longer. Now I feel it anew. I am going to die. There is no way out, the sky is black with bombers, we haven't got the smokescreen going. No sign of the Luftwaffe coming to help us either. And I can't even swim.

JAMES | God, never let me know what damage and suffering my Tallboy bomb is giving those down there who are fighting for their lives.

I am trained to keep thoughts like this away, but it doesn't help, the smoke which is rising up from Tirpitz, the moving dots of men in the telescope sights, no training can take that scene away, and suddenly I feel so lonely in the plane.

Hands keep on waving, but now I am away and don't see them anymore.

KASPAR | *"O Crux Ave Spes Unica"*, O cross, hail, my only hope, it will say on my grave if I don't get saved. I have sent Hildegard my last wishes. Just have to wait a few minutes before I jump.

The brief moment when we are lifted up into life to exist. Then sink down, to die.

The God for soldiers in war has forgotten his job. He is lying asleep, undisturbed and peaceful, he sleeps. Don't you hear the screams?

ROLF | The sun has become a grave lamp.

OTTO | Is it the sky itself bombing us? God's insane rage!

RICKARD | Today Gudrun will become a widow, and she does not know it, it is still an ordinary day for her. Strange to know it before she does. The hull of Tirpitz has turned into a sarcophagus.

Ernst, greet those at home when you come on shore. Jump out now. It is over for me. I can't swim, but I can pray, I will pray for you too.

Gudrun! This is the end, I know it, dammit! Don't argue with me, Ernst, I can't swim, do you hear! The only thing you must promise is to look up Gudrun in Stuttgart and tell her that my thoughts clung tightly to her, and that the love we had was the only thing that was left of me at the end. Say it exactly like that! I have written a letter to her, had it in my inner pocket for a while, the address is on it, now you must swear on my coming grave that you will look her up when this hellish war is over. Jump now!

BJARNE | We curl up under the table when the bombs come, Father and Gunnar are out and shout that they will hide themselves in the basement. When at last we peep out, Tirpitz is capsizing. It does not take many minutes. Mesmerized I stand and watch. Will it be safe here again at last, I think as Father comes in. He says we must get the boat out. Quickly!

FREGATTEN-KAPITÄN BIELER | "Destroy all secret papers" is the procedure when a ship is fatally hit, I couldn't care less, because now we ought to be saving as many as possible. Off with boots and jackets. Save yourselves!

I give each of the nearest men a handshake in farewell. I hear someone shouting: "Long live our proud vessel! Long live our families and our country. Hurrah! Hurrah! Hooray!" As an officer I feel deeply moved by it. Now the order is: Save yourselves if you can. I see nothing of the ship's captain and staff, could they have been locked up in the command post? Then they are doomed, because now we are turning belly-up, and it's going fast!

Think about someone you love, that is my last order.

Irmchen, dearest, my thoughts go to you. The light nights when we were young and sat talking, drinking cognac with apple cider, and you told me all your secrets.

PETER | Father, why didn't you teach me to swim!

ROLF | Bernhard and I jump together. I am slowly pulled down by the uniform. Get away, far from the ship, so you won't go down with it! I hear Bernhard shout. We are only two hundred metres from land, we can manage to swim that far. Get away from the ship, think of all the ammunition that might be set alight. Perhaps more bombs are coming, I think that maybe, the Brits want to be sure that we are rendered harmless. Swim, swim for your life! roars Bernhard. That is the last I see of him.

The cold presses against my body. My lungs tie themselves up in small knots to avoid drawing in water and oil. It is death itself we are fighting, but still the sea gives up the living, still there is life in the waves, life in the heads which are sticking up. As the oily water washes over me, I see a boat coming.

LOTHAR | I was talking to Peter in the minutes before we jumped into the sea, and knew that he could not swim, so as we lay there in the water waiting for the rescue boat, I held him up. Thought about my son.

GUSTAV | On my brother's tombstone it says: "*Wer den Tod im heiligen Kampf fand, ruht auch in fremder Erde im Vaterland.*"

He died 2 February 1942, now Mother can write 12 November 1944 and add my name. We who are locked in will suffocate. One of the youngest here was beginning to panic, so now the most senior officer has given us instructions to lie down, not to speak unnecessarily and breathe calmly, so we don't use up all the oxygen at once. Some try singing a psalm, but it becomes so dismal that they stop in the middle of a verse. Might just as well think of my own grave. "*Mein lieber Sohn Gustav Heue,*" it will say. I would like a statue of an angel to guard the stone, a large, grieving angel.

The others can't even be bothered to knock on the hatch any longer, to tell them that we are here. According to the book, we should knock every tenth minute, but we have given up.

I am lying right beside my brother in St Marien and St Nikolai churchyard in Prenzlauer Berg. It is peaceful and dark here.

BJARNE | Calmly now, says Father, we mustn't hit the one lying there, is he dead? Help me to see, he isn't moving. But there is one, I say. While I am getting him over the gunwale, he points to the man who isn't moving and implores: He is my friend, save him! You must save him! If we take in any more now, we'll capsize as well, I hear Father reply. One more, I say, we'll take one more. Thank you so much, he moans when we get him aboard, I couldn't have hung on much longer.

I must have counted more than a hundred dead now, they are still floating about. One of the badly wounded soldiers asks: Are angels men or women? Can you see the angel of death who is standing at my right side? A woman, he answers himself, death is a mother in reverse. They sit close together, shivering, crying quietly, one has enough humour to ask for a cigarette, most are silent, only the sound of chattering teeth and someone who is consoling others confusedly.

ROLF | Oil in my eyes. What can I do with myself? How can I hide myself from the light which is so strong? I fumble around myself in the boat, perhaps I'll go blind? The pain takes my breath away, and the iron sky throws back my prayers.

OTTO | From D turret I stand looking at how C turret is thrown high up into the air when the magazine under it catches fire and explodes. C turret looks like a child's toy made of matchsticks as it is lifted from barbette and lands in the sea. At once I jump into the water, swim and save my life. From land I can see the ship which has been my home for several years capsizing. In a matter of ten minutes it turns completely upside down.

While I stand there freezing, I think of the psychic woman at home, the one who said I was not to be in C turret. Thankfulness warms me from within, although my clothes are dripping ice cold water. I must find shelter.

WERNER | I saw God. Now there is no possibility of doubt any more. Not when you have seen what I saw. I hurt my leg when Tirpitz capsized, and could hardly keep myself afloat. Then God showed himself. He simply stood there, right in front of me, in the air, or perhaps it was on the sea, without opening his mouth he said: Swim, Werner. Then a plank came drifting towards me, as if it had been commanded! Now I will cling to life, I promise!

GUSTAV | Waiting to hear the roar of planes again, so that the Brits will complete their assignment to bomb the battleship into splinters. We are a mismatched bunch sitting here. The highest in rank tries to keep up our courage. Saying that certainly they have only to go to Tromsø to fetch better equipment, that we will soon be saved, we must not panic. I do not believe him. I pray, the others are listening to me, suddenly I find appropriate words for what we are thinking about, I remind us to give thanks for the life we have had, and that if we die, then we will all come to Christ together. We try again with Morse code to get a message out that we are here, it is my turn to knock, but I am not hammering what I really want to: Don't abandon us. Save me too.

BOOTSMANN SPIEDEL | N 69° 38' 46,35"
W 18° 48' 18,21"

At 9.48 Tirpitz capsized at Håkøya, 971 men died.

Sunday and sun, quiet, such was the day when we were put out of action.

A shout which is still echoing, a charge of grief, "I am only nineteen, I want to go home."

\

PETER | As we sat shivering from the cold on the rescue boat, the officers shouted at us: "Don't sleep, boys, keep yourselves awake, then you will stay alive. Don't sleep, talk! Think about the film "*Triumph des Willens*", with willpower you will win and get ashore. Lothar warmed me, drew me close to himself.

BJARNE | *Es geht ein Braunschweiger, marsch, marsch, marsch,*
Es geht als Hagelwetter, Donnerwetter, stillgestanden—Halt!

That is the only thing he says, again and again, before he dies. He is no older than me. Father has to help me chuck him overboard. The face has almost detached from the skull of another one I manage to wrestle up into the boat, I open his eyelids with my fingers and see that one eyeball has burst.

OTTO | My teeth were chattering so loudly that I woke up from the noise. Lying in a hay barn or something, can't remember how I landed up here. After a while a young girl comes in with a cowshed apron and a hayfork, she jumps backwards with fright when she sees me. I smile at her, that makes her less anxious, and when I say Tirpitz she starts crying and runs out. Immediately afterwards she is back with a man who must be her father, he drags me out and pulls me with him into the main house, gesticulates that I must take off my wet clothes. The girl goes out, I can hear her clattering with something, the father comes with a dry change of clothes, I hope my face expresses all the gratitude I feel. Then the girl comes in with scalding hot coffee, it tastes of thoughtfulness—they save my life, Inger Johanne and her father.

GUSTAV | Less and less air. No idea how much time has gone. We resign ourselves to the final departure. Is life a preparation for dying? I will pray again, but I'll wait a bit longer. It will be the last thing I do. Say goodbye with everyone in my thoughts, go the way of memory, back. What was unsaid? Whom should I have asked for forgiveness?

Mother said she heard a cry when they slapped me to make me draw breath for the first time. Twenty-two years ago. How much air haven't I had access to since then? Air I took for granted and did not value.

Breathe in carefully. Don't be greedy. Let it stay as long as possible, even though none of us believe in rescue any more. The emergency lights are in the process of going out, tiredness is already becoming insurmountable. They will find me with folded hands.

In the end we sing "*Deutschland, Deutschland über alles,*" verse after verse until there is no breath left, we shall sing ourselves into death, relaxed and gradually indifferent, we allow it to come closer. It is not so painful, nor so sad either. We may be proud to die like soldiers who did not fail in their courage.

God, now it is me and you.

KARI | To bear the stress they had gone through, their brains had to abandon reality. They were in shock. One sat chewing his own tongue so the blood ran. My task was to get them back. Asking their mother's name seemed to work, and how much four plus four is. If I asked about what had happened, they pulled a curtain down over their eyes, and I lost contact.

Later I joined in taking care of the dead. Stretcher after stretcher of the dying came in. There were so many! No chance of taking a break.

"One time the flag will be at half-mast for you too, dearest, then we will meet again." He lay on the bed in the sickroom and died slowly the first night, he had neither ink nor pen, he wrote this greeting with his own blood. I found it in the morning, but there had been no time to find out who was to get the note.

GUDRUN | "Death, where is thy sting? O grave, where is thy victory?" The priest talked about these words from Paul's First Epistle to the Corinthians during Mass today. It was absolutely tasteless. We have been informed that Tirpitz has gone down, but not who are dead, and who are saved. I feel myself becoming quite cold under my woollen coat. Then sweat breaks out, it almost feels like a fever, and I feel myself getting up, hear myself clear my throat and say, much too loudly, in the middle of the sermon: Death's sting is what a wife feels when her husband has been killed in the war.

It becomes completely silent. Of course it becomes silent. Then I begin to laugh, I hear myself how sick it sounds, the acoustics in the church are good. I roar the laughter out. Then come the arms that had to come, they pick me up, drag me across the church floor, I laugh and laugh, lose my hat and laugh even worse. There sits Frau Braun, how can you be so quiet, you have lost a son. You shall inherit from your child. Think of that! Inherit from your child.

Yesterday I met an unknown woman in the meat queue, she was ill, and her husband was of course away. She coughed and looked up at me and said: If I die, who will teach Elise to read then? I laughed at her too.

HILDEGARD | Sister Death is coming with her wagon, she gathers bodies and souls on the battlefield or at the bottom of the sea. She pulls the heavily-loaded wagon through slippery plains in the east and over wet seas full of corpses. The souls she wraps up in her shawl and carries them close to her heart. Forever she will roll her cart, it will never empty, there is always room for more on the cold breast.

Kaspar, dear brother, are you alive?

PETER | I survived, thanks to Lothar.

Five other Navy sailors I heard of saved themselves, got to land near a small farm. The farmer who lived there took them into the cowshed, and without a word he showed them how they should droop themselves over the cows and get warmth from the big bodies.

CARL | Fortunately we have alcohol here where us wounded are lodged. Cheers for Hitler, I call out. That is the Führer's toast, gentlemen! Carl, can't you shut up, I hear Jochen say.

NO, I CAN'T DO THAT! Especially now that Tirpitz has been taken out. Now we must not lose hope!

Take that damned medal and hang it on my grave, Jochen roars back. My Germany no longer exists. It has gone to the dogs, you can greet your damned Führer and tell him that!

GUDRUN | I don't want to cry because you have drowned, Rickard, you shall not have to flounder through my tears on your way to heaven. Now you will be able to rest.

I can't drive away the thought of how you began swallowing water, how heavy the uniform became, how cold it was. I'm not able to stop imagining how it was for you when you went under, when everything became thick and black, and at last you could not struggle any more. While you were still thinking about me, you fought the waves, the oil spill, the water and the cold, I know that. That way I see for myself that you died, gradually calm, like a piece of driftwood. With your hair waving like seagrass, and, in the autumn sky, an opening.

"Mein lieber, herzenguter Mann," I don't get any further in the letter I should send round to the relatives to tell them you have passed away.

I think of the time when we dreamed the same dream, we were newlywed and took it as a sign that we belonged together.

We both dreamed that we were running around searching for each other on a large square with many people at a market or something, at last we found each other. It was so beautiful. You mentioned it in your wedding speech.

Perhaps we will meet again in dreams, now.

ROLF | Jens came on board Tirpitz only days before the capsizing, he sacrificed himself in the water, let another be taken up into the boat which only had room for one more. I saw it myself, through the film of oil. He was pulled under by his clothes and equipment, unable to keep himself afloat any longer.

I too was floundering in the heavy oil spill, couldn't do anything for Jens, my fingers were stiff with cold and my eyes full of blackness. First one had to take care of oneself. "Death struggle", the expression had a literal meaning that day. Seeing those who were fighting for their lives in the water. Standing on land, wet and freezing, but safe. What a vast difference.

WERNER | After a few days my legs began to go blue, then black. Gangrene. The doctors at the hospital in Tromsø saved one leg, the other was cut off in the middle of the thigh. Will Brigitta find me repellant? The wounds itch, to stop myself complaining I visualize in front of me God on the water asking me to swim. A brief glimpse of light.

I remembered nothing when I woke up in the hospital. Not even that Tirpitz had been bombed. I was restless, and a nurse came running with a syringe. The stab when she stuck the needle in me, followed by a warm darkness which flowed from the arm and out over my whole body. A lovely half-sleep allowed me to drift away, beyond pain, where no discomfort exists, where it became light again. I remained lying as if I was floating in the most divine water while I felt the sun warming my face.

I heard a shout from land, there were white-clad people who were obviously having a party, I swam over to them, they said the food was ready. A pretty girl with lively brown eyes, she looked a bit like Brigitta, came over to me with a glass of wine. She was so close that I felt her breath on my cheek, she said she was glad to see me, wanted to dance with me, yes, because there would be a dance afterwards, she laughed lightly and led me to the carpet where I was to sit. Hot chicken legs and white bread were sent over, the girl reached out for butter, as if she knew this was exactly what I wanted. Talk of disappointment when I woke up and that lovely young girl was exchanged for a grey-haired nurse, who brusquely commanded me to lift up my bottom so she could put the bedpan underneath.

They have informed Brigitta, will she be able to see that this cripple is still me?

ROLF | Have you heard that "Rigel" went down? Where? Off Helgeland. Are there any survivors? Yes, some burned bodies have been sent to hospital, but there were over three thousand on board, both Russians and Serbs, a few Norwegians, and certainly a hundred of our own deserters...they would have been killed no matter what.

GUDRUN | You must have handed over the letter just before you swam up to heaven, it came two weeks after Tirpitz had gone down, forwarded by one Ernst Neumann. You dreamed of coming home and sleeping beside me again, you wrote. I can't fathom that you are gone.

When I work in the garden, turning the beds, turning up dark earth, I see that other women are getting their men back. Ragged and wounded, but they come home, and lift the woman who runs towards them up in the air. They come home. Why not you? I can't cope alone. Without you my life can't go on, there is no point in carrying on in the garden if you are not here to enjoy the vegetables, fruits and flowers. You would say that I had been hard-working and thorough and sneak out on my birthday to pick the first strawberries and serve them to me with milk and sugar, even though they were still rather green.

Dear Sonja

Tomorrow at last the boat transport to Germany is beginning, then we will be sent onwards by train. Will you come and meet me at the station? I look forward to coming home. I hope not too much of the house has been destroyed.

Johannes

HEDWIG | Crazed by hunger, you see it in the eyes. People are eating cats, it is said. Cooking root soup. At night grief is something cold, an old horse blanket is all you can find, and food is a memory the stomach tortures itself with. Just spit on the flames when your house is burning, and see if it helps.

There is shooting all the time, someone tried to tell me the difference between light and heavy machine gun fire, gradually the sound has become as ordinary as raindrops against the windowpane. We hear them, but don't get wet.

We aren't able to sustain deliveries into Berlin any longer, says the milkman one morning. Farmers are fighting the Russians while we are standing here talking. Yes, but without milk, I stammer, without milk the children will die. He looks at me, then he turns and goes away.

Imagine if I could have prayed. "Dear God, I don't believe in prayer, but help me now, just this once". These prayers are not worth much. Trust Hitler and the Lord, they always said.

FRAU INNERHOFER | I go with Hedwig and try to get bread and potatoes on our ration cards, rumours say there might be a little today. She supports me when I don't use my crutches, she won't be able to buy my ration, I have to be there myself. Hedwig knows I can't run if we hear the siren, I hope she understands that she has to save herself, that it is what I want, not that she should die for the sake of my slowness. We get a few potatoes and half a loaf. Hedwig is clearly relieved when we arrive at our block of flats again. She gives me a hug, we managed it well, tomorrow we have to hunt again, she says and goes inside to little Alfred.

I have realized that God does not depend on my faith. He does not need me as I needed him. In my darkest hour he is not here. I am living in a place God has given up on, a place I did not believe existed. I have never experienced such a big betrayal from any person. I have buried two sons, then I got word that my husband was missing in north Norway, near the city of Tromsø. Tirpitz has gone down, the impossible has happened. Now there is nowhere to hide any more. No-one to complain to, because it is only God one can complain to, when one has lost so much, then it is no good blaming Hitler or the admirals or the Brits. Like an unfaithful husband, he simply ran away from all he promised when I gave myself to him.

The hand-cranked gramophone that was taken to the bomb shelter always used to give us a bit of festivity. Now it does not manage to drown out the Stalin-organ, the most eerie sound in the world. I have survived, even though it was said that someone who hears the Stalin-organ is lost.

Looting began long ago. Hedwig and I take everything we can carry with us down into the cellar, I am not much help, but I can tuck something under my blouse. The Russians in any case won't find anything edible or alcoholic, we are agreed on that. I am most afraid of the rumours of American block-bombing. If it happens, the cellar will be our grave. I think with horror about what happened in Dresden in February.

In the afternoon I hobble out into the street, and then along comes an old father wheeling a cart with his dead family in it. Four corpses are lying there, without a covering over them, stiffening children, a woman, white and still. I look, but feel nothing. I am as dead as those lying there. I want to throw myself onto the cart, let myself be pulled along with them, down to where all struggles are ended, and you are able to rest, white and still.

OTTO | The days after capitulation are a whirl of different instructions, often contradictory. Rumours and nervous outcries. I am prepared for any possibility, we are pack animals, carrying food, carrying medicines, carrying petrol, carrying ourselves. We survive with whatever we have in our hands. We are interned in a camp, not far from Oslo, for endless days. Nothingness stretched out over time. Picking lice, a little sport, a little food. Greater and greater homesickness, at the same time fear, as we hear little by little about the death toll of the bombings, hardly anything in Germany will be intact any more.

The menu is simple: cabbage soup for starters, cabbage soup for main course and cabbage soup for dessert. Some days twenty grams of tinned ham and komiss bread, three slices each.

"Self-confident but modest. Honest and faithful. In that way a German soldier should be an example for the German people in manly strength", it was announced during training. Now we are nothing but filthy rags and lost pride.

I survived. I am alive. It is difficult to believe what a gift it is. I am a flag at half-mast. In a barracks further away I hear someone singing *"Heimat deine Sterne"*, in the evening breeze, and I weep until I get cramps and throw up.

\

"Why didn't I rise up in the ranks?"

"Because you kept yourself in the middle. A Navy sailor in a sailor suit, like a little kid. You should have worked your way up, taken the shortcut like so many others."

"What if we go home and get to hear from the neighbours that the Russians raped Mother."

"Yes, if the rumours are true, it is so for many people."

"Grace lies in the bottle. Here you have floating medicine. Sit down on a wine cork and off you go!"

"Where are you going, did you say?"

"Where the myths go to die."

"What do you mean?"

"The murderer's mark, all of Germany
bears the mark of Cain now."

"Snob talk."

"Killing in war isn't murder."

"But it feels like it, before God.
A battlefield is the best place to
hide a corpse...isn't that what they say?"

"The Law of War, if there is such a thing,
Does it override all laws?"

"No."

"Can one speak of the turning-point of suffering?"

"Stop that priest-talk there!"

"My connection with God is like an eternal
handshake,
When I want to let go, he holds me tight."

"Is death an act of love from God.
Like when a child is
born?"

"Yes, because in death we are born into another
world."

"Shut up, dammit, that's enough now!"

"My uncle's a doctor, he worked out in the country when
he
was young, once he told us that before they began doing
Caesareans, they used to have to cut living babies to
pieces
to get them out and save the mother. Carved up. To be
born dead, in pieces."

"How disgusting, come on, let's have a smoke!"

"Where do soldiers go after death, is there
a special place for us?"

"Hitler, where did he land up?"

Winston Churchill:

"It is a great relief to us to have this beast where we so long have wished him to be."

III

Germany, 1945-1955

FRAU GOESSNER | Have you seen my child? Have you seen my child, he is five, brown-haired, in short trousers. I was holding him by the hand when the bomb fell, he is gone, have you seen him? Can you help me search, please.

HEDWIG | We have got to see them at last, drunken Russian soldiers everywhere, they are actually just as bad as we heard they would be. Shameful that these barbarians have conquered us. At the same time people are laughing in the food queues, saying that now, after the Führer's suicide, the 'Heil Hitler' greeting means: the heap of ruins has become as high as this in Berlin!

The atmosphere of the End Days. Trains stand still for hours at the station. Everything is eerie, feverish. Brief encounters in a hallway. Love before you have to die. A conifer which has been damaged sheds an enormous number of cones before it dries up and falls.

It is actually more dangerous in Berlin now than during the war, every day buildings collapse, or somebody steps on undetonated grenades. Women have it worst, the Russian soldiers rape nearly everyone they see of the female sex, it was especially bad on the eve of the thirtieth anniversary of the Russian Revolution. Then it was not safe anywhere if you were walking in a skirt. Ivan is everywhere, everywhere he can do exactly as he pleases. And so he does. Several times I have taken the little boy with me and hidden in the clothes loft, behind the huge roll of cloth. The Brits and the Americans at least pay for what they get. There are many rumours going round about cannibalism. I have seen an old married couple cut into a dropped-dead horse with penknives and eat the flesh raw.

Two days ago parts of the district were on fire, but the postman walked around with his bag just the same.

INGE | Work away fear, go, go, go. A new Zündapp goes by, the driver is a Russian, he asks in sign language if I want to sit on it, and I have no willpower any more, I climb up onto the motorcycle and let myself be driven away, like a feather without a bird, bobbing on dirty water.

I can't bear to touch myself, can't stand my own skin.

ROLF | We who came in the first transports from Norway met a silent Berlin. I walked towards the goldfish pond in Tiergarten, it was here I was to meet Bernhard. He got away from me in the chaos after Tirpitz went down, now nobody knows what has happened to him. The goldfish pond is filthy and filled with algae, there are no fish there anymore, and most of the trees have been felled, used for firewood. Completely silent, gloomy even in the sunshine. When I ask about Hannah and her grandfather, there is nobody who knows anything about them either.

GOTTFRIED | Should I tell her about them anyway? Everyone says one should never admit unfaithfulness, that what they don't know can't hurt them and such glib sayings, but will *I* be able to bear my disloyalty, can I live with myself?

I love Elsa, but I also love Berit...and Laila I simply had to have, and Anne Marie is like a good friend, she understands me. Imagine that I should survive this hellish war which yielded all these opportunities, which brought Berit, as she came walking by with her pail, looking like a butterfly, one quivering hot June day in Drontheim.

When the war did not break me, my immorality will, because it is not easy to love several butterflies, one at home and three far away, close to my heart.

JOHANNES | She who is standing at the station and is going to receive me, at the same place where I left her four years ago, is heavily pregnant. Her face is oddly white, foreign, and yet so familiar. She is standing completely still. I hug her tightly, and she begins sobbing. You came home, I hear Sonja saying between the sobs, I thought I would never see you again. No, that is obvious, I say, she flinches, and I spoil everything before we have the chance to try.

JOSEF | It is high summer, for the rest of the world it is the summer of peace. There are many of us still waiting in Norway. How long are we going to stay? People who walk by spit at us and shout abuse. We have to dig up the graves of Norse resistance men behind Akershus Castle, half-rotted bodies. Slimy pieces of bone. Almost liquefied flesh. I see maggots nibbling at pupils; the corpse-stink, damp and something else, wettish. You have to become a machine. Disconnect all the human in you. When I come home, I will never tell anyone about this, they are not to know that for several weeks I was not a human being.

ROLF | Two who had hammocks just beside me and stayed together most of the time, we didn't get to know them very well, they wanted to keep a distance in a way, I don't know what it was, perhaps a form of class subservience, or the opposite, that they thought Kaspar and some of us were stuck-up pigs. The last I saw of them was, they held each other in their arms before they both jumped into the sea, hand in hand, it looked like,

I wasn't able to register any more before I did exactly the same, only seconds later I too was in the ice cold sea, spitting salt water and spilled oil and almost furiously making up my mind to hang on until the rescue boat came. I never saw them again, they must have gone under and drowned, both of them.

MARTIN | The train journey to Magdeburg takes a day and a night, the rails are damaged in several places. I sit gazing out of the window, can't sleep, smoke cigarette after cigarette, how will it be to meet Sabina again, will she think that I am old? Will we manage to live as husband and wife again, what has she been through in these years, what lay between and under the lines in the few letters which reached me on board? What does she look like now, has time wasted her away as well?

Suddenly I wish the journey home would be twice as long, I who have longed so volcanically for my wife! Is everything ruined, not merely the houses and tanks and battleships and planes, but people too? Has a smile become a grimace, a kiss a bite, and a loving caress a blow? Was it the war which conquered the peace and not the other way round? My Sabina, I am putting armour on before I dare to meet you.

HERMANN | Something was wrong. Mother and Father were lucky, their house hadn't been bombed, but just the same. They would sit silently for hours, and then there was something about the smell, the dirt, but more than that, a rotting, a dead crow in the pipe, what the hell, it didn't stink like that when I was growing up.

Then I understood that it was Mother's foot that smelled. She had got a shard of grenade in it. We have to cut it off above the knee, said the doctor. In the evening I see her lifting up her full, red-checked skirt and staring down at her foot, she is bidding farewell. Tomorrow she is going to the hospital. The healthy part of it has hardly any effect on the diseased part. Mother does not cry, the stink of dead flesh, perhaps she can't smell it? Perhaps it has become one with her.

What are you looking at? I hear Father saying behind me in the passage. Then he comes up beside me and sees Mother in the bedroom. He says nothing, but he may be thinking about all the dances they have danced together, they were good at that, even the tango, or all the times she has wrapped her legs around him, and laughed, when they were young. All the walks they have gone together. Now they are going to cut off a part of the leg.

Father clears his throat, says: I'll go in with her for a while. Mother is so pale against the green wall, I shift a little so that Father can get past, he has some pear brandy for Mother. A milk glass full. My gaze moves to the tapestry on the wall, the one with the woman on the horse, she has two legs. At Mother's side the dog she will never take out again is sleeping. I call it, it leaps straight from sleep to running and we go out of the door before Mother gets to put her face on and say anything.

JOHANNES | What could I say? How should I have replied? Sonja sobbed and told me about rape after rape. I couldn't stay around her and went out. Drank myself drunk. Behaved like a Russian. That must have been when I lost her. I don't know exactly what I was feeling either. She had become someone else.

You, she said and looked at me, just go away, you don't need to be here. Go: I can manage alone, I've had to learn that. Now no man is going to control me anymore. I am finished with shitty soldiers, of whatever nation.

KASPAR | My cactus had survived in the cellar bedsit in Hamburg, and scarcely a month later it flowered, white and strongly-scented. I took that as a good sign, the desert is blooming.

CARL | The smell of poverty lingers in the clothes, in the walls, I have been away so long that I had forgotten it. On board Tirpitz we had meat and bread. At home there is nothing, only porridge. Father doesn't even have coffee, I realized it suddenly when I wondered why he hadn't put the kettle on.

GUDRUN | Perhaps you didn't die, but lost your memory? Is that why you haven't come home even though it is nearly autumn and the war has been over for months? Perhaps you don't remember our address, are you out there somewhere searching for me?

WILLY | Surreptitiously I water her garden at night. Gudrun doesn't want help. All the same I know I have to do it for her, keep the garden in shape, weed and water, remove dead leaves, and scatter chicken manure over the roses, in the dark. I can often hear crying from her flat, it does not go away if I close my window.

PETER | I think a lot about the oath I swore to Hitler, am I released from it since he is gone?

THERES | Suddenly he is standing there, in the middle of the hall. He sees only Mother. Goes straight over to her and kisses her. For a long time. It was always those two first, then it was our turn. I know he loves Mother more than us.

JOSEF | Wilhelm does not recognize me when I come home, I wouldn't have been able to pick him out in a school playground either. He only wants to listen to his mother. Theres hesitates too, but then she throws herself at me like she used to. It takes a long time to get used to being a family again. We struggle, I have become loud-voiced and coarse from my life on board. Gretha is not the same, she has become accustomed to managing by herself, won't let me decide everything any more. I should have understood that better. Simply been pleased that we have each other, been pleased to be alive. I have been so angry with that war which took nearly six years. But it did not take my life.

LOTHAR | We must keep in contact, Peter, promise me you will write. I will be happy to come and visit you, you have been my only friend on board. Thank you, I said when we parted.

I am not getting any letters, don't understand why.

KURT | When at last I came home, I went first to my brother. I didn't have the energy to go straight to Mother and Father. All the questions, Mother would be sure to cry and make a fuss. I couldn't face it, but after a few hours rumours had gone round, Mother came flying in at the door. She did not say a word.

MARGOT | We took the girl in when she was five days old. Her mother had been raped. A half-Russian lay there kicking, but we couldn't think that way. She had sugar water every three hours, little by little she wanted to drink milk too. Unnaturally calm, almost as if she didn't want to be any trouble, as if she had felt her mother's hatred towards the swelling belly, against the small movements. I grew to love her more than I could have imagined. Her eyes are German-blue, now she smiles when I pick her up.

She is sure to win Leonard's heart soon too. There are so many consequences to the war, some good ones as well. But Uwe will not come back, nor Katharina. It is Uwe's room the girl has. Between football clothes, prizes and pictures from his Navy training, the little girl lies laughing.

BÄRBEL | Before the war began, I modelled for an artist, it wasn't anything nasty, he had been a little bit famous when he was young. He painted and told stories, and the pictures didn't look at all like me. Then he had to go back into the Navy, he must have been an officer or something. Now it is several years since I have heard of anyone who creates art. So long as we carry bricks and build up our houses, nobody carves sculptures or paints pictures.

It was the artist who told me about the old doctor and the young, fatally ill girl. She had asked him to lie with her, she didn't want to die before she had made love with someone, he was to represent the lovers death was coming to cheat her out of. I don't know if this is true, but nearly all the younger soldiers I talked to said things like, "I can't die without having fucked", yuck, how they nagged when they were on leave.

PETER | The shipwrecks we saw when at last we came to Kiel, they were large ghost ships, stranded for good. The houses bombed out and no trees, absolutely not one single tree, all must have been used for firewood. The children were obviously hungry, some of them got a loaf of bread I had in my bag, they couldn't even say thank you, just ran off. The happy feeling of survival and homecoming quickly ran out of me, and I had to go into the Russian Zone. Perhaps it wasn't so clever, said someone I met, but I had to go home to Mother and Father after all. When I mentioned that I would go through Dresden, everyone became so quiet.

Mother couldn't believe it was me when I came home, Father wept, I had never seen him do that before. He had become small, old, almost frail, my father, something must have broken him, and when I asked about Erwin, I understood what.

A couple of days later it was Midsummer, I thought we would be sure to celebrate at the bonfire place as usual, nothing is as usual, Mother tried to warn me, but I had a wash and went. It was a forlorn gathering that stood there, hardly anyone I knew. Mostly girls, and when somebody came at last with an accordion, they preferred to dance with each other. Young war widows who had never even been married. Angry with me because I, and not their sweethearts, had survived.

I couldn't bear to visit Lothar. Couldn't become the son he had lost.

CARL | They called it peace, but it was a daylight robbery of Germany. The plunder was shared. Carved up like a slaughtered animal. A forepart to the Soviets, a thigh each to the Americans and Brits, and laughably enough an *entrecote* to the Frenchmen, which they can fry with garlic and tarragon, with the false victor's smile on their faces. As if those cowards had had any share in the victory.

\

Dear Hildegard

How are you in Berlin? I hope the days are good, here it is dark and silent. "In your light we see light", I try to say encouragingly to myself, but I constantly catch myself humming Chopin's Funeral March. There is a lot of funeral music when an entire nation goes under and tries to drag the rest of the world with it. Goethe should have said that "Germany in itself is nothing, but every single German is a lot".

That was what we forgot.

I miss you very much, come and visit!

I will write more soon.

Warm greetings

Kaspar

GUSTAV | Almost forty men were imprisoned together in Tirpitz with me, many I knew slightly, but then we got entwined in another way. We sang. Were silent. Waited. Prayed. Then we heard the sound of metal on metal. The blowtorch. Soon we could see it. The opening! In the moment they hauled me out, I looked up at the sky, the multitude of stars.

It was a religious experience, I cannot see it any other way, it was then that I decided to train to be a priest, to learn to give thanks. To be close to this, the wonder of survival, the stars I fixed my eyes on. We had been locked in for ten hours, we came to know it when we reached land. I felt the life in me living more distinctly, my pulse beat, the water in the corner of my eye, the sight that was made for the stars.

HEDWIG | The pastor told us about a woman who was sitting embroidering a christening robe when the news of death came from Norway. Another widow dyed her bridal dress black and wore it at the memorial service.

GUDRUN | Being a war widow is cold. Cold legs and no warm body to press them close against. This autumn I have not once made apple cake, Rickard's favourite. My warm apple cake, with crumbled butter, the taste is strangely different when you melt the butter instead of crumbling it. Now there is no butter to be had, and the apples have been left on the trees. There they hang on show, large and red. Look, she hasn't the energy, she is about to lose her grip, she can't even do the gardening. We are freezing out here, nobody is coming to pick us, or dip us in boiling sugar and caramelize us. The birds and the neighbouring children may take us. As windfalls we will be food for small animals and worms, there will be maggots in us, like in corpses, listen, we are too good for maggots. You need the vitamins for the winter. Eat us, harvest us, take the trouble, have the energy.

Everything is demanding. Everything gives me a bad conscience, and I can't cope with picking up the knife, fetching the pail, picking the tree clean, I'll never be able to do it, at all. Sniffling, I try to cook a little mashed potato. There aren't any sausages, and I cry a little for that as well.

If only I had been able to borrow you for a single day more, Rickard. One day together in the summer house by the sea, we would have made love for most of it, I would have memorized your face, and we could have bid farewell to each other, made it something solemn, like when we married.

OTTO | In October I first managed to pull myself together enough to take the trip to Steglitz, to meet the young widow and the two children. The block of flats would be behind the park. I cleared my throat, rang the bell and suddenly they were standing there. Now I was to say everything that Matthias had wanted me to pass on if I came home and he did not. I sought help in the surroundings, the hat stand on the right, a little serving trolley on the left. Further inside the flat I glimpsed a sofa. Your father loved you very much, I began. He thought of you every single day. The children aged eight and six looked at me with serious eyes. Suddenly I became violently ill and couldn't manage to say anything for a while, that frightened them, I saw. Mother, he isn't saying anything, was the last I heard before I fainted.

JOSEF | Almost shy in my own home. We have become strangers to each other. My wife's laughter from the old days is heard no more. Home is not home. I can't find my way around the house, don't hear the pearls in the laughter of hers I loved.

It feels as if I have two animals in my stomach, two wild ferrets which crawl around fighting for space, biting and ravaging.

They are called Anxiety and Courage, and I don't know which one I am feeding the most, which one is growing the biggest, which one is going to win in the end.

GRETHA | He couldn't sleep without the light on when he came home. He told us nothing. Theres asked: Father, what was it like when Tirpitz was bombed? He did not look at her, only took his jacket and went out until he was quite sure she was asleep. When he came home, he looked at me with a look that implored silence, let me go, love me anyway. And that is what I have made up my mind to try to do.

BOOTSMANN SPIEDEL | On 17 January over two hundred British bomber planes dropped several hundred tonnes of explosives over Hamburg. That was when Mother was killed. I got the news only when I came home after having survived the attack on Tirpitz and being in captivity in Norway for several long months.

In March the block-bombers had come, 1,800-kilo bombs which pulverized the whole city centre. The neighbour girl Ada told me she had tried to get down into a bomb shelter, but it was full. She could see the planes getting nearer, and understood that people were shouting "Alarm!" She threw herself under a cart that was standing nearby, the air was knocked out of her lungs, and her mouth was filled with blood. She could hear nothing, she said, as if sound had disappeared with the gust from the firestorms, she saw only building dust and smoke.

Both Mother and Oskar are dead. How will Father get along, and me and Regina?

PASTOR RUHLAND | I don't even get to open my mouth before Frau Sachenbacher begins talking feverishly about the potatoes which should have been bought, about the windows which ought to get a new coat of paint, the child who is so good and gentle, call me Lisel, we will come to church more often, Pastor, and at last: He is dead, Pastor, isn't he? Yes, Lisel, we believe so. In Norway Tirpitz has gone down, and according to my papers he has not been found. Not a sound comes from her, but her strong bloodless fingertips dig themselves into her temples as if they are trying to prevent the words she is hearing through her ears from getting to her brain. She simply sits like that, completely silent.

At last I have to go. I will never forget the red marks her fingers made on her temples, soon they will go blue.

ANSELM | I kept myself afloat by clinging to a dead officer who had a lifejacket. I couldn't pull it off him. As we lay there, I spoke to him, told him what I would do when I came ashore.

When Hannah returned home, she didn't want to have any contact with Rolf. Probably didn't want to remember her old life. It did not seem to trouble him, I believe he has met a new one. Hannah could not explain why she chose to come back, or how she had survived. People were friendly and asked where she came from, they had already forgotten what Jews looked like.

She wanted to join in building up the country, she said. That summer her thin arms got visible muscles, she carried stone after stone from the collapsed buildings. Back and forth, she worked the hardest of all of us. Wanted to build instead of curse. If you carry enough of them, the stones become light in the end, she said. To be totally without a family must be a form of freedom too. We won't have children, she said. I don't want to.

David came anyway. The child gave her a weight which also grounded her. You could see it in her body. She had given birth, and that had given birth to her.

INGE | Behold the handmaid of the Lord; be it unto me according to thy word. Suddenly this sentence came into my head. Could I manage it, surrender myself, avoid the shame. Stefan my son is half Russian.

LISEL | A man is walking slowly down our street, it is just after lunch-time, and nobody is out to see who is coming. He knows where he is going, makes his way straight to the house, remains standing outside for a moment before he opens the door.

I hear myself screaming. A high scream and tears too, laughter and more tears. Bernhard came home! My husband came home, he had been in a prisoner-of-war camp. I just wanted to run to Pastor Ruhland and shout it out. Bernhard is not dead! He has just come home!

BERNHARD | Rolf belonged to the stern section of the ship, I in the fore part, every evening we used to meet, had a meeting-point just under the main flag. My best friend. I was so pleased when I saw him being taken on board the fishing boat which came towards him. Just afterwards I was hauled up into another boat, I had not got oil in my eyes and could see, most who were picked up were blinded by the oil, for many it lasted for weeks. Just after the wreck, I and some others were put on a boat to Narvik, I had to go in front of the group like a white stick. I was never able to find Rolf and say goodbye.

In the final months of the war I served on a cruiser in the Baltic, I believed Lisel had been informed. When we were torpedoed, I ended up in a camp for prisoners in England which was called London Cage. The interrogations and conditions were tough. Brutal. I got to hear that Rolf was alive when I came home, I became so happy and wanted to visit him at once, but Lisel didn't want to let me go.

ROLF | Navy sailors always kept matches in waterproof canvas, it is basic training, that was how Christian was able to light a fire to dry wet clothes when he, I and a few others got into the uninhabited hut or whatever it was, which had a usable stove. That saved my life, it is quite certain, the others said I was blue and white, shaking, half-fainting with cold. I searched for Bernhard for days, went from sickroom to sickroom. Now he has come back. Has the war continued inside him as well?

HILDEGARD | The second summer after the capitulation was the hottest since I moved to Berlin, we often went to one of the nearby lakes to bathe. I had inherited a swimsuit from Elfride, she and her mother died when their apartment in the city was bombed, but there was no fire, all the clothes were intact, and I was allowed to take whatever was suitable. It felt so wrong to be able to cycle out and swim, while Elfride lay rotting in the ground. The war could not be forgotten at the lake either, we looked straight at a soldier's grave with a cross made of two nailed-together branches and the helmet hanging over it. Yet another who should have been out bathing. Look you people, how unfair it is that you are alive, shrieked the grave.

Grandmother was from Archangelsk, and her family moved to Hamburg during the civil war; they settled down permanently there when they realized that the Reds had won and many relatives had been killed. She insisted on teaching Kaspar and me Russian. You will come to love the great literature was her argument, so every Sunday afternoon, before she began drinking too heavily, we had to have two hours' Russian conversation with her. That was what saved me when the Soviet army came to Forster Strasse 36, where I lived. They came running into the backyard, while I was standing pumping air into the bicycle tyres, shouting and screaming and wanting to take me. When I snapped back and swore in Russian, there was a sudden silence. They asked pardon, went out of the backyard and never came back.

I wandered about in my own area of the city and looked at all the signs written in the Cyrillic alphabet, little encouraging posters for the exhausted soldiers who were moving in and taking the city.

"Forward, brave Soviet soldiers, victory is near! Look proudly ahead, soon the heart of Berlin will be conquered!" we could read. In a way I was pleased that the Russians came and put an end to the war; at the same time I saw what they were doing to people, and it was terrible to see Berlin fall to pieces.

JOSEF | The boat is disappearing away from me, I thrash about with my arms and feel my mouth filling up with salt water, I am slowly sinking, and then suddenly I wake up sweating in bed.

When I came home, Gretha used my helmet as a saucepan, others used it as a potty, there was a shortage of everything. Now I feel sick if I even see helmets.

She also sewed a tablecloth out of my puttees. First she dyed them, then she embroidered the material. She wanted to transform my suffering into something fine.

BJARNE | I dreamed about dead bodies in the sea, about the screams for help, about all the ones we could not save. They don't let me rest, they don't let me go, the corpses, the dead soldiers in the bay, they keep me awake tonight and other nights. I know we could have saved more, if we had got the boat out earlier. I watch them as they drift further and further away, the waves bury them and wash them away, rinsing the sea of people, of wreckage. They are gone, but their screams do not fall silent.

HEDWIG | Herr Geiger, can you lend me ten marks for food? You will get them back on Thursday. Alright, no, excuse me for asking, have a good day.

BERNHARD | I came in at the door after having been reported missing after the destruction of Tirpitz, Father was not able to say anything. He simply stood for a long time looking at me, then he went quickly to the bookshelf and took out the family Bible and read aloud to us:

> *Bring forth the best robe, and put it on him; and put a ring on his hand, and shoes on his feet: and bring hither the fatted calf, and kill it, and let us eat, and be merry: for this my son was dead, and is alive again; he was lost and is found.*

ROLF | Today it is three years since Tirpitz went down. Soon we will gather, we who live in Berlin. Perhaps forty to fifty men. We have wondered a little about how we can commemorate the day, and if we are allowed to do so. Probably the Brits will show the most understanding of such an arrangement, we figured out, so we shall meet in the British Sector, bringing wreaths, a priest has promised to say a few words.

The wreaths were thrown into the Spree, they drifted away swiftly, to where they belong, in the sea.

MARTIN | I had fractured one of the knuckles in my hand when I shielded myself as the bombs struck, and I didn't notice the fracture until so much time had gone by that it had healed awkwardly. It was so trivial in those days, while we were still doing roll-calls and counting the dead. Every time I see that little bump on my hand, memory beams at me, as if I had Tirpitz tattooed on my arm.

KASPAR | The first country the National Socialists occupied was Germany. Don't forget that, I say, the others stare at me, don't understand, won`t understand, I hurry and take a large gulp of beer. One of the others around the table, one I don't know well, tells us that he had had a cyanide capsule hidden in a cavity in a tooth, that it was usual in the SS. There were dentists who made the hole and inserted the capsule. If you were caught, you had only to tug it out and bite the tiny little pill, before half a minute had gone you would be dead. He laughed and said it wasn't always fun to eat rusks.

JOHANNES | Mother took me aside that time and said: It is now that Sonja needs you, you can lift her life back to dignity. Yes, she actually said that, Mother, and I decided to bring Sonja back to life again, as they sing in the opera.

Her boy is growing up, we think he is wild and demanding, sometimes I manage to stop thinking about his origins. It is good to have someone to hate.

OTTO | The worst was the rats which came on board together with the supplies. You never saw them in the daytime, but at night you heard that gnawing noise. Helmut grabbed one and threw it at the wall, I haven't forgotten how it yelped.

No, the worst was the lice. Not only on the head, but under the arms as well, now and then we got delousing stuff which stung like hell, but after a few nights they were back again. One of the old boys said we had to put our pillows out on deck when there was frost, then the lice die, he said, but I didn't think it made much difference. You had to think the itching away, that was the only thing that helped.

JOSEF | The children are yelling, it must be the lunch break, I am tired of the children's racket. Give me the railway, large vehicles, trains hooting, just not children playing. I did not sleep at all last night either.

The house has a fire escape. If I let myself go from the top, I will die. It is exactly that easy.

BERNHARD | After the capitulation there were over ten million Germans in various prisoner-of-war camps, many of us share that experience.

Lisel said afterwards that she too had been a prisoner-of-war right up until I came home, a prisoner in my mother and father's house. It was so crowded that she and the little boy even had to sleep in the same bed as my sisters. Five people shared one room, the overcrowding must have been just as bad as your time in the prisoners' camp, said Lisel. Not until I began to tell her a bit about what it really had been like did she become quiet. I had tried as hard as I could to send money home from Norway, and even smoked herring, before we capsized, but it must have got rancid before it arrived.

KURT | Yesterday I met Herr Müller, my old teacher, in the library. He smiled and said it was nice to see me. You never quite managed to get the hang of doubled consonants, I certainly remember you, he said, laughing.

He should have seen me the day I dived in and saved Rudolf. He couldn't swim, everyone knew it, but it was I who stripped off and jumped. And I found him. That led to a medal for bravery, that did. Would you believe it, old teacher-devil?

ROLF | You are welcome home again, Rolf. Strong words from Mother. I had never known her to say such fine words to me before. But she was not smiling. I have thought about that a lot. She did not smile at me. Maria is asking when she may be able to meet her, says I must not feel betrayed if she likes Mother. Maria is so wise.

KASPAR | Mother insisted on the family going to the photographer before I left. He positioned us, Hildegard and me on either side of Mother, who had Helga in her lap. Serious. Mother tries to smile a little, while Hildegard and I knew why she wanted to have a picture of us. If I died, this picture would have pride of place. I found it in Mother's cupboard today, I took out my penknife and cut out my face, then there was a grey hole in the picture, only now does it resemble me.

THERES | The hours in the bomb shelter at night, half-conscious, so tired that I thought: Just let the bombs come. The thin nightdress with a woollen jacket on top, the slippers which absorbed the damp, the poor light I could not read by, but not sleep in either. The bad-smelling pillows, and the red juice that Frau Stehle from staircase B always brought, even now I can't bear to drink red juice. I quite simply can't get it down my throat. All the hours while we waited for the all-clear signal, that was our war.

HEDWIG | Alfred said one day: "Mother, can't we find a ladder that's long enough to reach up to heaven, and climb up to Father. Bring him down with us, home, so he can take care of us." How does one answer such questions? Now and then he has exactly the same smile as Fritz, and then I am not always up to smiling back, but have to swallow and swallow away the tears I don't want him to see. I grieve most that Alfred is fatherless, but my own grief sometimes wants to have a place too, and then I usually hide myself away in the closet. There I can bite one of Fritz's sweaters that I have left unwashed, and howl as soundlessly as I can, not to frighten Alfred. Breathe sorrow in short breaths. Then breathe out, go down again. Smile.

OLAV | While I am in the German Army, I meet Werner, my "friend" from Tirpitz, again. Unbelievable, but one day I see him in the street in a wheelchair, he has lost his foot. I shout after him, he is so pleased, and he asks for news of Fættenfjord. He is most pleased when I slip him a couple of boxes of tinned sausage and some chewing tobacco, then the tears come. Oh yes. I can see how wan he is, almost transparent, it is not the first time I have felt sympathy with a German since I came here. A crushed people, no doubt about it. They are grey. Never a smile. Empty, mostly empty eyes.

\

Dear Hildegard

Are you well? I very much hope so! Myself, I think too much, torture myself with pictures of all of us who dressed up as soldiers and officers; ordinary men, with normal lives, teachers and bus drivers, dentists, bricklayers and singers, suddenly all of us were to play at war. Now when we are home again, it is also a masquerade, then we have to play common men again. Behind the mask we are not crying, we laugh when anyone hurts themselves. Hit out. Sneer when someone dies. So lonely that we no longer feel ourselves to be a part of humanity. Am I sick to think like this? I can't talk to Helga about this, only write to you. Iron sharpens iron, as Solomon says. I have never seen a more precise description of war. And what it did to me.

Hoping you will come home for my birthday.

Yours affectionately,

Kaspar

ROLF | In June 1948 we got the new D-mark, but not in Berlin. That was the beginning of the end for a whole Germany, and then came the blockade, then it was obvious.

At the most 58 planes an hour landed in what was called an airlift. We stood looking on while the planes came in over our bombed-out city, like mother birds bringing insects and grubs to the young in the nest.

OTTO | The best thing about life on board was that nobody asked what you did in civilian life. Nobody knew who I was, or what my father was called. The anonymity of war, in the uniform, I will always miss it. At home I am indistinguishable from the farm and the family.

PETER | All who died in Tirpitz are a lost dream.

Bruno, Franck, Oswald, Gregor, Heinz, Horst, Mathias, Fritz, Uwe, Rickard.

GUDRUN | Nothing in the world can alter death. I have kept the letter I received on 29 November 1944:

> *We regret to have to inform you that Naval sailor Rickard Stock died when Tirpitz was bombed outside Tromsø, Norway, 12 November.*

That was all.

BOOTSMANN SPIEDEL | The Nazi party showed great psychological sense by not telling us what really happened to the Jews. We would never have said yes out loud to that. They only let there be rumours, rumours we could brush aside as unlikely because they were so grotesque.

I conducted myself according to Hitler's three demands for his officers: 1. Capability which matches their rank; 2. To report correctly on the situation; 3. Obedience. These I felt were quite appropriate expectations, I had no problem with following them. Hitler knew that a big lie always works better than a small lie. We were cheated.

"Would you define guilt as being responsible for breaking a moral or judicial law?"

"I think that sounds right."

"Are you guilty of anything yourself?"

"What shall I say, we were in a war, after all."

"But do you feel guilty?"

"Yes, I do, every single day, every single hour, I was about to say, but that is a bit of an overstatement, yes, often. I know what I have done."

"It must be painful, I mean, it is a heavy burden, or what should I call it?"

"Regret is a condition. A place to be. Before forgiveness, perhaps, if I ever get there I can forgive myself."

"What has your guilty deed done to you?"

"Nothing in me is light. I often think of the word 'carefree'."

"What's the worst?"

"That I was part of a system which thought it was fine to use millions of people to achieve a goal."

"Would it have been better to sit in jail? In a prisoner-of-war camp? Do you think you would feel differently if you were able to expiate it?"

"It seems so distant now...besides I am sitting in an inner prison, with a life sentence."

"In war it must be legitimate to take the life of the enemy?"

"Is it?"

"Would you like some more coffee? I can sit a little longer, it's okay."

"Yes, sit a bit longer, by all means."

Germany, 1955-1975

ROLF | In the rest of Europe there are celebrations that it is ten years since the end of the war. Commemorations. Flowers and orchestras. Guards of honour. How would we have celebrated if we had won?

GUDRUN | Grief is a triangle in the breast which turns round and round and shatters and damages the heart, right up until the triangle is worn down to a ball. To a gold medal of love: You were loved and loved yourself, therefore it was so painful to lose. I often think about Chekhov's story 'Champagne', which says something like: "What more painful thing can happen to a fish which is already caught, fried, laid on a plate and served with sauce?" Yes, I want to reply, it can be eaten, crushed between teeth, kneaded in saliva, swallowed and shat out again. Sorrow can always become even worse, even more painful. The triangle comes back and has to be worn down anew.

BRIGITTA | It's a pity for me too, I thought, but never said so, pity for me because my handsome husband has become repulsive, disgusting, unsavoury. I have to leave the bathroom if he comes limping in, of course he notices that, I see how unhappy he is. When the nightmares and phantom pains tortured him, I should have been there, helping. Now it is the morphine which comforts him.

His doctor prepared me to be strong, but I wasn't strong before he came home either. It was always he who took care of me. He is brave, but it affects him that everyone stares at the missing foot, that I hide myself behind my glasses, the book, practical things.

I wish he had died in the war. That it was all over from one second to the next, a bullet between the eyes. That I shouldn't have to witness the whole process, the breakdown of the body which had given me so much pleasure. Dagmarr has become afraid of him, does not want to go into his room when he calls, I can't force her, I understand her so well, but it must wound him.

If he asks for too much morphine, I think he should get it. Just as well that we don't talk to each other any longer.

WERNER | "Before, when I lived in heaven, when I saw the house with you and Mother in it, I wanted to come here." That is how Dagmarr explained exactly how she came into Brigitta's belly when she was small. When does the soul enter the foetus? I felt very humbled that she chose us. Now she just wants to get away.

GUDRUN | I don't know how I'm going to manage it, but I have promised myself that no matter how bad it is, I won't let the flowers in the garden die. Willy helps me. I force myself out to do the watering every morning. Afterwards I give myself permission to go back to bed again and sleep it all away.

PETER | Mother was so proud that I travelled, like Kaiser Wilhelm, to Norway, but I was more preoccupied with Amundsen and Nansen. The adventure of my life, yes, one can put it like that, I never got to travel again, so the nearly three-year long voyage to Norway was my only journey abroad. I remember so many details, and the album from that time is among my dearest possessions. I still know a little Norwegian: *God dag og tusen takk. Jeg elsker deg!*

\

Dear Sister

To save Germany, Germany had to be destroyed, as Klaus Mann said, there is no shame in this defeat. The Nazis were shameful. Think of what Goebbels said after Stalingrad, in the speech about Total War. About giving oneself to the Führer body and soul, with the motto: "Now people, raise yourselves up, storm and tear yourselves loose!" And we replied as always: "Führer befiehl, wir folgen!"

There were twice as many civilians who died in comparison to the military. It was more dangerous to be at home than in the war.

We should have learned from the Jews, about what they call Shalom Bayit—peace in the home. Peace at every dusk, the family gathered, quiet and strong. Out of all we killed, I think now and then about Shalom Bayit, how it was destroyed forever for just about all the Jewish families.

Don't feel sorry for me, dear Hildegard, I know you think I am stuck in this, but I can't let it go.

Miss you, hope you are living well.

Kaspar

ULRICH | A straight bow, that was Hitler's theory. We made the bow straight, he brutalized all that was fine.

BJARNE | There were drifting corpses coming all the time. We struggled to get them on board. Gradually we had to throw some out again and give priority to the living, those who were shouting. Who are still shouting.

OLAV | We met in the Norwegian Independent Brigade Group, I and Kåre from Kåfjord, we had both had Tirpitz as a neighbour, and we became good friends, oh yes. What made the strongest impression on us was Ellen Mari, a Norwegian woman who had accompanied her German husband there after the war. She was malnourished, that was obvious, and they had two little children, she told us. Her voice cracked when she said that she no longer had her Norwegian passport or citizenship. "But I am just as Norwegian as you two, I am from Skedsmo. I should have been allowed to come home again. It isn't liveable here," she said, even quieter. "He wasn't worth it."

Kåre and I wonder now and then how it went with her and the little family, if she ever got to go home. Every time I hear talk about Skedsmo, I think of Ellen Mari. Her war began when ours ended.

JOSEF | Grandmother said she wanted to talk with me before she died, are you ill? I said, surprised. No, but I am eighty, it is time I made a will. My philosophical testament, I mean, the ornaments and art they can fight over when I am dead. I won't stick my nose into that, but I see you are worn out, I see that the war will not let go of you, I see how Gretha tries, but that you don't let her make you happy. You are carrying guilt and fear, that is clear. I think I must try to speak plainly to you, and not keep silent, as we usually do in this family. Grandmother's voice was strong and clear, hardly weakened at all by age, it came out of the lipsticked mouth, the little double chins and the towering frame. I let her speak, said nothing, even though it was not quite correct, about Gretha and me.

You deserve a richer life, Josef, said Grandmother, and suddenly I felt so exhausted. Tears came into my eyes, good heavens, are you going to cry in front of your grandmother, as if you are a whiny child, I thought, swallowing and swallowing. You must be more attentive to daily life, take part in it, do you understand that, said Grandmother. Yes, I whispered. Now it was going better, this was so unspecific that it was possible to hang in there. You have to understand yourself, Grandmother went on. That is everybody's task in life. One has to change *oneself,* not others, one can't demand that. Growth comes when one listens inwardly. Let the basis always be friendliness, said Grandmother gently, directed towards yourself as well. Then I felt the tears coming again, pathetic self-pity, I thought before Grandmother said: Worthiness and love, respect and understanding, are most important for all people. The four great virtues. Let go of your bad conscience, Josef, then you will make progress, go further. Remember to give to yourself, give yourself what you are missing. Serve yourself. Give something *good*. Accept and bring out what has been difficult. Hold it in your hands, pour it into the stream, your sins can become as white as snow, as it says in the Bible. Overcome people by forgiving. Forgive, and be grateful that you survived the war, many millions never came home to their Gretchen. Gratitude that you are whole, that the wounds are located in your head, so that you can work on them. Now you will learn to be happy. You *are* happy, but you have forgotten how it feels. Grandmother shifted a little, and then I did as well, feeling how sticky my thighs were against the leather upholstery of the chair. Don't let the war be redoubled in you, continued Grandmother insistently, allow the civil war in your head to end in peace. I saw that she was tired out now, it was hot in the room, and the monologue had taken a lot out of her, but she still had more she wanted to say. Now she focussed her gaze upon me again and said: Create something that is reliable in yourself, she took a small pause, her gaze faded, but she continued in a clear voice: Build an enduring confidence which survives outer disturbances. It is possible to live in love and safety. It is possible to live that way, believe me, dear Josef, for you as well. Then Grandmother got up and opened the window, just then it was as if a wind swept through me and I felt something being drawn out of my body, it was almost as if I could see it, a dark breeze blowing out of the window. Something lifted, I was relieved inside. I could feel it, good God, I felt it.

Grandmother, I said, thank you! Thank you, dear Grandmother, there was something that I've let go. Go out, said Grandmother hoarsely, go out to Gretha and the children, play with them, laugh with them, and you will be fine, but now I have to lie down, I have become a little tired. I helped her over to the bed. She smiled at me, I see it, she said, you are feeling better now?

Grandmother died that night, her doctor did not understand anything. I knew, she had used up all her spiritual power on me, got the heaviness to pull itself out, it had cost her all the strength she had, drawn the life out of her, but she saved me.

BJARNE | "The cock crows over a corpse," Grandfather always used to say solemnly, and I remember how much those words frightened me.

When Ole Petter came on a visit, he wanted to take our cock with him in a rowing boat and go back and forth over the area where Tirpitz sank. The cock crowed and crowed, that is for sure, but then it was not used to being in a boat either. We should never have done it. "The peace of the grave," was one of the other expressions Grandfather used seriously.

BERIT | In the post-war years you were not allowed to forget, no. Rumour ran before you, the punishment is not over, *you* get only half your wage. No accommodation is free when *you* phone. You are not to serve the customers in the shop, no, not *you*. I haven't killed anyone, you feel like shouting, but you can't do that. Not *you,* then you will get a beating, and that's exactly what you can't bear. No more blows, please, don't hit me! Shut up, *you* have nothing to say. Disappear, slip away home, creep, creep, you Nazi beetle, or bleed, they said to Morten, nearly every day he came home with a nosebleed and black eyes.

OTTO | The conclusion of the speech General von Falkenhorst made at the memorial service for the death of "Blücher" was quoted in the newspaper, it was terrifying to read. I still remember parts of it: "Let us put sorrow behind us. Our slogan shall be: Over the graves—forward!"

I froze up when I saw that, we sailors were worth so little. But I had still wanted to participate when I saw the uniforms, heard the songs, read about the bloodthirsty and swinish enemies of Germany. I understood that the greatest historical event of my life was only as far away as the recruitment office. I did not think any further.

I have read that Himmler ordered 30,000 deserters to be shot towards the very end of the war, just before everything was over, war-stressed men who knew that capitulation had to come soon, who only wished for peace, who so much wanted to survive.

The hobby became my salvation; after taking care of the cowshed work, I switched over to the big twenties car I inherited from uncle. Collected old car magazines. Swapped and sold parts, wrote letters to other collectors. It took time. Fortunately. And Dora then, the war widow from a neighbouring farm whom I hastened to propose to. Thus, both the farm and Doris, as I fondly called her, grew bigger. Before a year had gone by, she gave birth to a great big boy, with fists like a woodcutter!

HEDWIG | The thing I will never be able to understand, already early in the fifties German women began to say yes to rearmament. Mothers without sons, young widows, they knew how deeply the madness struck.

MARTIN | My home is Tirpitz, us sailors always used to say. It became my home after the war too.

Sabina always says I am so distant. Where are you? she asks often. On Tirpitz, I reply.

Come home, she says. I can't, I say. In dreams I float in the water until it feels warm to be there. The water closes around me, combs my hair, which has turned to seaweed. My bones will turn into corals. From the sea you have come, to the sea you will become. Martin, stop that! Sabina always goes out into the garden when I start something like that after a few drams.

GUDRUN | She, who is me, fetches the bicycle from the storeroom, puts the wreath and the lamp in the front basket and cycles slowly towards the churchyard. It is Hallowe'en, and as always she lights a lamp at the large memorial at the western edge of the churchyard with other widows. She can hardly remember any more what Rickard looked like, but to the churchyard she must go, that's the way it is, year after year, until she becomes so old that she can't manage to cycle there. Fortunately there is nobody at the nearby graves, quickly she gets it all finished, it is a duty, an obligation, she, who is me, feels nothing. A green and brown wreath with a few red autumn leaves from the garden, and a light, they have to do, she can't afford anything else. He won't notice anything, after all. He doesn't even lie here, but in a war cemetery somewhere north in Norway, where she will never go. Why should she go, she can't remember his face any longer, but the smell of him, that she can recall now and then, and that thick hair. Wait, now it is coming, his eyes were light blue, and his beard became red if he let it grow. His nose was small and straight and his eyebrows prominent, imagine, now he is coming to me! This evening I will be able to remember him, so you still exist in me, my dear, so the whole fuss was not in vain, this evening you are on a visit.

PETER | In a photo I have kept, from 1943, I am twenty-one years old and in uniform, you can see the apathy in my eyes. In another picture Tirpitz lies with her belly in the air, like a dead whale. I used the pictures of myself and the ship when I wrote an article for *Der Scheinwerfer*, the members' magazine of the Tirpitz Veterans' Association. I had never believed that writing would help, but it did me good, and reading what others wrote too, again so conspicuous: Nobody else understands.

KASPAR | In a book about the fate of the Jews, I read: If there are more than thirty-six righteous people left on the Earth, it will survive.

Perhaps there were only just enough?

OTTO | It gradually dawned on me that I had been a part of the killing machine which would not have come to anything without all of us who were in it. As a result fifty million people died. I was in it, I have to acknowledge my responsibility.

Not much differentiates one soldier from another, but people don't want to listen to me when I talk like that. Dear Otto, you are so kind, you could never have killed a Jew. No, I reply, but others could not have done it either, if it were not for us who supported the Führer's plans.

LUDWIG | Ellen Mari and I married on a cold June day in Oslo in 1945. The District Court judge was not exactly welcoming. Ellen Mari came with me the day I was released. First on a boat to Kiel, after that we had to use our legs. If she had known what she was coming to, she would not have said yes to me, even though we loved each other so much. Bremen is an ugly city, was the first thing she said when we arrived. I understood her, everything that had been beautiful had gone, the fine old buildings, in the parks the trees had been chopped down for wood, and in the flowerbeds turnips were growing. We had only to roll up our sleeves, to tell the truth. But it went well. Everything goes well when it has to, as my grandmother used to say, she was still alive when we came back, and glorified God in loud songs of praise. Ellen Mari thought she was crazy, but it was not that bad, even if nothing was as before, not even Grandmother. Little by little we got ourselves organized, and in 1957 I had already brought my own car home, and our two boys were so proud that they became completely quiet when we put them in the back seat and drove around the district. A brand new family car! Imagine that I, the poor boy, owned a car. We are many who have done well since the war, I often think.

The first journey we took, we went to my cousin down by the Weser. Ellen Mari asserts that I looked prouder at the wheel than in the photograph in which I am holding our elder boy on his christening day.

HEDWIG | Dieter was not among them when the other men in the street began popping up, one by one, grey and bowed, after imprisonment in Canada or France or other places. In the end Lily travelled to a psychic woman in Düsseldorf. Lily got to hear from her that Dieter was alive, he was not wounded, but sitting in a Russian work camp and would come home within two years. She often went to the hairdresser's and always had fresh flowers in, the wine lay ready in the cellar, cheese and sausages, all for him to come. Nearly three years had passed since we tried to talk sense into her, but she clung to that explanation. In the end we played along with her, but thought it was a pity, because she never remarried and had no children, and at last she became very lonely. We couldn't bear all the talk about Dieter who would soon pop up. We should have taken the matter up, written and found out what had happened to him, so that Lily could have gone on living, not only longing. We betrayed her. It is not grief I feel as I walk behind her coffin, but shame.

KURT | I was born on 12 February, confirmed on 12 April, engaged on 12 June, 12 November Tirpitz went down, and 12 January Adelheid was killed. Now when the twelfth of the month approaches, I am not able to relax.

12 December I met Inge at an early Christmas party at Otto's farm. She is a midwife and has a son called Stefan.

WERNER | Little by little I had ruined everything, I saw that in the looks Brigitta gave me. Dagmarr shrank away from the roars that came out of my mouth. The doctor told me plainly that I would not get any more morphine. I swapped some in trades with another veteran. Brigitta did not find her gold bracelet, nor the ring with the amethyst either. No doubt she quickly suspected me, but she had promised 'for better or worse', I saw how determined her mouth became, buttoned-up, tight-jawed, locked. In the end I stuck the needles in openly, straight into the veins of my arm. Brigitta went away, taking Dagmarr with her, saying we can talk to each other when you have become yourself again. I laughed, she does not know about the dance of colours, the glimpse of the divine.

FRAU BRAUN | The degradation is smashed glass, cigarettes and ash turning into earth, weevils, leftovers which have hardened, stink. There is nothing to be said. I dig out cloths and run water, pour in soap. I start in one corner, wash away stains, air the room, clean the windows, throw out rubbish. I can't look at the broken vase which was a wedding present from Mother and Father. Dead pot plants, flies. The clothes can only be chucked out. Werner, my boy, why haven't you said anything? The only thing I can do is to let in the daylight and insist on dignity. This is only shit, and shit can be washed away. It will be clean here. Light. Light, I say it like a refrain while I am scrubbing and scrubbing at a burned-in mark in the oven, but I do not see the light, as the tears are blinding me. It is my son who has been here, who has slipped so far down that he no longer does credit to the life I gave him. On the contrary, he longs to escape from it. What was it the war took away from you, Werner? What became of all the strength I tried to impress in you? I have to sit down, suddenly I feel so faint. I can't cope with it. I won't be able to get it clean, and then who is to do it, who will keep up dignity for you, if I can't manage it?

It was painful giving birth to you, it will be impossible to abandon you.

GUDRUN | Many years went by without my hearing anything from Willy—at one point he got up and left—then he came to me and asked straight out whether I would marry him. It is enough for me that I love you, he said. In that way my life became a novel, almost, with brown tears and purple life and all the shades in between, which I can't think about without crying.

ANSELM | After the war I was preoccupied with finding out the details of what is called the Holocaust. I read that towards the end of the war, trains with Jews on their way to the gas chambers in Poland had higher priority than supply trains to the front. In the summer of 1941 came the gas Zyklon B. It took four or five minutes to tear apart the lungs. I studied the poster which had been in the gas chambers: "After the bath you will get hot coffee. Fold your clothes nicely, and tie your shoes together." Small children were thrown in through the windows when the room was crammed full. People were used as living targets for bayonet and shooting training in the camps.

I read about Dresden too, about the firestorms there. In the centre the temperature was so high that the oxygen was sucked out and tens of thousands suffocated in cellars and bomb shelters. Those who fled into the streets got stuck fast in the melting asphalt, or blew up in the firestorm.

Hannah didn't want to hear anything about this.

INGE | I met him through Otto, who understood that both 'Inge my-favourite-cousin', as he still calls me, and Kurt needed somebody. Kurt had been a lookout, he told me proudly. Purely an arranged marriage, I thought, but after a few years I notice it was there anyway, love. That I had not recognized it, because I believed that love came without choosing, like something you get caught up in, and can't wriggle yourself out of. Now I saw that between me and Kurt there was a mature love, in which the love-project is no longer like a life-project, in which my life was to grow out of the relationship. Now there was a different repose in our life together, it was unforced, I could choose Kurt, I did not have to. I was free, and so I could tolerate distance, and with that closeness came over us. Now we are so good together that people laugh. If only Stefan, my son, had been healthy and happy.

In May every year we travel to the veterans' gathering for the Tirpitz survivors in Heiligenhafen. It is important for Kurt. He was the eagle eye, as he calls it, on Tirpitz. Only others who were there can understand, he said to me earlier in our marriage. I accepted it, refrained from asking, but listened when he wanted to tell, in snatches, about the bombs, the shouts, the ship which capsized, his friends. It is only the other women who were marked out by the Russians who understand me too. The conversation can go in any direction, but I can see it in their eyes, we have something in common. I can talk to them about Stefan's problems. Afterwards Kurt and I stay a few extra days at the Baltic. In peace and quiet. Our life together is blessed with peace and quiet.

WERNER | I was lying in my own cold, stinking urine when Mother came. She did not implore me, did not cry, just brought out the large zinc bowl of warm washing water. I gave birth to you, she said. I am going to keep life living in you.

Now it is finished. Never more morphine. I'll stay here as long as necessary. She managed it. Mother is so steadfast that she managed it. Kept me at home, fed me with veal soup after the seizures, a cold cloth on my forehead. She gave me time. And it took time, but I survived and am living, suddenly I smelled the scent of the roses in the garden. Only humans enjoy the scent of flowers, I remember thinking. I have become human again.

Brigitta came back. For a while I had been in my own war, but we won it, Mother and I, and Brigitta.

HEDWIG | When you were little, you called all men in uniform 'papa'. You cycled after them in the street on your tricycle, and shouted papa, papa, wait for me. Some turned round and smiled, others were embarrassed, must have thought you didn't have a father, that you didn't know what he had looked like, that he was just a uniform in a photo.

CARL | It was England which came out with the declaration of war. An England which during the past three hundred and fifty years had made war in one hundred and fifteen of them and colonized large parts of the world and subdued a quarter of the population of the world. Europe must not forget that the Brits started it. They fried our children in phosphorus!

To my dear Hildegard

I moved some boxes of books today, and heard myself singing 'Heida, Heido, Heida'. The refrain means nothing whatsoever, but it made the work lighter as we scrubbed the deck of Tirpitz with coarse sand and cold seawater. The banal things from the war have stuck. Or as Carl, in the last veterans' gathering, put it: No large perspectives, only athlete's foot and boring dried food. Wanking. Days of useless waiting. A little laughter. A dram and a dream about a woman.

When I went to university, life was divided into four: love, politics, aesthetics and philosophy, I sketched out schematically for Carl. It was so easy in those days. Good grief, said Carl, you had it good in the war! What do you think, Hildegard, did I?

Is it good weather in Berlin nowadays? Here it is warm and spring-like now. Kiss and hug from Helga and Mother, as always.

With love
Kaspar

PS
Hope you are all right, will you phone soon?

KONRAD | When the youngest one moved out and I got a better position, I invited my wife to come on a car trip to Norway. At last she should see the lovely landscapes I was surrounded by in the long years on Tirpitz, the places I have talked about so much. I don't know if I have the strength to go to Håkøya, where I swam ashore as I heard the shouts behind me, but we can go to Fættenfjord, Bogen and maybe all the way up to Kåfjord.

We set out with the old Mercedes packed full of tents, tinned food and a storm kitchen, fishing rod and woollens and raincoats. I know the weather up there, ugh, how cold it could be even in summer! Proud to show my wife that we too can afford a holiday abroad and not only trips to my parents in Niedersachsen. On the autobahn northwards, it all goes by quickly, then we take the ferry from Kiel, and suddenly I am in Norway again. I am not prepared for it, it's hard to hear that language we had around us daily, to be aware of what my country did to these people, so many who had their lives destroyed. No, I must shake it off, my wife is so happy, as she seldom is usually, and I know how far it is up there, we just have to get going and tick off mile after mile. The next day we arrive at Fættenfjord.

"Tirpitz lay here."

We parked right by the beach. So strange to see the place again without the huge battleship. My body remembers nature here, the low mountains, hills mostly, the narrow valley, the fjord with the little islands, white and red houses, cows grazing outside. It is exactly as idyllic as I remember it, maybe even more beautiful, and now I don't have to keep watch for bomber planes. I dare not make contact with the people on the farm which lies close by, tell them that I have been here before, don't know how they feel about Germans. I take my wife with me and go for a walk towards the site of the quay we constructed, try to tell her what it was like when the whole narrow bay was filled up with battleships, cruisers and destroyers. This peaceful spot was for a while Germany's largest shipping harbour in the north. So different it all is now. Almost unreal.

My wife is in a marvellous mood, talking together is easy. I had dreaded it, lots of long hours together in the car, will we have anything to say to each other when it isn't only a matter of who is going to fetch the children from the sports ground, and whether we have saved enough for a new TV, and other practical things like that. When we met, she was never interested in what I had done during the war, maybe she was afraid of getting to know something she could not bear, it is better not to ask. Many people must have thought that way. Maybe she herself wanted to avoid questions?

After a few days in Fættenfjord, we go into Trondheim, and I am able to show her the cathedral and the river and Munkholmen in good weather. We buy prawns straight from the boat and sit in the sun with seagulls who beg. Then we head northwards again. I have forgotten how far it is, it must of course be quicker in an enormous ship than in a clapped-out car. We see Bogen and Ofoten and are going to drive only a little further this evening before we find a place to stay overnight. I ask my wife to look out for campsites, it has become really late, we drive and drive, at last she shouts that she thinks there may be one here. I turn in and see huts and tents and a little house where it says 'Reception'. Just as I climb out of the car, I notice the sign: "GERMANS *NOT* WELCOME". I feel myself going red, throw myself into the car again and reverse as fast as I can, what is it, asks my wife. Full, is the only thing I can manage to say.

MARTIN | Our son went to Norway on so-called 'Peace Service', he worked for nothing at a home for handicapped children, the kind that had been gassed to death here only thirty years ago. In Norway they were well cared for, our son wrote. He is ashamed of being German, says he should have had a T-shirt saying, "It wasn't my fault."

I have started thinking that perhaps he is with this appalling thing the newspapers are writing about these days. Baader-Meinhof Gang. These radical young people from West Germany who kidnap people. I know they get help from here to hide members who have to go into hiding. The signs add up, the more I think about it. Something is terribly wrong. If he comes home this evening, there is no alternative but to confront him. Perhaps I am wrong, but why is he always so secretive? And who were that man and woman in his room last night, I saw them sneaking out in the twilight.

How could well-informed people have believed the State's lies? he asked me the other day. That the Jews were plutocrats who owned the largest banks, that they were behind a worldwide conspiracy to dominate the whole world, that they were "the Jewish Problem". Bloody hell, Father, it falls apart with its own absurdity! How could you all have ended up believing it?

THERES | At the edge of the beach, straw and stone, damp sand. All these trips to different places on the Baltic, nearly every summer. The little holiday flats, the hot weather, the idyll that remained until the fathers had had too much beer, which was more or less at eleven on Fridays and Saturdays, and in July nearly every evening. When all had drunk so much that they began talking about the war, then everything quickly unravelled, and they became a group of soldiers grumbling and reminiscing. Back in their rooms they beat their wives, the children lay silently pretending to sleep. Later the whole bitter rows between the war generation and us, their children, who stood yelling: "Father, you are a murderer! Don't touch me, you have blood on your hands! Don't try explaining it away, the Holocaust can't be explained away, do you hear?"

Little by little, I understand too that not everyone in the Wehrmacht was a monster, and that my father was only an ordinary Navy sailor who had to go out in the war. I missed you, Wilhelm and Mother, he used to say, all the time I went around missing you, while the war ravaged the days of my life, and I hated that threadbare uniform, the bad jokes, the cold, darkness and meaninglessness. It was worse for Ebba in my class, she found out her father had been in the SS and worked at Birkenau, then there were no excuses. She was never really happy again, Ebba.

Mother

Now you can stop pretending you have to love me. I know what happened. Frau Weber told me about the rape a while ago. The union of victim and abuser in me can only be resolved by suicide.

Stefan

WILLY | Rickard's clothes are still hanging in the wardrobe. His papers are lying in the bureau. His shoes dirty from the garden are still standing in the hall.

OTTO | When we came home from Norway, Germany was sitting in a wheelchair, begging for pennies, but you won't get me to say it was better during the war. As they say: The dog knows what to expect when it steals the meat.

For many years after the capitulation I caught myself matching my footsteps with whoever I was walking with. Marching in step seemed most natural to me.

CARL | I get so bloody furious when I remember when the Wilhelm Gustloff was torpedoed, more than 9,000 people drowned, nearly all women and children. It's the biggest shipwreck in history, and five times as many died than when the Titanic went down, which they are always going on about, but hardly anyone mentions the story of the Wilhelm Gustloff. It must have been because they were Germans, then, and Germans weren't worth much at the end of January 1945. That tragedy on the fringes of the war ended up in the shadow of what we are permitted to grieve. Because now Gustloff is no longer considered to be the hero he was when he was killed in 1936. I remember something Gustloff is supposed to have said, it was quoted often in the Hitler Youth, I believe it was something like this: "Those I love most here in the world are my wife and my mother. If the Führer ordered me to kill them, I would obey him."

WILLY | He sits in the square every evening, near the big theatre, on the benches by the ornamental bushes, and grills seagulls. He went mad after the war, or in it, nobody knows much about him, but he keeps mumbling something about Tirpitz, Tirpitz, as he turns the gulls on the spit so they get cooked on all sides. One late evening I walk past and he calls out to me: “Do you believe in fire?”

THERES | Once Papa didn’t come home at the agreed time, Mama became frightened, I can no longer remember where he was, if he was with Uncle, or if it was something at work, we were so small then. We had never seen her frightened before. She should of course have said it wasn’t serious, but now she was anxious, it terrified us. I remember she gathered us round her in the big bed and said we should pray to God together. She didn’t usually pray, had never spoken about God with us, nor taught us evening prayers. She seemed a bit uncertain as we solemnly prayed that Papa would come home safely. I can’t even remember him coming back, but the prayer, the picture of my young mother with us children by her side, I will never forget.

\

"And now Günther is dead too."

"Here lies one who does not need to be afraid any more, I thought when I saw his coffin."

"Do you remember what the priest said in his talk:
'The light from his star has not yet stopped shining on us.'"

"I read once that simple African tribes believe that a person is not really dead until all who can remember him are also dead. Not until one is completely forgotten is one dead. The war will continue like that, we still have many we remember."

"I stood watching him die, there at Håkøya, it must have been heart failure on account of the cold water."

"I bit into the Bible in the field hospital, I was so frightened. I took care of it, the toothmarks still show. Now it would no doubt be called an anxiety attack."

"People seek not only safety, National Socialism taught us that we also seek self-sacrifice and struggle, loyalty and comradely feelings, to be gathered under one banner, with drumbeats and speeches."

"Hitler thought it was better to have a terrible ending than an endless disaster."

"Ugh!"

"I was set to collect the identification tags from the corpses which had been dragged up on to land. So far away from the dream of the Iron Cross."

"Will we always dwell on these things?"

"Don't know."

Germany, 1975-1990

OTTO | Let's see, I remember it still, I believe, yes: "I swear by God the holy oath that I will render to Adolf Hitler, the German State and the people's Leader…" what was it that came next, something long and difficult, I'll try again: "people's Leader, the Defence Forces' Supreme Commander, absolute obedience, and that I as a brave soldier will be prepared at all times to give my life for this oath." Yes, that was how it went, imagine that we accepted that we would give our lives, be willing to die for the sake of that rigmarole. We must have been mad, completely out of our heads. So many died on account of this, several million young boys who are not able to stand here like me, with grandchildren and everything, but instead lie in nameless graves which nobody visits.

BOOTSMANN SPIEDEL | Old comrades, what rubbish! No, I didn't want to have anything to do with the other officers after the war, didn't want to sit talking about this and that occasion when this and that happened, I didn't want anyone to remind me of what had been done wrong in those years. Now it is the Thirty Years' Commemoration of the end of the war. In the news one sees all the British veterans with medals on their chests. Just the word 'veteran' makes me upset. I kick out at the bitch which is scurrying about obscuring the TV. Regina says nothing. Just looks at me.

CARL | Having a low membership number in the Party became a mark of honour, and I had that. We went through a race test and were declared pure after a series of biological investigations. Bloody good breeding material.

We were encouraged to make children with Aryan, Norse women. I know that Magda gave birth to a son at a maternity home somewhere in South Norway. It did not have much to do with love. Breeding. I was the stallion. It was—devil take me!—not worse than other jobs, hee hee.

Hitler made us into Masterfolk. We had lain with broken pride, humiliated and ruined, in 1918. He raised us up to dignity. Obviously we were willing to work hard to get Germany on its feet. It is just such a pity that we did not reach the goal.

We celebrated the Führer's birthday in secret until well into the seventies. We fixed sheets over the window and hung up portraits, brought out uniforms and rifles with bayonets. There were always six courses. Vintage wine. Old songs. Old toasts. At last we let it die out without speaking of it.

THERES | Father disappeared into the bedroom and stayed there for days. He became much better for a while, that was after Great-grandmother died. Then it came back again, he just lay in his room and didn't go out. Mother carried in sandwiches and coffee. Carried out the half-empty cups. Silently. Once I had a glimpse of him. He was sitting in his bed, looking without seeing. Stiffly erect, he stared into the silence. A torso.

I catch myself thinking that I ought to phone him now. When he died, I opened the window and let out his soul.

ROLF | What did we talk about all those evenings on board, we were together for several years, doomed to each other's company. Now I can hardly remember a single conversation. The time just went by, disappeared. Later I had that feeling again when I was depressed. I had only to wait until it was over, after a few minutes under a blanket of silence, as Maria used to call it. She is the best thing that has happened to me, what a blessing to get a life companion like her. She understood, didn't fuss. She never tried to make me act happy. Go for a walk. Visit friends. Go shopping. Eat. If I had been able to, I wouldn't have been ill, it's as simple as that.

Hang on tight to what is healthy in you, she whispered in my ear on the heaviest mornings when there was no question of getting up. Remember that you are more than your heavy thoughts. When it got too bad, she put her hands over my eyes and shielded me from the light. Waited beside me. Maria fell down with me, but she always managed to get up again, gradually she got me up as well. When better days came, she filled them with good things, the cinema, car trips, cream cake. Maria was given to me so that I could cope with my life, this much I know.

Maria, Maria, suddenly it was reversed. Now it was she who was quiet. With eyes that begged to be left in peace. Leave me alone, said her shoulders when she turned away. Don't talk to me, mumbled the dark rings under her eyes. The tumours were discovered too late, they were in her kidneys and as big as fists. They simply sewed her up again, saying that there was nothing else to do here but say goodbye. Three or four weeks, they said, perhaps a little longer.

Now I have nobody to set me straight when I am stranded in pitch darkness, nobody to say, come, we'll take our coffee out into the garden, smell how sweet the jasmine smells, as she used to say, listen, the blackbird has a different song this year, look how the thuja has grown, the one we planted on our silver wedding, do you remember? When she said things like that, it was impossible not to smile.

Maria, without you I have no protection.

INGE | My breasts are full of the milk of sorrow. Stefan drank depression out of me and into himself, I have realized in the aftermath of his suicide. I couldn't stop crying, even when the baby smiled. All I saw was his father bent over me in the rape. They should have taken the boy away from me, protected him from me and the stubborn pain I lived in before I found Kurt. Should have let Stefan have his smile, his eternal light which I extinguished.

REGINA | In the evenings, when the spirits have a good hold on him, then he becomes an officer again, and I am no longer wife but someone he can bash around. Swear words are spat out: *Schiesshund!* Bring beer. You devil, what are you dawdling over? *Schwein!* The evenings always end with both of us crying, and I have to console him because he has been so horrible to me. I promised for better or for worse, it's my own fault.

HEDWIG | The last division of the Wehrmacht was us women. We, who fought at home, got no medals. The luckiest ones got back some remains of a husband that had to be put together all over again. Perhaps it was just as good to be alone?

ANGELA | I was only five years old, but I remember that Mother, Mathilda, Jenny and some other women were running away from the Russians. I was in my Mother's arms, she tried to jump over the stones and bricks which lay scattered in the streets. Mathilda said: Follow the railway lines, follow the rails, go after the other women. I thought I was hindering Mother from running. This memory comes up every time I feel I am a bother to anyone.

We did not get far enough, the Russians caught up with us, and I don't know what happened, I have repressed it, as it is called. Father had gone down with Tirpitz, Mother had told me so, but I didn't remember him. We had not heard from Grandfather or Uncle since they had been called up into *Volksturm*. I thought it was such a splendid name.

Mother was afraid we would never find them in the chaos, but when we came back to the old flat after two months, we had a letter from Uncle, he was in hospital in a small town I have forgotten the name of, but he was going to get well again. We still have no idea about Grandfather. He must quite definitely be dead, he was far too old to be a soldier. Mother is bitter, but so many lost several of their own. I did not miss a father, it was normal to grow up without one. The flight in Mother's arms, through dark streets, is my only clear memory from the war years. That bottle-green coat of hers, the shawl she tied round me, the large bag of the most important things, and in my pocket the prettiest marble I had, so blue that it could blind you if you looked at the sun through it. I still have it. My daughter asked me if she might have it, but for once I said no.

OTTO | The domestic films which were shown after the war were so idiotically sentimental that people loved them. The focus in the film was on us, on the sufferings of the German people. Suddenly all Germans became victims of Nazism. I thought it was sickening, but God help anyone who said something like that in the grocery shop, few wanted to think about what had actually happened. Let the horse use his head, his is much bigger, Grandad used to say.

Now it is "Reconciliation" which is the correct way to relate to Nazism. Reconciliation between victims and molesters, but also reconciliation with one's own past, one's own family's war background.

A family is memories, isn't it? Every day and special events, stories about broken legs and birthday celebrations, the hand-reared lamb which lived indoors, weddings, visits to relatives, gardening, the family doctor, the silver cutlery drawer, the rhododendron behind the house which we all reverently ran out to see the first lilac-coloured flower on, a ritual as powerful as any. Or the story about when Mutti fell down the stairs, but saved the eggs on the tray she was holding in her hands, about Inge, my favourite cousin, who always got five freckles, exactly five, never more, or the first day after school was finished for the summer and she and I went to the lake to swim. The family code when we talked among us, I often think about it now, how fine it was, how ours, now when there is no longer anyone who understands what I mean if I simply say 'bumblebee' or 'fartingmiss' or 'father's thermometer'.

ROLF | If one travels around in Europe, one constantly comes across memorial cemeteries and monuments and memorial plaques with the names of soldiers on them, but we don't remember our fallen. Not all were brutal Nazis, many were like Father, like Uwe, Andreas, Fritz and Jochen. Our men are not to be remembered. We are denied the right to pay homage to our dead. A lot is suppressed in Germany, both pain and of pride. That war was only a dress rehearsal, Maria used to say, I am afraid she was right. The premiere will happen the evening the atomic button is pressed down on both sides of the stage.

GOTTFRIED | "The doorbell rang, outside stood a grown man who said: 'Hello, you don't know me, but you knew my mother in Norway.' Behind me I heard my wife asking who was there," Felix tells me as we sit over a beer. I become red hot, I've just had a letter from the Red Cross, Berit had also had a son. He is called Morten and wants to get in touch, it said. I can't bear to sit here any longer, excuse myself from Felix and go home. I become heavy with shame when Elsa smiles at me and says: Are you home already, how nice.

THERES | Just after the war I used to be woken up by Father shouting: Help me up out of the water, help me, help! Towards the end of his life he could not go near the sea, nor even a river. The sound of water, everything brought back memories from the war. After the electric shocks he could remember nothing of what had just happened. We were at a wedding in Ingolstadt, and when everyone was standing on the church steps afterwards, I heard Father asking Mother whether the bridal pair had said yes. The despair in the look Mother shot me then.

OTTO | If you didn't have a wife who understood, like Doris, or friends to talk with, it often led straight downhill, the regular dance between drinks, dismissal, eviction, then the gutter.

ANSELM | Adolf Eichmann is supposed to have declared in Argentina that he was sorry he had not managed to kill all the Jews in the world. When the trials of the crimes in the concentration camps began, nobody could deny the Holocaust any longer, but many still murmured that the Jews themselves were to blame for their fate.

Mischling—half-Jew or mixed-race—our child identified himself by these terms for a long time, says Hannah. The language of the abusers sticks. "Look, there goes one they forgot to gas." Such calls could be shouted after me on the street far into the sixties, continues Hannah.

I shall never forget when Willy Brandt fell on his knees in front of the monuments to the Warsaw Ghetto in 1970. He said: "By the abyss of German history and under the burden of the millions who were murdered, I did what people do when language fails." He was a true statesman.

BOOTSMANN SPIEDEL | Over the fireplace hangs the picture of Tirpitz, from the day she was launched. Turn, I think when I look at the picture, turn back, don't set out.

GUSTAV | It is always worse when it is somebody you know, they don't think of that, the widows who phone and tell me that yet another veteran is dead. Helmut threw himself in front of a train.

The wind makes it impossible to toss earth into the grave. I can hardly get any earth to land on the coffin, the rest flies onto the shining polished shoes of the mourners. The churchyard has seldom been so inhospitable. It was like that when Helmut died. Even the weather mourned.

OTTO | I discovered the phrase "survivor's guilt" in a newspaper interview with a psychologist. Then many things fell into place. I just hadn't known what it was, what I was suffering. Why did I get to live, is as big a question as why another died.

I survived, nearly a thousand drowned. Is it so simple, that one can explain it as luck and bad luck, or must we form larger words in our mouths, like fate or God? I have pondered this a lot. Not that the thoughts get anywhere, it isn't given to humans to understand these things. In any case, it's not what saves you from a situation, and then exposes you to another, with deadly consequences. I think about Rudolf, who died in a car accident in Pomerania, only a meagre year after he had been picked up out of the sea. Or the fellow from Cologne who had a brain tumour and died in December 1945, he must already have had the tumour while he was on board, why should he have been saved only to die?

MONICA | When the war was over and Jochen came home, I got a letter from him. He had never dared to send it from Tirpitz. Now he has gone. The days are long, with the children and grandchildren in Hanover, so in the later years I have busied myself with documenting German resistance work during the war. Many people, particularly abroad, have the impression that it hardly existed, but it isn't true, my history shows that, and the letter from my fine, loving soldier:

Dearest Monica

How I miss you! If you think my handwriting is bad, it is because I have to use my left hand, I have hurt the right one (nothing serious), I fell against one of the cannons when there was a strong wind (it was almost a hurricane).

I am tormented by the fact that we here north of the Arctic Circle don't know enough about what is happening in the rest of the world, and about how all of you are amidst all the bombing. I constantly feel more opposition to the whole war and Hitler's and Himmler's ideas, but it is difficult to know what is actually going on. We get no proper news here, everything is censored. Just the same there is reason to believe that a very large number of soldiers on both sides have been killed, and then on top of that, all the civilians as well. I have heard appalling, and I mean appalling, rumours from Russia about how our people are behaving there. It leaves us scant honour, one must not forget that "honour" too can lead one straight into the abyss.

So terrible what you told me about the Goldstein family, that they were discovered, dragged out of the house and sent away! That must be the SS, I suppose, they are hooligans and executioners, the lot of them! I shudder both at them and the Gestapo. No, now I am writing myself into anger and sorrow, dear Monica, and I think this letter will be more dangerous both to send and to receive the longer it gets. So then I can hardly ask about how it is going with the man your parents are hiding in the gardener's house? Is he still equally careless? You must not let him expose all of you to danger, but I understand the wish to help someone who is in such a desperate situation. Promise me you will run down into the cellar every single time there is an air raid siren, never hesitate, drop whatever you have in your hands and get yourself to safety! Don't be nonchalant. It could be your death and consequently mine, because I can't live without you.

And Erich, whom you wrote about in the previous letter, who is he actually, how do you all know he isn't a spy? Can you vouch for him? One can't rely on anyone these days, remember this, my dear, you who like people so much, you could easily be led astray. I don't mean to sound like a misanthrope, but I am so afraid for you, you understand that, don't you, don't become irritated now, after all I know you, my Monica. A tip, see whether he goes armed, if he does, you must keep far away! Be careful, sweetheart, think of our future, better times have to come after these horrible years. Now I am saying it straight out, someone must make an end to this hell! I know that Hitler has survived several assassination attempts, as if he is immortal, but there will certainly be more. Germany still has courageous and clever men, particularly among the officers, I believe many are beginning to have had enough.

Burn this letter! Now I see how dangerous what I said here is. Burn all photos of us, everything! My nerves are jumping outside my skin these days, I struggle with sleep too. The knowledge of being part of a filthy war with such an objectionable goal as world domination, is wearing me down. I have to finish this letter soon, it is late, my rosebud, my sugar bowl and everything that is sweet, I am exhausted, and it is clear weather, and then we always have to look out for bombers. Now I must sleep, but first I want to say that I love you more than ever, us forever!

A few days have gone by, I got your letter before I got round to posting mine (the truth is that I didn't dare send it, there is so much dangerous stuff here that I hardly dare to read it myself) and it is terrible to hear that they have arrested your parents! Is it because of Erich? I knew there was something suspicious about him! Have you been called for interrogation? In that case, vigorously deny everything, act stupid, lie, whatever, but never admit anything, then you are lost! Lord Christ, how frightened I am for you. Hurry up and write to me, even just a small card, a sign of life.... Go to Switzerland, if you can, I will find you there after all this is over, I promise!

Once again, don't ignore a single air raid siren, because I love you.

And once again, I love you.

Yours, forever
Jochen

PS I kiss you all over your face, light, light butterfly kisses over your forehead, and over your red cheeks and sweet nose. Write back quickly.

MONICA | After my parents were arrested, I went into hiding. It was chaos, people were imprisoned for the slightest wrongdoing, and hanged with guitar strings, butcher's hooks or whatever bestialities these monsters could think up. My friends disappeared in turn, and at last I was also discovered and brought in for questioning. They tried to break me down, one in particular. He was like the devil himself, twisted everything I said, and showed me pictures of people tortured to death, saying I would be next.

But I got through it, in solitary too. I kept myself fit in both brain and body. Conjugated strong verbs and did press-ups, recapitulated the periodic tables and ran in place, lay down with high knee-lifts. Declaimed poems and hopped on one leg. The most important thing was that I scratched a calendar into the wall with a sharp stone, so that I could keep track of the days, it helped a lot not to go crazy. They were called solitary cells, but there were millions of bedbugs there, fleas and lice which kept on making me even more insane than the chief tormentor in the interrogations. It was a long, cold autumn and winter, but in the end I was actually released, the earth under the Nazis' feet was starting to burn. The Red Army would be at hand, even us inmates knew it. The prison wardens were afraid of the Russians, and suddenly one day us political prisoners were set free. Free in a doomed city. Berlin was bombed to rubble, and in the silence after the bombs we could hear artillery fire and soon marching feet as well, Russian troops.

When I came out of jail, I had no idea whether either Jochen or my parents were alive. Tirpitz had gone down in November, but Jochen had survived. Father could tell me this when he astonishingly popped up in our flat, where I had only just recovered a little and got rid of the lice from my hair. He had had a letter from Jochen only a few weeks before. Mother we knew nothing about, still we used hope as a candle, even though the flame got weaker and weaker. I tried not to lose any more weight, but we had so little food, I weighed only forty-two kilos when I was released, and felt like the skeleton of a bird, without any buoyancy.

Jochen was lucky and came quickly to Germany after the capitulation, while others were still sitting in Norway for months. We married as soon as he came home, only three days later, in fact. We happened upon a priest quite by chance. I was not a white bride, there was no white cloth to be had in Berlin, but Jochen picked an enormous bridal bouquet for me, with flowers from a garden beside a bombed-out house. Grief and joy, they go together: a few days after the wedding it became clear that Mother was dead.

OTTO | To think that it would be the swimming practice every summer which saved me. Learn to swim, boy, for God's sake learn to swim, I have said to my grandchild a hundred times. He just looks at me, resigned.

Today we are to deliver young animals to slaughter, mostly bull calves and a few heifers my son doesn't have faith in. I think now and then that everything that was done to the Jews and others in the camps, we do to animals every single day. Kittens are drowned, while the mother cat searches and meows with teats full of milk. Pigs castrated without anaesthesia, and if a lamb looks weak it is killed. Many of the animals are not outside in the summer, and at the slaughterhouse there is death on the production line. The Jews were transported in cattle trucks, now there are cattle again in the trucks, on their way to a place they will not come back from.

It is good that my son has taken over, I have become far too soft-hearted. One can't think like this, but for the animals people are SS.

CARL | You arrogant little shit! We went to war so that the likes of you would be able to live in a Great-Germany, in prosperity and wealth, and then you stand here shouting that we have not had a confrontation with ourselves, what the hell do you know about it? What do you know about being under attack, have you been close to dying, perhaps, dying for your country? Only the situation decides who does what! Don't think I am ashamed, you ungrateful schoolboy.

HEINRICH | In the Ukraine, we often used to heave female prisoners up into the truck and take them in turns and then throw them out of the vehicle again when we had finished. I never thought about Renate at such times, it wasn't like being unfaithful with the secretary at the office back home. This was something completely different, at any rate then, now I am not so sure. I have begun to startle when I catch the word 'rape' on the news or read about it in the paper. Suddenly I hear all over again the fear in the voice, the feeble prayers to be let go, I always used to pull their skirts up so high that I didn't have to see their faces while I was doing it. If I go all the way down memory lane, I can smell the odour of semen and sweat and remember how slippery it was where several men had already emptied themselves. Afterwards we used to laugh and have a smoke together, a little bothered that we had watched while everyone fucked themselves to kingdom come, we were not bothered by what we had done to the prisoner. When we came home, we became ordinary husbands again, none of us went on with killing and raping then. We never spoke about it either when we met at the veterans' gathering. We could talk about fighting and ships and bombs for hours, but not about this. Never. Imagine, Renate does not know that for so many years she has lived with a rapist.

My job on Tirpitz was killing, that was why I was sent there when the attacks accelerated. They knew I would manage it, the officers, when they saw how I had served before. I was to hold the gun, direct it against the enemy. Whether it was a submarine, a battleship, a plane, whatever it was, I was to shoot until I myself was hit, shoot as long as there was life in me and the enemy. I remember the first plane I took out. While I felt the recoil, I understood that it was a great hit, and immediately after I saw the back part of the plane beginning to burn, it quickly lost height, before it disappeared over the mountain. Then there was an explosion, mass of smoke, and I felt my heart searching for its rhythm. Since it was my first plane, I cut a wing into my belt as a trophy, along with all the marks from the Ukraine.

At the Forty Years' Commemoration of the end of the war, a British journalist asked if he could track down the pilot, if he had survived; I remembered the number of the plane. Now I am standing here with an invitation to London in my hand, the pilot is alive and willing to meet me and my wife. He ejected himself in a parachute that time and got away.

I cannot meet him.

OTTO | The one who was to be on the night watch was now and then given 'panser chocolate', then one was awake! Couldn't get to sleep after the watch either. Light-hearted, yes cheerful, that's how I remember I felt.

After the war a friend who is a pharmacist told me it was metamphetamine we were given, or speed, as it is called today, which the young take before they go to party and dance all night. Now I don't touch anything stronger than my pipe, which is lying with a faint glow on the rolled tin ashtray.

MARTIN | "Arisen from the ruins and facing the future," the delusion in the very first sentence of our national anthem. The Party chiefs want us to identify ourselves with the Soviet victory rather than with the German defeat. It implied quickly becoming a communist. Otherwise came Stasi, "the Party's sign and sword". Now our republic is coming to an end. Will there be war again? When the neighbour boy tried to escape, the guards shot at him, he bled to death in the border corridor.

GOTTFRIED | I ought to have understood that about Berit, that she was pregnant. She enjoyed our hours more, was not so restrained or careful that I should pull myself out. And the way she looked at me when we said goodbye that last night. She did not cry, oh no she didn't, she was far too proud, indeed that was what I liked about her, she was no coquettish young girl who had to be taken care of. She did not come and wave when we went northwards either. I may have had my suspicions, but it was easiest not to ask.

Now I am scared every time the doorbell rings, even though I said no to the Red Cross woman. Nothing is to disturb Elsa, the lump in her left breast has come back.

ROLF | In an antique shop I come across something that leaves me quite rattled. The pictures from the Ukraine show a man who was called 'The Butcher', and it is Heinrich, he who came on board Tirpitz when we lay in Kåfjord! It says here that he used an iron bar to kill his victims, Jews in particular. On the ground lie several dead, and our soldiers are standing around him, watching. Imagine pounding away at a living person with an iron bar, seeing them turn towards you and scream, imagine being one of the spectators. Where has the soul gone when such things happen?

Dear Hildegard

How is it with you? Do you have good days? Are you coming to visit soon? Promise me you will. It would mean so much. I don't need anything, don't bring anything because I go for a walk to the shop every day. Only a little company, that is the only thing I miss.

And you must hug me, without any body contact I am going to die, I have realized. Nobody has touched me for months. My skin can't bear it any more, you must hold me, dear twin sister, let me stroke your arm, so my fingers may remember how warm skin feels. Do you know that skin is softer in the morning? It is true, I remember that from when Mother was alive and we were children. Soft morning skin, warm, close to Mother.

As you can see, I need a visit, hoping to see you, soon, Hildegard.

Live well.

Kaspar

BJARNE | Bodies come drifting, the half-dead shout: Help me, come over here, can you see me?

Going out in the boat that day destroyed my life.

OLAV | Not very many know it, but Hitler's private yacht Aviso Grille came to Fættenfjord just before the end of the war and lay at the quay there until peace came. Yes of course, some people speculated whether Hitler was on board, he and Eva Braun, that they had fled to North-Trøndelag when the Soviets came close to Berlin. Had I known that Hitler was there, I would have sunk the yacht myself. Imagine being the one who killed Hitler!

An island by Djupvika is called Storholmen. Here there was dive-bombing practice. Many of the names there are hardly in use any longer, nobody has any business out there now.

WERNER | There is light in only one window in the block across the street. It is probably a war-invalid, who can't get to sleep at night either. The local government has installed us cripples in single-room flats, far enough away so they don't see us every day. We queue up with our wheelchairs and crutches to get our social security, and when we have fetched it, we buy coal and coffee, and then nobody sees us again, unless they are up at night and notice the light in our windows. Dagmarr doesn't come here to visit. Never.

God, how I miss going fishing! The Veterans' Association tried to organize some events for us handicapped ones, but they were not much fun, and now we are too old, all of us. Better to let it be, think instead about when I used to haul cod after cod up from the depths. I used to do that once. Throw myself into the water, dive and swim. I used to do that once.

CARL | The Veterans' Association has changed, it is no longer acceptable to talk about the war as the best years in one's life. The war years *were* the best years in my life, no doubt about it. Bring on the storm, you devils! This old sailor can't sleep without hearing the sound of breaking waves.

THERES | When will I be able to cry over my father, I still wonder.

OTTO | I came in from the ploughing and caught my six-year-old grandchild playing war at sea. He was in the middle of a big battle and was playing both the Brits and Germans. I did not know what to say, the only thing I wanted to do was to tear the toy ships out of his hands and throw them away, give him a book or a ball instead.

God forbid that you have to be a soldier, I said to him, he looked at me with big eyes. I believe he understood. In any case, I never again saw him playing war. I often think about this. No new world war has come yet.

MARTIN | Imprisoned in one's own country for decades. Now when it is allowed at last, I hardly have the energy to travel, but I will go to Norway. One can take a boat called Hurtigruten, from Bergen and all the way up to Kirkenes. Just to be on board, like before.

KASPAR | Gustav comes to visit, he has started walking with a stick, he laughs almost apologetically, yes, it's beginning to be a long time since we capsized at Håkøya, he says. A long time since I was cut free after hours in the dark, so close to death that it breathed next to me, in a room where the air began to empty itself. That wasn't yesterday, he says. It is only I who still hang on tightly to my memories, I mumble.

GOTTFRIED | We are sitting under the plum tree at the end of the garden, Elsa and I, the plum tree is in blossom and drops white petals over us as if it was snow.

When the plums are ripe, she will be dead, both of us know that. Perhaps for the first time we have a heart-to-heart talk with each other, we who have been married so long, and I tell her I have a son in Norway who is called Morten, that I had a letter from the Red Cross a while ago. She goes quiet, then she asks me to reach out to him. I feel how strong it is, my love for this woman, she who has been closest to me in life, so painful to know that her part in it will soon be over. You are going to need somebody else, she says, when I am gone. Go to Norway and look for your son, the family we never had, maybe you will find it there? It could very well be that you are a grandfather, she says quietly, and I see the tears that moisten her eyes and make her so beautiful.

\

Dear Gustav

It was so nice to have you visit, good to reminisce together. After you left, I thought a little more about what memory is, what ontological status it has, so to speak. What is it that happens when we remember, and to continue our conversation I want to say that to remember is to magnify, maintain and not least to increase. One supplies something, the memory is generous, it adds nuances, and perhaps loses others from sight. All this makes recollection something new. Remembering is an investment. When you remember me, you are also remembered, one may suppose. To remember is to come in contact with each other, to cross the distance in time and space. I remember you, you exist like that.

Dear friend, you will hear from me again soon.

All the best

Kaspar

KURT | On the night of 12 November it is difficult to sleep, the night will not bring rest, only thoughts, waves, bombs, shouts. Tirpitz goes on capsizing, an eternally overturning arch.

OTTO | Someone has made a film about when they found the wreck of the Bismarck in 1989. Seeing our sister ship in the depths is enough to give me a sleepless night, even with two sleeping pills I am on my way down to the waves and the terror again. Doris puts her arms around me, it is the only thing that helps.

We shall never forget you all.

OLAV | Here lay Tirpitz, I still think every time I drive past Fættenfjord. Now I can admit that I would have liked to have gone on board. Only once, to stand on the deck. After the war Einar Høvding's ship scrapping business paid 30,000 kroner for the whole wreck, corpses and all. Oh yes.

One summer I was in Oslo, and by chance went by a construction site at Alexander Kiellands Square. A deep hole had been dug for the water and drainage-system installations, and to get cars and pedestrians safely across they had laid out an enormous steel plate. I went over and asked: Does that come from Tirpitz? Well now, you know that story, replied the foreman. Yes, this plate here is from the inner carapace, he said, and it has not worn out either, even though we have used it for years. Special grade steel this, both flexible and hard, German, you know.

A couple of days later I read in the paper about a man who was out for a walk with his dog on the stony beach at Håkøya, just at the spot where Tirpitz was bombed. Here he found an old leather boot and inside the boot a leg bone. It must have come up with the very high tide in winter, says the man.

The leg is to be buried in the German cemetery in Narvik, and the boot will end up in a museum. What will the next high tide bring up?

BJARNE | Just the other day a German-registered car came into the yard. It turned out to be one of those Father and I saved. He is called Bernhard, and he had his wife, Lisel, with him. It was a fine evening. I saw pictures of his children and grandchildren. They would not have been alive if we hadn't taken out the boat. I saw he was thinking the same thing.

\

INGRID | During the Literary Festival in Tromsø in the autumn of 2009 I say that I have been thinking about going to the place where Tirpitz was bombed. Carl-Michael Edenborg becomes interested and wants to come with me, so we take a taxi out to Håkøya. The taxi driver says he knows someone who hid in the manure cellar when the air raid began. He phones her, Helga, puts her on his mobile's loudspeaker, and we listen to her telling us how frightened she was. Then we arrive at the memorial which is engraved on a steel plate from the ship's hull.

Tirpitz lay here.

In the postbox which hangs there, people have written greetings. RIP, dear Grandfather, you will never be forgotten. A last greeting. Pity I never got to meet you, Great-grandfather.

I stroll a little way over to the beach, look at the huge basin which the driver says is the crater from one of the Tallboy bombs. As I walk, I notice a chain with big links and some other scrap iron. I realize that it comes from Tirpitz, and take a piece of the chain with me in my purse. I go onwards, there is low cloud cover, drizzle, I can no longer see Carl-Michael and the driver. Suddenly a young boy comes walking towards me, how could he pop up like this? I thought there was nobody else here.

I gaze at him. He does not speak, but I feel there is something he wants to say to me. He comes even closer, I can see the green tint in his eyes, the hair which looks wet. Now the face is so close that I could have touched it, but I am not able to move.

"Ich bin nur 19 Jahre alt," he says. *"Ich will nach Hause."* Slowly, the face completely vanishes.

I am only 19 years old, I want to go home.

\

The Tirpitz coat-of-arms

Construction of the battleship Admiral von Tirpitz was begun on 2 November 1936 at the shipyard in Wilhelmshaven and it was launched on 1 April, 1939. The 250-metre long ship has a crew of over 2,500 men. Hitler is present at the launch. The crew go on exercises in the Baltic and Gotenhafen is their base for some time.

On 12 January, 1942 Tirpitz is let through the Kiel Canal after leaving the naval base in Wilhelmshaven in secret. On 17 January the ship turns up in Fættenfjord, a small arm of the Trondheimsfjord. The ship remains here until 2 July, then it goes to Altafjord.

While Tirpitz is hunting for convoys in the Arctic Ocean, it is exposed to an unsuccessful attack by the Russian submarine K–21.

On 8 July, 1942 Tirpitz moves to Bogen in Ofoten. It stays here until 23 October the same year, then it goes to Fættenfjord again for repairs. Here the ship is exposed to attack.

On 11 March, 1943 Tirpitz returns to Bogen. Then it goes on to Kåfjord, where it stays until it goes on a raid to Spitzbergen with Scharnhorst from 6-9 September, 1943.

On 22 September in Kåfjord there is an attack by British mini-submarines as part of Operation Source, which leads to great damage to the ship and its seaworthiness.

During Operation Tungsten on 3 April, 1944, Tirpitz is exposed to a massive attack by more than 100 British planes, which take off from an aircraft carrier off the coast. The battleship is hit by about 15 bombs and peppered with machine-gun fire. In the bloodbath 122 of the crew are killed and 316 wounded. Extensive new repairs have to be done.

Several attempts to strike down Tirpitz in July and August the same year are unsuccessful, but on 15 September comes a raid with 27 long-range Lancaster bombers, each of which carries a 5.4-tonne bomb of the Tallboy type. One of the bombs inflicts great damage to the prow and forepart of the ship. Tirpitz is no longer seaworthy and is towed to Håkøya outside Tromsø in October, where the battleship stays anchored like a floating battery to ward off a feared Allied landing.

On 12 November, 1944 comes the end. 27 new Lancaster planes go into attack and hit Tirpitz with 3 Tallboy bombs. The battleship capsizes. 971 men are killed, 806 survive, 82 of them are blown up out of the ship's carapace.

In addition to this, the Norwegian war hero, Shetlands-Larsen, made an unsuccessful attempt to capture the ship in Fættenfjord in the autumn of 1942.

IN MEMORIAM TORUNN BORGE

Torunn Borge was for a long time not only my very close friend, but also my best reader and greatest support.

Torunn died on November 17, 2014, just 54 years old, and my gratitude to her comes with *An Eternal Endurance*.

Oslo,
5 December, 2014
Ingrid Storholmen

ABOUT THE WHITE NIGHTS SERIES

On behalf of Vani Book Company and Vani Prakashan, we're happy to announce, retrospectively, the formal launch of the series White Nights with the publication of the English translations of the celebrated Norwegian poet and novelist Ingrid Storholmen's novel *Here Lay Tirpitz* and Hans Sande's *Black Calf @ White Snow*. Though we hadn't given the series this name earlier, White Nights, is nevertheless, already a substantial series rolled out by Vani Prakashan, of Scandinavian literature in Hindi translation. It goes without saying that we've been building up the series, straw by straw, first in Hindi, since the beginning of the millennium, with a major and voluminous publication of Swedish poetry and the works of the Nobel Prize-winning Norwegian novelist Knut Hamsun. The series also includes plays by Henrik Ibsen followed by several titles of contemporary Swedish poetry and Norwegian fiction. It is a labour of love for and our recognition of the significance of writing from these breathtakingly beautiful countries of northern Europe. So it's not that writers like Olav Hauge and Jon Fosse are with us because they are iconic names the world over, but because, in our view, their appearance in the Indian publishing scene is likely to have immense discursive value too, apart from introducing to Indian readers authors whose works bring incomparable, brand new and infinitely enriching reading experiences.

The series may well be regarded as a tribute to Fyodor Dostoevsky whose story "White Nights" inspired its name. The young female protagonist of the story is shocked to hear that the man she happens to have befriended on a particularly magical white night is not in possession of the story of his life. When he asks her equally surprised, "But who told you there was such a story?" she asks another baffling question: "But how did you manage to live, if there's no story?" Between these two questions from "White Nights", contemporary Nordic literature unveils its Janus-faced existence: the wholesome classical story-telling and the infinitely evocative fragmentary writing, both of which seem to possess an equally compelling incantatory quality in most texts we've been taking up for publishing. What might distinguish Nordic writing further is the utterly mysterious blending of these faces, at times, in the body of the same text, when in the mystery of an un-dark night or a dark winter day illumined only by snow-light, the faces slowly turn around to face each other!

I am happy to find a publication team that chose to be counted among the pioneers in Indian publishing in their willingness to venture into the Hindi as well as English translations of significant works from Norwegian and Swedish literature. The Hindi already occupies decent shelf space and enjoys considerable readership in our country warranting many a title to go into subsequent editions. Now the English translations are also lined up for publication, and, in some cases, we have the same authors or/and titles that will appear in both languages. The Nordic series in English translation is in the making and that's what seems to matter most of all to us at this given moment in the history of Indian publishing.

Teji Grover

Series Editor

ALSO IN WHITE NIGHTS

BLACK CALF @ WHITE SNOW
an email novel

Hans Sande
Translated from the Norwegian
by Marietta Taralrud Maddrell

'[This book] is amusing, risky and absurd, but also painful and serious. Recommended to everyone who likes something heartwarming, bizarre and astonishing.'—*Aftenposten*

Black Calf @ White Snow is an existential novel told through a series of emails between Mother and Son. The headstrong Krollalfa (Curly Alpha) has run away from the farm, up to the free life of the summer pasture. His mother Krollbrura (Curly Bride) tries to coax him back to the safety and warmth of the cowshed—but Krollalfa refuses, knowing the fate that awaits young bull calves like him.

Despairing for her son, the powerless mother hopes to protect the child from afar. She tells him of her own visits to the pasture, grazing on clover, dreaming of strong bulls and keeping away from scary wolves. Krollalfa learns to wag his tail from his sheep friends—Where and Wherefore—and feasts on the same clover meadow to his heart's content.

However, it will soon be winter and impossible to survive in the snow. Will Krollalfa come back to the farm? *Black Calf @ White Snow* is a tender, whimsical and illuminating fable about parental relationships, freedom and truth. Available for the first time in English in an evocative translation—with vivid illustrations—it is a book all children and adults must read.